All the characters in this book are fictional and any resemblance to actual persons, living or dead is purely coincidental.

All rights reserved. No part of this publication may be reproduced, stored in a retrieval system, or transmitted, in any form or by any means, electronic, mechanical, photocopying, recording or otherwise, without the prior permission of the copyright owner.

COPYRIGHT©2014

PROLOGUE

Late April, 1945.
Battle ravaged Europe and the culmination of the Second World War.
The Allied nations are finally regaining control from the tyranny that had taken a malevolent hold in the last six years and as the resilient and valiant soldiers pushed the weakening Nazi Armies back to Berlin, its capture was imminent. Bombs continued to rain down on many of the German towns and cities in a tumultuous and destructive retribution.
The skies above the dissonant battlefields and burning buildings were continuously bruised and blackened from the ever raging fires and billowing columns of grey smoke drifted upwards from the devastated land below.
It would be the largest conflict the world had ever known - the war to end all wars - and when the dust settled the estimated lives lost would be fifty million.
To the west, the North Sea was calm and subdued; a world away from the madness. There was none of the crashing waves and fierce winds that typified these waters; it almost seemed respectively solemn and bereaving to what was taking place on European soil.
A hundred and thirty feet beneath the sedate surface a submersible cautiously approached the North East coast of England, steadily and patiently skimming the rising seabed.

The men inside listened keenly with their trained ears for any tell tale sounds of enemy vessels but all that could be heard was the steady hum of the engines.

The sub was easy on controls and very manoeuvrable despite its size and being a two man submersible, the crew of three were still able to cope with the lack of space in the tight confines amongst a maze of pipes and wiring.

Two of the perspiring men stared through the bulkheads at their own imaginary fears while gripping their instruments with a steely nerve.

'Steady.' The third said. He was not perspiring like the others but he stooped awkwardly.

Despite the overbearing mugginess of their confines, he appeared cool and reposed but Captain Lucas Huber was not. He had had enough of this war. He itched his pallor skin beneath a thick and tangled black beard. At six foot five he always wondered why he joined the Kriegsmarine and after twenty-seven years and it being all he ever knew, he still asked himself that question.

He was too tall for the low confines of a submarine and since then it had given him a permanent stoop. The other reflection that invariably followed was what was he doing beneath the sea when he always longed for wide open spaces? Maybe it was because of that fact; spending most of his life underwater that he would naturally yearn for the great outdoors, yet deep down he knew it was much more complicated than that.

Since the war had taken over their lives he had not done much rambling - back in the autumn of '43 was the last break he had had, a one week leave in two years.

The irony was he often felt like a prisoner of this war.

He was born in 1902 and was a twelve year old boy when WWI broke out. From then on his life never knew peace. At

the age of sixteen - just as the First World War was ending he enlisted when the German Navy was in its infancy. He, like many, thought it would be an uneventful and noble employment and yet here he was again at the end of another war and once again on the losing side.
It felt like someone was telling him something.

The tension was worse now the closer they approached.
The lengthy journey up to this point had not been without its stresses, it was always going to be difficult, and they knew that. They had done it a hundred times before on countless other patrols during this war.
The increasing fear of being detected by the enemy vessels was prevalent but this crawl and the threat of the sea bed rising too quickly was unbearable. This was an altogether different kind of mission.
As their clothing became damper from their continuing perspiration, they were convinced they heard their sweat splashing the deck.
'Sea floor climbing sir, thirty-two fathoms.'
'Four knots' He ordered, looking at the Helmsman.
'Thirty, sir.'
'Two knots.'
The Helmsman squatted over his controls.
'Watch propeller.' The captain cautioned.
'Rising quickly sir. Twenty-five, twenty-one…..'
'All stop Helmsman.'
There was a drawn out shudder throughout the submarine as it groaned to a halt.
'At sixteen, sir.'
They nodded at each other as they eyed a packet of cigarettes by the console. 'Soon!' they kept telling themselves.

Huber moved to the periscope, raising it slowly. Eyes to the viewer, he began to move it left and right in measured motions, back and forth.
A few minutes later he said 'Fore and aft.'
'Fore and aft sir.'
Underwater, the sub slowly turned into position in readiness.
'Closest ever for me.' Huber said with his thick eyebrows raised. The sea bed put him on edge. 'Easy now.'
Eventually satisfied he looked at his watch, brought periscope down and addressed his men. 'Now we wait.'
If his two men had groaned, he would not have minded. He saw the looks on their faces despite their tough demeanour. They were two hours ahead of schedule which was testament to their submariner skills. His trust in them was well placed. Never doubted it!
'At ease lads.'
There was Jerome; his Second Officer/Chief Engineer, his very own 'war hog' as Huber nicknamed him. Taking into account wartime rations, Jerome still looked as well fed as a spoilt king yet despite his portliness he was as robust as a bear. He had on his cherry chubby face one of those curling handlebar moustaches that were had by all in the late 18th century but now were only spouted by the old guards of World War One. There was only five years between them and Huber had as much respect for him as he did for his father and had insisted on him for this venture. He would not have entered into it otherwise. In his eyes, Jerome was a true hero from the First World War - they had served together on the same U-Boat the last three years - and it should have been Jerome with his very own command and boat but was considered by his superiors to lack leadership. He was never promoted and Jerome would not have wanted it any other way.

Grien was his Helmsman - the kid – and had enlisted like a lot of youngsters when the war started. He had previously served with him for ten months and Huber requested him for this mission simply because of his acute abilities. Though he was twenty-one he looked ten years younger and like death warmed up. With big bewildered eyes and being clean shaven all the time it made him appear even more childlike. Sometimes Huber wondered like many others whether Grien had even reached puberty yet, never once had they seen him shave. Yet the young lad followed orders well, with a maturity and instinct that put sailors with twice as much experience to shame. There was a future for the Heartland.

Still they eyed their packets of cigarettes anxiously; the craving for a smoke had become nearly unbearable since arriving near land. It would also represent a well earned reward of sorts, symbolising the conclusion of their journey. Such simple pleasures were more appreciated during the difficulties and hardship of war.

Taking their minds off cigarettes, they occupied themselves by preparing for the long awaited exit by getting together their equipment. Checking again and again in nervous anticipation yet knowing there was only so many times they could be ready.

They limbered up too with stretching exercises and chatted in good humour about their first smoke, drink and hot meal once they got out of this suffocating tub. It was often said, you never got used to it no matter how many hours you spent under.

The Nazi German Navy's - Kriegsmarine - 'Seehund' type XXVII was a two man crew spying submarine based on the designs of two salvaged British X Class Subs that were originally designed to lay dynamite underneath enemy ships. With diesel engines and electric motors, it could dive to

150ft and make up to 9 knots. The Kriegsmarine had reproduced the configurations with espionage capabilities and this particular vessel had operational apparatus specifically modified for this significant mission. It was designated the UC55.

Most of her armaments and stores had been taken out during the refit and all the torpedo aft tubes and stowage discarded, making more room and conditions a good deal easier. Anything not essential was torn out. Dry and cold storage, unneeded auxiliary equipment and machines, all unnecessary parts, fixtures, pipes and conduits, hand wheels and cranks were all dismantled and removed from the sub before leaving dock. The bunks too were thrown as there wouldn't be much time for sleeping on this trip.

Ballast is the weight added to a vessel that is in a light condition - displacement it was termed - so because the interior of the sub had been stripped down considerably, the weight of the precious cargo that had been placed throughout the cramped confines of the submersible compensated. Even the fuel tanks were partly filled with what they estimated would be all they needed for the voyage. It was only going to be a one way trip.

They had started the crossing three days ago. Departing still occupied Denmark after midnight from the small harbour of Saeby; part of the Jutland peninsula on the north east coast and veering north westerly to Norway, following the coastline around to its west at cruising speed. Passing Stavanger and Bergen they raced out at full power west to the deep waters of the Norwegian Sea, eventually in patrolled waters they headed south at a depth of 110 ft towards the North Sea and the tip of Scotland.

Still avoiding the Allied patrolled English Channel at depths of 140ft they reached the eastern coast of England, hugging it close as the sea bed began to rise and signifying journey's end after a distance of over 470 miles from their embarkation point.

The comprehension he was AWOL did not bother him. Would he be missed or his fellow comrades, he didn't think so. Many soldiers were fleeing now, trying to find their escape from the collapsing reign. It had become a shambles and orders were now being disobeyed and disregarded.

He, Jerome and Grien had felt the same way. They knew a lost cause after all the blood and tears that they had been through. Like so many of their own.

It was a losing battle and far too many good men were dying; men that would be great doctors, architects, engineers, teachers and fathers too. All of them wasted in a war that was becoming completely redundant. Hitler had pushed us too far, overreached himself and it was the German people that were now paying for it with their lives.

He could understand why the rest of the world joined in the fight against them. We had corrupted the dream, lost the plot. Our nation and Europe needed reformation but not as tyrants in a grievous domination and if the rumours were true about the Jews, well, we were only monsters. That was not the rectifying future that was promised. It was not the original vision and some of us no longer wanted a part of it. No wonder the Allies were winning the war. It was an unimpeachable right over wrong.

Like so many; his men and himself had been loyal and tough and in the end they did not deserve to be fighting this war anymore. They had remained steadfast all those months under the sea while death constantly threatened from above, wondering if you were going to perish at the bottom of the sea in a steel tomb from a mine or torpedo. Often those boys out there under the sea were the forgotten heroes of the war.

By undertaking this, he hoped the final assignment would give his men and himself a better future; a future without war and death and payback for all their unsung efforts.

A drawn out hour and a half later, Captain Huber upped the periscope and once again began scouring the beach area that was ninety feet from their position.
Nothing yet.
Behind him Huber heard frequent movement. His men were becoming restless, eager to get moving. The waiting was nerve wracking for all of them.
Fifteen minutes later the periscope emerged again and began slowly moving left and right, eventually lingering on a jetty a few hundred yards away.
The sea still remained unusually calm and the light from the near full moon from time to time shone brightly through the breaks in the overcast clouds.
No other light was seen from a house or building, the village was nestled further back inland above and beyond the steep road that led to it from the beach. To the north a wall of black stretched miles into the distance, its cliffs marking the end of the North York Moors.
Then a flash to the left!
Swinging the periscope back towards the wooden jetty, he waited again for the signal.
A few minutes later there it was, this time three bursts that seemed to hover above the jetty like a winking star.
The rendezvous had made it.
Huber uttered the words Jerome and Grien had been waiting forever for. 'There's the signal. Take her in. Ahead close as you can Helmsman.'
He did not have to remind Grien about the keel. 'As far and as gently as a dingy please.'

Still at periscope depth they slowly moved aft until they slipped up out of the shallow depths; its grey hull low in the water, creeping at half a knot.

'Lee side and bow.'

There was a gentle bump as the sub nudged against the wooden jetty.

'All stop. Engines off.'

What little air there was in the submarine seemed to let out a relieved sigh.

'Well done lads. I would recommend each of you for an Iron Cross if I could.' Huber extolled. 'But we are not at home anymore. We are objectors. So I can't.'

Jerome and Grien grinned at the light-hearted comment, while accomplishment showed on their pale and tired faces.

Smiles and hand shakes all round followed with an eagerness to get out of the submersible UC55 that had been their dwelling for the last three days. For now their tiredness and the fact that the mission was far from over and that they were now in enemy territory was forgotten.

As far as they were concerned they had completed the worst of it and the thought of open spaces, fresh air and a cigarette was all they wanted now.

'Lets be free again gentlemen.' the Captain ordered resoundingly. 'Topside!'

Opening the hatch, he courteously let his diligent crew go first, slapping their backs cordially as they made their exits.

Emerging into the fresh salty air invigorated them. The relieving cool, breezy weather began to fill their stuffy lungs and take the weight off their leaden hearts.

Grien secured the line.

Ambling on deck in triumphant completion, they lit up those much craved and well earned cigarettes.

The North Sea was still as placid as a lake and the familiar harsh winds were all but non existent. There wasn't a star to be seen in the sky, it was a blanket of milky clouds. The beach that stretched out before them was a mixture of sand and rocky platforms that gleamed like mirrored pools.

On the coast of North Yorkshire, Robin Hood's Bay was nestled in a fissure between two steep cliffs and above the contrasting beach nestled its small fishing village five miles South of Whitby and fifteen miles North of Scarborough. The origin of the Bay's name is uncertain and it is doubtful that the man himself was ever in the neighbourhood. Legends come about easily when stories are passed around like hearsay, yet the town always had a tradition of smuggling and it was rife during the 17th century. Vessels from the continent smuggled contraband of tea, gin, brandy and tobacco to avoid paying the tax duties.

Huber lit another cigarette; his first had finished too quickly for his pleasure.

He scratched at his beard thinking he needed an overdue hot shave.

The wide open outdoors at last and it was putting him in a pensive mood. He was looking forward to the future, to finally settling down and having a family. This war got in the way of all that and there was never time to do what pleased him most, which was rambling.

There were many beautiful places in England for walks, he had seen the photos and it seemed so peaceful, away from everything untroubled. He couldn't do that at home anymore; his country had been ruined, spoiled. Maybe he could settle down with an English girl and she would understand his longing, see past his wrongdoings and walk with him too. That was all he wanted.

Interrupting his thoughts, he spotted three figures emerge from behind an outcrop of rocks and hurriedly make their way towards him and the jetty. Immediately he and his men became alert.

As soon as they treaded onto the creaking jetty, the head of the group had his arm outstretched, 'Captain Huber....?'

It wasn't so much a query but more confirmation. No one else was expecting a Nazi submarine in a small English fishing village.

Huber shook his hand and nodded.

'I'm Frenchy and this is Ludo and Adam.' The stranger gestured to the two men with him who remained silent.

Huber knew that their names would not be their real ones. It was standard operations but at least they were not the real Home Guard.

They certainly looked the part with their field caps and black polished boots and attired in the 'Denim' issued uniform of the Home Guard, though it was the older version he observed. Maybe they couldn't get hold of the latest uniform which in some areas the volunteers waited months for. These were probably the cast offs which were more easily appropriated.

Carried on their front was their Haversacks, unique only to the Home Guard and it would contain standard equipment like a water bottle, rations, soap, wound dressings, a knife and their all important gas mask. Weapons were only allowed to a select few Home Guards and certainly not to those in areas not considered at risk of invasion, like this back water. Huber was certain without a doubt that these men's Haversacks consisted of more than the standard issue equipment.

Frenchy was French, that was obvious but he spoke almost perfect middle class English. He was tall and noticeably slender under the bulky uniform and had a jet black pencil moustache.

His partners were big, stern men that looked more like steel workers than soldiers. He wondered whether they were chosen specifically for the work ahead.

From what Huber had been briefed - and it wasn't a lot - these men were double spies enlisted for this part of the operation, yet another few colluders that were cogs of the bigger scheme.

'Well done Captain Huber. And your men.' Frenchy's praise was curt. He immediately got down to business. Huber could understand the urgency.

Frenchy turned to one of his men, 'Ludo. Go bring up the truck.' He ordered and turning back addressed the captain again.

'I know you are tired my friends but we must load this truck quickly now.'

'Of course.' replied Huber.

Jerome and Grien finished their cigarettes and slapped their hands in readiness.

Two hundred feet away where the village road ended at the beach, Frenchy's man Ludo reached a truck that was barely visible in the shadows. With its lights remaining off, it slowly reversed to the jetty's edge, its engine purring quietly as it rolled over the hard sand.

They all got stuck in. The longer it took the more likely they would be discovered.

Being free of the sub seemed to revive the three men who were willing to take on most of the heavy work with a renewed optimism and strength.

All around the coastal area remained tranquil; the only sound was the gentle lapping of the subdued tide. They felt like the only people in the world.

It was hefty work that progressively became more back breaking as they carried on. Nevertheless, ninety minutes later the truck was loaded with its important cargo.

Not a word had been uttered by Frenchy's colleagues during the transfer from submarine to truck; even eye contact was avoided, so Huber did not know if they were French, German or even British. That did not matter though, alliances were changing every day and he did not expect everyone to be sociable in these times. It was hard to trust anybody.

Even Frenchy had become subdued Huber had noticed, but he put it down to probably the work load, an urgency to finish and the constant dread of possibly being caught by the real Home Guard or any suspicious locals.

They were now waiting for Grien, who had left loading a little earlier to perform one last task; the scuttling of the sub. Frenchy had also sent his other man Adam down with Grien to assist.

While Ludo started the truck up again and moved off, Huber, Jerome and Frenchy followed behind until the truck stopped at the beginning of the steep road.

Ludo got out of the truck and joined them.

Frenchy said, 'Once your man and mine are done with the sub, be ready to get into the back of the truck.'

'Another smoke before we set off?' Jerome suggested.

'Good idea.' Frenchy encouraged. 'We have a long journey ahead of us.'

Silently they lit up, contemplating their own thoughts while they waited for Grien and Adam.

They watched the submarine as it slowly began to move away from the jetty towards deeper waters and then slip beneath the waves.

Both Grien and Adam had the unpleasant job of evacuating the sub and swimming back to shore in the cold waters but waterproofs were already provided in the submersible. They were probably suited in them now.

The men on land could see across the voluminous North Sea to the south east where a thin strip of light was spreading on the horizon. Day was beginning to wake.

As Huber looked eastwards towards France and Europe he could still visualise the death and destruction that they had left behind. Out of sight perhaps but for as long as he lived he will never forget what he had seen, witnessed and regrettably been part of.

'What will we do if we really do lose the war?' Jerome asked them all.

'We will prepare for the next one. That is what this is all about.' Frenchy said as he pointed to the cargo in the back of the truck. 'This is our future.'

Jerome flicked his finished cigarette into the air and it flew off abruptly in another direction.

The wind was picking up.

'What's keeping that boy?' Jerome asked irritably as he buttoned his coat up.

Jerome was getting anxious Huber noticed. So was he.

The kid and Frenchy's man should be swimming back now.

'Grien will come Jerome. Not long now.' Huber reassured.

'I'm afraid he won't be coming back Captain Huber.' Frenchy declared. 'If my colleague has done his job, your man's body is sinking to the bottom of the ocean with your submersible.'

Both Huber and Jerome turned in bewilderment.

Frenchy and Ludo had pistols aimed at them both.

'BASTARDS!' spat Jerome.

So those were the weapons they had concealed in their Home Guard Haversacks, Huber regarded gravely – High standard HDM's based on a .22 calibre pistol and fitted with a sound suppressor.

He did not like the feeling he had now. It was a dreadful acceptance of what was going to happen to him and he was afraid. Afraid and disappointed for his men and their hopes too.

It wasn't fair after all they had been through.

Frenchy and Ludo had their orders and they carried them out.

1

20th July 2009

A wedding reception was in full swing and the merriment of the event was enhanced by the hot July weather. Without a cloud in the sky, the airy and cooling breeze was refreshingly welcome.

In the grounds of this vast estate, a Palladian forty-six bedroom manor with a verdant four hundred acre gardens and woods in Schloss Bruck, Austria was the venue for the marriage of Mr & Mrs Markus Lochner.

Dotted throughout the rear of the property's green were giant gazebos filled with food and drink galore that the bustling waiters and waitresses continually provided and which the guests who were garbed in their finest attire, consumed heartily.

A stage had been set up on the lawn where the music from the live band played and people danced. Shrieks of excited children filled the air, enjoying the playground funfair that had been provided for them.

Floral white confetti still sprinkled the ground and colourful day-glo balloons reached for the clear skies.

Two figures moved unhurriedly away from the social mingling, making a casual stroll further into the multicoloured gardens. A tall man in a distinguished Army uniform was pushing an elderly man in a wheelchair whose deteriorated legs could not support his eagerness to continue moving about as they used to. Despite his stubborn determination, his limbs and bones were not strong enough anymore. It was an old war wound, he told people but that was not exactly the truth.

Undeterred by his disabilities, the ninety-two year old man still had all his other faculties that were as strong and acute as he was many years ago. There was something still youthful about his sharp features and his ice blue eyes that pierced with unwavering spirit. He had a rounded face with a squat nose above a constantly grimacing mouth and his shaven head gleamed in the daylight.

He spoke with a smokers rasp, 'Push me down over there Jan. We will have some privacy.'

The man in uniform pushing him continued to do so with mild disdain, he wanted to return to the party. Actually he wanted to go home; family gatherings were never his thing. Even if it was his son's wedding day.

At six foot three, he appeared lanky and lean but underneath the military attire of a colonel, his body was at the peak of robustness. His posture and confidence exemplified his authoritative demeanour which conveyed all his years of a soldiered disciple.

At forty-two Colonel Jan Lochner of the German Army was as sturdy as any marine in his prime. He had short cropped blond hair with knowledgeable dark eyes hiding behind mirrored sunglasses. A protruding square chin showed the white of an old scar on an otherwise unblemished tan glowed face. Very rarely did he smile but when the lips turned uncommonly upwards, it always seemed condescending.

They found a spot enclosed with high immaculately trimmed hedges and in the centre a grey stone fountain cascaded sparkled water. The ornamental fishes around its edge interminably mouthed an 'O' in futile expectancy.

Jan positioned the wheelchair next to the end of a white marbled bench, facing it towards the water feature. He remained standing a few feet away.

There was an awkward silence between them as the sun warmed their backs. Neither was saying anything and the soothing trickling of the water fountain were spoilt a little by the faint pounding of the party music and the distance cries of children.

The elderly man reached inside his suit jacket and pulled out a copper coloured flask and swiftly downed a dose of its contents.

He exhaled satisfactory and said, 'How is the situation in Afghanistan?'

'A drag.' Jan replied stoically.

'I know. It saps the endeavour and spirit of any soldier that war.'

'It's not a war anymore,' Jan stated, shifting the weight on his feet. 'It's like chasing rats. Ceaseless! If I had my way I'd bomb the whole country. Finish it once and for all. Too many good men killed.'

The old man nodded.

With UN obligations, the German Army had a presence in Afghanistan too. Situated in the comparatively quiet North of the country in Kunduz, they still had had nearly a hundred soldiers killed and a few hundred more injured in hostile activity. Not many casualties compared to the many losses other occupying forces suffered in this long drawn out war against terror but nevertheless, one was too many.

The two men regarded the fountain as silence fell between them both again, mulling over their own awkwardness that had brought them together after so many years without contact.

Eventually the older man said, 'It's been perfect weather for a wedding. Just what the bride wants for her special day, for everyone else's too. She must be overjoyed at this splendour?'

'She is.' Jan replied curtly. Small talk never interested him.

He had been granted a week's leave for the wedding; Jan's one and only child from his twenty-two year marriage and it only reminded him of the banality. It was a nuptial of convenience that the Army encouraged in their soldiers - domestic stability - and he had gone through the rituals of courting, engagement and marriage to an uninteresting plain Jane and then a few years later, parenthood in an almost nonchalant routine. The whole family thing never enthused him and he was barely ever home. In the early days, his wife would wonder if it was always the Army that kept him away but soon learnt that her husband and father of their only child simply did not do domesticity. She came to realise that the one thing of importance in Jan's life, was the Army.

The silence and idling between him and his senior was irritating him, 'What do you want old man?' He snarled.

'Show some respect Jan. I'm still your elder. Take off your glasses.'

Seething inside, he reluctantly obliged. Only to get this over with!

'You used to look up to me Jan, even loved me. What happened?'

The question annoyed him and his sable eyes seem to become even darker. Why did he have to bring this up? He had an urge to just walk away.

'You were never there as I got older.' Jan answered impatiently. 'I saw less and less of you. We grew apart. I then saw you for what you were and I did not like that anymore.'

Despite his intention to skip the subject, there was always a denial that history was repeating itself. He would never be able to shake the truth that what the old man had done to him; he had only been repeating it with his son. A classic case of 'like father, like son' and he was only passing it on.
'You have grown to despise me, I know. See me as an imbecile.'
'I'm glad you're aware of my feelings for you.' He replied glibly. 'Yes. You're an old reprobate from an out of date time. Not even my real father.'
'Ah, Jan…' he pleaded. 'That's hurtful. And to my sister too who brought you up with so much love as if you were her very own. That's disrespectful. Would that mean I wasn't there for you anymore then you are for your son?'
A twinge of anger blazed across his face but was quickly rebuffed as a feeble emotion. Playing dirty now the bastard, he fumed inside.
'You manipulated my youth. I was only a child.' He hissed back.
'I wouldn't quite say that. We gave you a future that most of us never had.' He reminded him.
He had been found left outside a hospital on a freezing January night. Left by whom, no one knew. Nurses guessed his age to be about one and a half and appropriately named him Jan after the month. His parents were never traced and he was then raised by Engel and his sister care of an adoption agency.
A group of excitable children came running in, interrupting the tension.
They watched as the kids chased each other around the fountain, stopping to splash themselves with water until the old man suggested to them, 'Who can get out of the hedge maze further down in the gardens first?'

They immediately scampered off, shrieking with excitement. Not once had Jan turned his head and given the old man eye contact. He just did not what to encourage him anymore then he had to. Returning to the inane socialising of the occasion was more appealing then this trying conversation!
'Stop wasting my time. Tell me what you have to say.' Jan said brusquely.
'Never had much to say, did you Jan? A man of few words. Curt and to the point.' He shrugged his shoulders, amused at his own statement. 'Come. Sit down....'
Jan stared with aversion at the hand beckoning him.
'This will not take long now. I know you want to go.'
He reluctantly sat.
'First thing first......'
'Should have known.' Jan grumbled inwardly.
'.....You must know why I am telling you this....' He seemed to pause for dramatic effect.
'....I am to be put on trial for my involvement as a Nazi during World War Two.'
He looked over to Jan for a reaction but he continued to stare at the water in the fountain.
The old man took out a cigarette box from his jacket pocket and pulling one out, lit it.
'I was a foot soldier of the Third Reich and am the last of the old regime. One of the few that have remained uncaught for many years. Until now.'
He blew out smoke ambiguously.
He was enjoying this, Jan thought. The most attention, he's probably had in years.
'New evidence has inevitably come to light and this time will be damning. A testimony from a Jew.....' the epitaph spat like an insult. '....who has recognised me after all this time. Can you believe it?' It wasn't so much a question but a

statement. 'It's true when they say; you cannot outrun your past.'

If Jan was nonplussed earlier, now he had to admit - if only to himself - he was a little curious.

Was the old man finally going to make some kind of apology? Maybe even clear his conscious and finally admit to his past and the things he regretted.

Growing up, Jan had heard rumours that his foster-father was a Nazi officer but he had always took it as hearsay and the questions were always avoided. Until he asked the old man one day before he left home to join the Army but he denied it as nonsense and vicious rumours.

As far as everyone knew, he was a teacher that was imprisoned for his views against Fascism during the war. Yet Jan did begin to have an inkling the older he got that his foster-father was involved somehow because he was always so detached and taciturn in character. Jan always felt deep down that he was hiding something.

The old man continued, 'I have a secret to tell you Jan and soon you and everyone will know my past.'

He paused, tarrying like he was relishing this moment and he was. This would be his final hour.

'There is gold Jan. A vast amount, untouched, unforgotten and it is yours.'

The words surprised him but he did not say anything. He waited.

The old man was mired in his own reverie. After so many years, it was going to be a relief to finally share this secret with someone he was convinced would take up the struggle again. All those years of planning would finally come to fruition by the one he nurtured. His foster son, the protégé; the only one left with the power and influences to resurrect the Reich.

'This bullion is in England, beneath one of the capitals most famous buildings and still it remains undiscovered by the British. They are completely unaware of it.' He smiled at that, as he continued to smoke.

Jan had thought that the revelation would be a confession or an apology, not ramblings about hidden gold. This sounded like delusional attention seeking to him. The old man was senile; reliving past glories that were simply failures.

He carried on, 'By telling you this secret, I am giving you the means to bring glory back to our cause once again. Now it is your time Jan. You have kept your political ambitions hidden well from those that still oppose and repress. It's something you do not speak freely of. But I know you strive for change in our country and Europe.' He shifted in his seat, leaning forward with significance.

'My notes and details have been dispatched. You will receive those tomorrow. I could not risk handing something over to you here. They may be watching.'

Jan asked disdainfully, 'Who and what are you talking about old man?'

'The past is still present like a vengeful ghost.' he divulged. 'Interpol will apprehend me in a few days time for war crimes.'

At least he had his interest, Jan allowed. He indulged him by letting him continue.

'They are no fools, yet I have remained free till now. I had to protect myself. Us and the project too! I was incredibly fortunate you could say but it's been torturous, every waking and sleeping hour, always fearful of who would come. The lie has lived with me and been my bane for a very long time. That's been my punishment. I've done my time and I have lived long enough with this burden. I cannot go on trial and I will not go to prison. That is why I have told you this now.'

His body seemed to empty of all air, as he sighed and sank back into his wheelchair.

He's hanging onto some old dream of Nazi glory and the guilt of what they had actually committed had driven him deranged, Jan assumed.

The excited children could be heard before they spilled back into the enclosure. Squabbling and taunting each other over who was the first to complete the hedge maze.

The old man hushed them down and said 'I've just been told that the cake is now being served. Lets all go get some.'

With that, the children scrambled out and ran back to the house like excited monkeys.

The old man took one last drag on his cigarette and flicked it disregardless into the fountain.

'C'mon Jan....' he beckoned to be pushed back and Jan eagerly obliged. '... You too can have cake. And eat it.'

He chuckled at that, feeling appeased. He couldn't remember the last time he laughed so candidly.

As Jan pushed the old man back to the party, he was sure this conversation would be forgotten in the morning. That they probably wouldn't see each again, even if what he claimed about being arrested was true. Nothing would have changed.

Yet something niggled like a gut feeling. The old man could be telling the truth, no matter how absurd it sounded and for the rest of the occasion he couldn't shake the notion from his mind.

Jan never did see the old man again.

2

The blind was closed, shutting out the midnight and the kitchen light spotlighted everything on the table where he was sitting. Scattered on it were the eight separate pieces of his Luger pistol.

After all this time, it still worked perfectly because he had always maintained it. Occasionally throughout the years he had even fired a few rounds from it but now he was cleaning and checking it for the last time.

An old crumpled box of bullets rested to the side.

It had been a few hours since one of the guests had driven him back from the wedding reception to his rented villa and he was still dressed in his grey suit. He didn't see the point in changing.

He had managed to get out of his wheelchair and slowly and painfully walked from the hallway to the kitchen using a walking stick. When the time came, he did not want to be in that contraption.

It had been good to see Jan and he looked very well - though a twinge of guilt did pull at him when he saw him. Resplendent in his uniform, it had given him a surge of pride. His foster son was in the prime of his life and he took some satisfaction at the man he had grown to be.

It seemed a lifetime ago when he had encouraged Jan to join the Army as soon as he turned sixteen and they had not seen each other in over twenty years since. Jan certainly made that clear.

He could now sympathise with his foster son's ire but then he deemed it prudent to have less contact as the years went by, so the authorities would not become suspicious of Jan and what he would become to represent. He had had to distance himself for his protection and the project's. One day Jan would understand that.

Nevertheless he had at last passed on the mantle. The weight of it had been like the tonnage of the gold itself.

He was Udo Engel despite living under a false name since the end of the war and was born in 1920 in Leipzig. It was the age of seventeen when he started a life of crime and eventually enlisted with the Nazi party in his twenties and achieved the rank of 'Hauptmann' – Captain. He was exalted of that fact even if to some, it did not amount to much after all that had transpired.

Sixty-five years he had in a sense been on the run. To last that long un-apprehended was a miracle and a curse but now he could finally rest in peace. The war never really ended for him and he had remained faithful right up to the end, a loyal and diligent soldier. His Fuhrer would have been pleased.

The reek of polished metal gun parts hung in the room, the antique weapon had been meticulously cleaned. He wiped his hands of blackened and grey grease onto a dirty rag and then began to re-assemble the gun one last time.

Slowly and methodically going through the motions as he had taught himself many years ago; a disciplined soldier always kept a clean and functioning gun; it was a matter of life and death.

Though Jan's reaction was discouraging to him, he knew when he finally retrieved that gold, Jan would then believe.

Seeing him today, he believed German's future would triumph. The original plan that was envisioned back at the end of the Second World War could finally be realised after all this time. Germany will have Europe again. Third time lucky, he could not help but reason.

A part of him savoured that moment when he had divulged his secret to Jan, the most excitement he had had in a long time. It would be a glory of sorts but to witness the look in Jan's face; that would not happen. He would never see it. That would be his final regret!

The last piece of the gun finally clicked into place. It was now fully assembled again.

He took out a single dusty bullet from the old ammunition box, wiped it and then loaded it into the gun.

There would be no more freedom, if you can call all those years looking over my shoulder, salvation. He was tired now. All the energy he had had was spent on the burden and secret that he had carried for so long – he realised it was the only thing that had kept him going – and now that he was relieved of it, he was exhausted. There was nothing else for him now.

Those coming to arrest him will never again let him wear this suit, clean his gun, let him see his foster son and ultimately witness the glory of the 'Phonix aus der Asche.'

He put the Luger in his mouth and pulled the trigger.

3

News article from German Newspaper 'Faz' dated 22nd July 2009
'NAZI SUSPECT SENT DEATH CAMP VICTIMS.'
A wanted Nazi suspect who allegedly participated in the murder of more than 5,000 Jews, Polish, Russians and enemies of the state was found dead yesterday. Ninety-two year old and former Nazi-German Udo Engel, who had lived undisturbed in the village of Kottenforst outside Bonn for many years under the falsified name of Konrad Schroder-Kopf, was responsible for sending victims to numerous death camps during World War Two. Was twenty-one years old when he allegedly started working as a captain in the SP (Secret Police) Division of the Nazi Party in January 1941. Known and feared as one of the notorious Gangster Nazis, Engel had been on a list of possible suspects for many years but statements were never conclusive. It was rumoured that an arrest was to be made shortly after implicating evidence came to light. Suicide was the verdict.

So it was true. The old boy was dead, Jan reflected. He had only seen him two days ago at the wedding.

Putting down the newspaper, he opened his desk drawer and found the brown envelope that had arrived in the post that morning.

He was home alone and in his study. His wife was out mollifying her existence with some 'Coffee morning' with other bored housewives in town.

He opened the envelope using a WWI Fairbairn Sykes fighting knife. It was a boyhood emblem given to him when the old man had sent him off to the Army.

I should be sad or even grieving but I don't feel a thing. It's as if I really did not know him. Is this how it will be when I pass away? Will my son have the same indifference towards me?

Contained in the envelope was a hand written letter, a sheet of paper with a list of names and contact numbers, some worn and folded photocopied blueprints of a building and three old grainy black and white photographs. One of them showed what looked like gold stacked in a bricked chamber. Another was a group of men in a line passing what again looked like gold bars to each other into the back of a truck. The men looked tired and haggard and some were dressed in the old British Home Guard uniforms, the background showed what appeared to be a beach. The other photo showed the truck parked by a road sign of opposite arrows with the destinations, 'Robin Hood Bay' and 'London.' One of the men from the previous photo was pointing at the old wooden sign.

It's getting more and more intriguing old man, he said to himself as he began to read the three page letter. There was no initial or formal greeting, not even a 'Dear' or date and address.

My time has run out Jan….. It begun. …. *It's not because I'm well into the fading twilight of my life. I've been very*

lucky in that sense after all the things I have done and it's not the fact that I have become so weary and full of physical pain that I'm ready to give up the ghost but it's my persistent pursuers who will soon catch up with me after sixty-five years with incriminating evidence of my secret.
It was that Jew's testimony that was the last straw.
Putting together the OSI's (Office of Special Investigations) previous evidence and with the involvement of the still active Wiesenthal Centre and it's 'Operation Last Chance' - a final opportunity to bring Nazis to trial before their deaths, they now have the evidence and power to arrest me and they are coming.
I have been forewarned by a contact in Interpol, a member of the Phoenix Project……

Ah, the Phoenix Project! The influential group and many subjects benefactor, including my own, Jan recollected.

The letter continued …..*but first let me tell you who I really am. You deserve that.*
During our country's depression after the First World War, I was a young orphan on the streets and desperate. My Mother and Father had both died from malnutrition and disease caused by the disruption and embargos of that war. Without money and unable to feed myself, it led me, like many of us, to crime. It was survival of the fittest and fiercest.
Eventually working for gangs, I learnt I had a knack for ruthlessness, eventually making a business of it myself. From racketeering, trafficking of weapons, drugs and blackmail and in work like that, it inevitably led to the removal of certain people. I murdered notorious characters, dispatched of political persons that were a threat to influential parties. It became easy for me, hunger overcame the remorse and I could finally provide for myself.

When the Nazis Party began to gain popularity and support, I was given an opportunity in the brown shirts - the S.A. They gave me a role with my criminal talents to do their bidding. They told me they admired my efficiency and brutality. So for me it was business as usual but this time with immigrants, ethnic minorities, foreign citizens and whoever got in the way of the Nazification of Germany.

Then the war began and they made me a Hauptmann for the ruling Nazi party and my orders had not changed. The only difference now, I was sitting behind a desk in a government building signing orders for the arrest of the same people I used to hunt down myself.

Interesting, Jan mused. Was the old man telling the truth? Was he really in such a position to be a 'Liegeman' of Hitler's regime? I always thought the rumours were true about his involvement with Nazism but did he have such a decisive role? If anything, I had assumed he had been but a mere foot soldier.

He resumed reading with a new persuasion growing for the old man.

History of course informs us of the two failed assassination attempts on the Fuhrer's life and his retribution that followed but some of us still remained elusive.

We the conspirator's grew, as more and more respected officers began to join. Disillusioned with our leader's egomaniacal behaviour and his refusal to listen. It was unheard of for Hitler to ever stand down from his design or change his strategies. The success of his early triumphs in Europe convinced him that his way would still always prevail even when later campaigns failed. No one, not even his most trusted officers could draw attention to these facts. He became mistrustful of new ideas even when his policies began to fail.

We were going to lose the war and this caused us much concern.
So finally we acted. At least this way, we could prepare for the future.
Our plan was to obtain an achievable amount of the gold that we had looted from all the conquered European countries and relocate it to a safe hiding place until we could regroup. Months later our spies in London informed us that the British were preparing to invade. As early as 1939 the Abwehr - Nazi Intelligence warned us that England could possibly enter the war against us and just as the British were amassing its troops, an opportunity presented itself to us.
That location would be right under the nose of Winston Churchill himself. The one man who had known from the very beginning the threat of the Third Reich. We enjoyed that fact. It would be the last place anyone would look.
No one really knew how much gold our regime had looted and amassed. It was approximated we stole over $500 million, equivalent to billions in today's worth. A lot of us knew it to be much more, because even today, some still remains unrecovered.
We planned a daring operation to secretly ship the gold to Britain in a reconfigured submersible and a crew of three. Evading Allied patrols, they made it without incident to the coast of England.
We had to eliminate the sub crew who had completed their part of the undertaking because we could not leave a trail. Nothing could be left to chance. Captain Huber and his men were only more collateral in this war.
Common knowledge now but one of Briton's many precautions before joining the war on Nazi Germany was to remove its national treasures from all their museums,

galleries, government buildings and royal residences and evacuate them to the remote country side of Wales for fear of repercussion bomb raids destroying the priceless collections. At one point there were rumours about them moving the irreplaceables to Canada but this idea was firmly rejected by Winston Churchill who said 'Bury them in caves or cellars, but not an antiquity shall leave this island.'
Thus the slate quarry at Manod, North Wales was requisitioned for the country's treasures.
Frenchy was one of the staff's truck team that made the journeys back and forth from Wales to London and he had access to the building. Since the outbreak of war, the opening hours were not consistent, the country was at war, resources and men were needed in more vital places. We took advantage of that.
During the night our men secretly built a small chamber to the existing foundations of the building under the guise of emergency reinforcements, should the bombs strike. With expert engineers in the team who were Frenchy's two men - Ludo and Adam, all was accomplished skilfully and safely so the foundations and stability of the building was not damaged or weakened and most crucially, the gold was concealed.
From Berlin, Germany to London, England we had successfully transported our consignment without mishap or discovery and straight into the lion's den. Quite a feat!
Then the outcome of the war which was so final. We never expected it to be so swiftly annihilating.
Many of us were hunted down, some took their own lives and it was becoming impossible to continue our plans, difficult to regroup.
Because of the Nuremberg Trials, many of us were apprehended. In the end, executed or imprisoned and yet

those that were captured and knew, never revealed the secret.
Towards the end, I eloped by placing myself into one of the concentration camps.
'Belzec' it was and with a fabricated history and a new name of Konrad Schroder-Kopf, I passed myself of as a German teacher that objected the Nazis. What you and everyone else were told.
I convinced myself it was the perfect cover. No one would believe a Nazi Officer would hide in such an awful place and there was a certain irony to it. I sent many people to their deaths in those camps and there I was consigning myself.
The lie had kept me alive though, even if it meant that I had had my own concentration camp experience.
The stench and wailing of those dying around me was horrifying and everywhere the crawling of lice. Epidemics and contagious diseases prevailed. Spotted Fever was the common disease rife in all the camps. It was easy to catch, even by the guards and for me, it led to meningitis which over the years had gradually destroyed my leg bones and joints.
That and the starving, the thirst and the humiliation I had to go through to survive the longer than expected weeks until Europe was liberated. I guess I got a taste of my own medicine and it was very bitter!
To this day, I refuse to believe it was some form of fate or punishment for the things I did and I refused to let the indignation wear away at me like the scourge in my limbs. I don't regret the decision to hide in the camps. It meant my freedom.
After all this time, it became easier on my conscious but the stigma of being a Nazi was viewed as depraved and yes, we did some terrible things in the euphoria of absolute power

but that is war! My belief was that I was still serving my fatherland and I did no wrong.

Of course they, the Nazi Hunters had their suspicions. Always suspected me but they could not find sufficient proof because many records were destroyed. Without the evidence, they could only act within the law. They were no fools though. While continually watching me over the years, the International Criminal Courts gradually put the pieces together.

This letter, it's a confession too, Jan considered. This is the most he has ever disclosed to me.

He lit a Corona Gorda Honduran cigar. His one and only vice that he allowed himself from time to time and it was the only cigar he would smoke. Its distinct aroma became wispy clouds as he continued to read the letter.

Can you not see that is why I sowed the seeds in you about National Socialism since you were a child?

I taught you of our constant struggle as a nation and what it was to be a German Nationalist. Your young mind soaked it up like an education and that's what it was. Just as it was for all of us when our Fuhrer spoke to us. He was our liberator that united us with his uplifting words, gave us back our identity and pride. Never before did anyone give us so much hope and determination to become our own nation once again after all the oppression. We believed and we followed.

All your achievements and honours you cannot deny that I have been a part of. I helped nurture you into the man and soldier you are today.

So this is where my inclinations came from. Jan again paused reading the letter.

He always believed it was his own freewill but he could not get away from this undeniable heritage. It wasn't all his own decision. He had always had the notion but to read it now in this letter only emphasised the truth.

Many years of hardened training, he had become a well drilled soldier. It was his one goal he focused on and finally earned it along with the respect and revere from his superiors and it was his blood and sweat that had progressed him up the ranks diligently, becoming a second lieutenant at a young twenty-six. Eventually eight years later attaining the rank Oberst: Colonel. Many of his superiors envisaged him as a future general. He was feared, respected, a wise head on a young body; the ingredients for a perfect leader. He was still his own self made man but he had to admit, he had been influenced and subconsciously steered into the military by the old man. That road had already been laid.

We are not completely defeated, they still whisper our names. The belief thrives in the hearts and minds of The Greater German Reich. We are not forgotten, we are a power still to be reckoned with and our enemies know this. They still respect our inherent potential because they are afraid. Why do you think they are still hunting us down so relentlessly after all this time?

We are not just phantoms in the history books. It is because they fear the 'Phonix aus der Asche.'

The insurrection will begin as the thousands of loyal soldiers of our country's army are waiting for the rallying cry, including thousands of wealthy, influential patriots from around the world that share the same ambition and ideology of the Fourth Reich, who have been patiently planning and building for this day.

You are a respected man and soldier with a political future too. In a sense, you... It was underlined in the letter .... *are the 'Phoenix Project!*

Get our gold back Jan. Resurrect the glory, for it is our time again.

This is our hour! Do it for us and our Fuhrer's legacy. Most of all do it for Germany, this generation, your generation and the destined German supremacy. The new fatherland.

I only wish I could be there to see it. To be able to share that moment and gaze upon the golden glow of our wealth and legacy and witness the dream finally realised.

Remember I told you at the wedding that 'The past is still present like a vengeful ghost.' Well that is true of Nazism too. We can be that vengeful ghost.

As one soldier to another soldier, 'kamerad viel glück!'

The scribble of his barely eligible signature ended the letter.

Jan sat back taking a few more puffs on his cigar, staring through the walls of his room, mulling over what he had just read.

A small part of him was beginning to believe those rumours could well have some truth to them. Was he a Nazi? Could there really be all that gold waiting to be discovered? Could this all be true?

I will do some research myself. Contact the names on the list, the old man gave me and the 'Phoenix Project' group too. Find out for sure.

Many questions still ran around in his head as he looked at the photographs again.

4

Present day.
If London were to have a capital of its own, it would have to be Trafalgar Square, where every day multitudes of tourists flocked here to this iconic landmark that was known the world over.
In the square's centre and surrounded by four giant black onyx lions, a column reached for the skies and atop stood the statue of Admiral Lord Horatio Nelson. Not at all interested in the throng masses below him milling about taking photograph after photograph, his gaze was directed southwards towards the Houses of Parliament and the River Thames.
The day was bright, clear but autumnal crisp and once the tourists had got their fill of countless snaps, they hurriedly and customarily pour into the Neoclassical Grade I listed building at the North of the square where internally the building's architects trendily echoed from edifices such as the Vatican, Victorian storehouses and ancient Egyptian temples.
The National Gallery welcomes over six million visitors a year to see the greatest accumulation of art in the world and was built in 1838 to house a growing collection that had amassed to approximately two and a half thousand paintings dating from mid-13th century to the 1900's. Overall the assemblage was encyclopaedic in scope with most major

European paintings from Giotto to Cezanne represented along with many other important works.

Concealed in a cramped maintenance shaft above a toilet cubicle in the men's public toilets were two men. After nearly two years worth of meticulous planning they were in.
Giving themselves enough time, they had entered the gallery separately as members of the public during opening hours. Both had worn baseball caps pulled down tightly on their slumped heads to avoid being recorded on the CCTV.
Advancing to the Portico toilets, they discreetly slipped into a vacant cubicle together when no other visitors would notice their odd behaviour.
'What happens if security finds us in here together?' One of them asked.
'Then we pretend we're lovers getting our kicks on.' The other joked.
Forty minutes before closing time, they noiselessly unscrewed the hatch above their heads - because the cubicles were totally enclosed when the doors were engaged, no one would see them working above their heads - and pulled themselves up into the maintenance shaft, the last man deftly releasing the cubicle lock with his foot and his partner quickly sliding the hatch closed after him.
'You didn't flush the chain.' The other quipped.
Now all they had to do was stay composed and remain undetected. The drawn out waiting game would be tedious.
A thin strip of light from the toilets below streamed in through the edges of the hatch panel, giving them enough light to partially illuminate their surroundings. Allowing for all the overhead pipes and cabling, the shaft area was only three feet high. With little space and restrictive manoeuvrability, the two of them could still without too

much discomfit, alternate lying flat on their stomachs or on their backs when they got restless being in the same position for too long. Considering the stifling heat and the lack of air conditioning, it was bearable but they would swelter in these stuffy and close confines. Anticipating this, some items of clothing had already been removed down in the cubicle earlier and packed away into their backpacks.

They began to settle down as best as they could, it would be awhile before they would vacate their hiding place.

From the initial stages it was decided that this would be the place to conceal themselves when the building was closed to the public. Here they could stay completely concealed, albeit somewhat uncomfortably for the three or four hours they needed.

Below them they heard the male public utilising the toilets, a hubbub of voices, slamming doors, paper dispensers tumbling, toilets flushing and hand dryers blasting.

'I could do with a smoke now. Doing nothing always makes me want to.' Joseph whispered.

'We just got here.'

'I know. I know…' was the reluctant reply.

'Keep chewing those gums.' Pawel encouraged.

'I am. It's all I can do.' He sighed.

Pawel Widzislaw and Joseph Poznan were both born in Poland in 1976 and brought up only ten miles, five months and eighteen days from each other in the towns of Wilda and Racot respectively. In another coincidence, they later discovered that they had even attended the same school in nearby Koscian but because of the five month difference in their ages, Joseph had missed the first term of enrolling so Pawel was always a year ahead. They would have almost certainly passed each other in school but in their own circle of friends they had been oblivious to each other.

It was years later when they both were on their way to London for work that they met for the first time, on the boat from France to Dover. They had alot in common apart from the obvious strangers in a strange land and so they swopped numbers, stayed in touch and became good friends over the eight years since. To this day, they were convinced that they were always meant to meet because of the coincidences.

Pawel had a blond crew cut and grey, greenish eyes. His face had always had an ashen pallor and all his features were slightly exaggerated in an appealing caricatured way. Years of working in inactive security roles had given him a scrawny body but he was not unfit. He did a lot of walking and running and at a short five foot six, he was still taller than his friend Joseph.

Joseph had black eyes under thick black eyebrows which met in the middle to form one long bushy line; it made him appear like he was constantly scowling. He had the typical shaven head that most young balding men had but it suited his stocky frame and short height, he was four inches shorter than Pawel and his skin had that red blotchiness that was usually associated with alcoholics but he never drank.

After many meaningless jobs, Pawel eventually found steady work in a gallery as night security and Joseph already a qualified electrician found plenty of work which also doubled as a way for him to check out potential properties in his other livelihood as a burglar.

Like most law-breaking opportunists, they were both hoping to retire sooner rather than later.

It was now getting humid and the drowsiness it caused was another obstacle that had to be overcome. It could easily send them to sleep and if anyone was certain to fall asleep it would be Joseph, Pawel smiled. He could sleep anywhere and through anything.

Pawel had only left the job six months ago and by then the plan was already in place. He had previously worked in this building for five years and then three years into his employment, he got an offer that was too good to turn down. He remembered the only two telephone conversations and the baritone English voice trying to pass itself off as Russian. It had introduced himself as Mr. Golyadkin and Pawel being an avid reader was sure that the name was from the Dostoyevsky's novel 'The Double.' It wouldn't be his real name of course but it did not stop Pawel from trying to imagine the man behind the voice. Perhaps some overweight Howard Hughes type character used to getting whatever he desired; a man who had more money than the world and filled his time with novel ways of spending it. Maybe he was one of those genuine and eccentric collectors of art and because certain pieces were unattainable, he would obtain it anyway he could.

'Do you not want an end to your mundane routine Mr. Widzislaw?' the put-on voice began.

'The day in, day out of just getting by and becoming more and more restless. Hoping foolishly for your numbers to come up in life's lottery and waiting for your life to really begin. Have you not thought this is that moment? You're one and only chance and to decline it now because you're not brave or smart enough to comprehend it? Only to realise it was this day that you would regret, this moment when it all remained the same, your directionless life unchanged and forever in bitter regret....' He certainly had an impelling way with words, '... and never forgetting this day, as the day you said 'No!' The day your dreams died. Everybody gets one unique chance and this is yours, Mr. Widzislaw. I can promise you a comfortable existence. Set you up for life. What I will pay you will be more than enough for your risks. Is it yes or is it no, Mr. Widzislaw?'

That was the moment, the crossroad in his life! The silence on the line was beckoning for an answer and the intimidating feeling of time stopped, underscored the importance of the choice.

His eventual reply led to the meeting of Mr. Golyadkin's associate Mr. Ipsen. A short roundish man, balding and with bespectacled eyes that watched you with the knowing of a condescending cat. The meeting took only twenty-five minutes with both Pawel and Joseph present - after persuading his best friend that this was an opportunity for both of them. Pawel knowing only too well, Joseph's other pursuits and expertise would come in handy.

Ipsen told them that they could not ask any questions, time enough when Mr. Golyadkin determines you have the job and they would have to answer all his questions honestly and promptly. His manner was polite and attentive like a doctor but his eyes interrogated calculably like a shrewd investor.

Mr. Golyadkin or Mr. G as Pawel and Joseph now referred him, called back for the second and final time, four days later.

'My associate Mr. Ipsen has verified you have an intention to do what I am asking of you and you are prepared to follow it through and that you both can be trusted. He believes and that makes me believe. Also, I'm impressed with Joseph's expertise and know I have come to the right men for the job. Regrettably we will never meet. I will not have the pleasure…' Pawel and Joseph knew that that was only civil business talk. They were paid to do a job and nothing more. '…. and this will be the last time we will speak to each other. Mr. Ipsen will still be contactable if you have any queries or problems but I trust all will go to plan and the only time you will be calling his number, is to say you have what I want in your possession. Do the job and you and I will be very contented people. Good luck Mr. Widzislaw.'

Later, Pawel would suspiciously mention to Joseph that it was as if Mr. G. already knew about both of them and Joseph's reply was, 'It's an unsaid word of mouth and not unusual to be approached like this in his game. There was still honour amongst thieves.' he had expressed.

The elation on getting the job was brief. The seriousness of what they were going to do sunk in. Now the hard work would begin.

'Just want to do this job. The more we wait, the more the doubt creeps in.'

'Patience, Joseph.' He whispered. 'You of all people must know that.'

'This is different. Usually I can be in and out very quickly. This is drawn out torture.'

He nudged him, 'Here...' and gave him three small packets from his shirt pocket. 'Gum! Thought you might run out?'

'You know me well.'

'Yes! When you can't smoke, you chew gum like a common prostitute. Plenty of it too!'

'Ha!' He said sarcastically. 'Always the Skaut!' It was Polish for Boy Scout.

'Someone has to keep this machine in motion.'

'I'm just as important.'

'I know, I know. That's why cogs need oiling too. Chew your gum.'

He smiled at that. Though he doubted Pawel noticed, it was mostly shadows up here.

A couple of hours passed and the restless yawns came more frequently.

Joseph felt like sleeping and all Pawel wanted to do was drink. It was the lack of oxygen and the humidity; effects of their confined quarters. They sipped water occasionally, wetting the dryness of their mouths. Too much and the toilets below would beckon.

At one point, Pawel was convinced there was a leaking pipe somewhere in the shaft with them. It grew louder and more irritating until he suddenly became aware what it was; the chewing motion of the gum in Joseph's mouth!

Maybe Joseph had the right idea, he nodded to himself. At least it was something to do. If you can't beat 'em, join 'em! He threw some into his mouth and tried to recall when he last tasted gum. The flavour gave him a gratifying recollection of those days back at school as a kid.

His fond reverie was interrupted by the announcement from the tannoy echoing throughout the building of the imminent closure. The Friday night late opening for the gallery was approaching the 21:00 shut down time. Soon they would hear the security staff as they inspected all the cubicles and cleared the toilets.

Friday night was rightfully considered the ideal time to do the job with the distractions of a lively and noisy start to the London weekend. The busyness of the gallery then on a Saturday could work in their favour.

The toilets below them were beginning to empty, the clamour was dying down.

The worst of the wait had passed. Yet they still had another hour or so before it would be safe to leave but at least it was bringing them closer to exiting their almost airless confines.

The anticipation began to win over the tedium.

Minutes later, a member of staff was heard yelling, 'Toilets closing shortly.'

By now their eyes were already adjusted to the darkness of the shaft and could make out more of themselves. Joseph could see Pawel's index finger against his lips and Pawel noticed Joseph nod his head in exaggerated acknowledgement.

They were fraught now, despite this being the easiest part of the operation. They were securely hidden and there was no reason that they would be discovered. The space above the cubicle would not be searched; it was never checked by the staff or even glanced up at. It was only ever used when maintenance work was required. There was nothing to give them away as long as they remained still and silent for the next twenty minutes while the building was slowly emptied and locked down.

5

Mr. Kaleem Kadel had arrived in the building and was getting into uniform. He was due to start the drudgery of the night shift over an hour ago but problems with a defective train had delayed him.

After twenty-two long years, there was nothing interesting about the job anymore and it was only his colleagues that made the routine passable. Every working day, he had carried himself through the motions and tried to not let the monotony get him down but despite the invariable grind, he was in good spirits tonight.

Changed into uniform, he left his locker room and strolled at an unhurried pace down the empty corridors. He never rushed no matter how late he was, it just was not worth the hassle – it always seemed to go against you and anyway, his sixty-one year old body wouldn't have any of it.

The staff area was deserted; all the daytime teams had already escaped the building and what staff there was at night, were all at their posts.

A mouse scuttled ahead of him and around the nearest corner.

The TV in the recreational room blared to vacant chairs. He turned it off.

It was always like this after closing time. The buzz and atmosphere of fellow workers had left and the place became like an empty station you saw in those post apocalyptic

science fiction films, seemingly abandoned and frozen in time.
Only a skeleton crew remained in the building and with so few in this desolate deployment – how he liked to term it - you could patrol around for hours and not see a colleague.
That thought reminded him, he had not done a radio check yet.
'Sierra three to Tango one, radio check please over.'
The radio crackled and a lethargic voice replied 'Receiving you loud and clear Sierra three. Glad to hear you finally turned up for the graveyard shift.'
He smiled at that and signed off with 'Got nothing better to do, Tango one. Out.'
Leaving the recreation area, he climbed a set of steps to a closed door. It needed a swipe from his security pass that was clipped to his waist band. All the doors from the main public floors that led to the staff areas had this system. It beeped and he passed through, the door swung shut resoundingly and securely behind him. They were specifically designed that way, to make certain they did close.
En route to the control room, he began his procedural checks of rooms, corridors, closets and doors.
Mr. Kadel was wondering if his colleague was up for another game of cards tonight. He was still beaming as he was when he went home yesterday morning at the end of the shift. Being eighty-six pounds flushed was almost equivalent to a nights pay. Gerard had lost badly and might want to win some of it; if not all, back tonight? He grinned greedily. Might even get some more out of him, if my luck continues.
Twenty minutes later his route was completed, all was secure to his satisfaction. He tried to recall when he last came across something amiss in his rounds and was sure it

was about seven years ago and that was only an unlocked cleaning cupboard. Nothing ever changed here, the checks were always done and all was as it should be. If there was complacency in the routine there was nothing to offset it.

Kaleem approached the Kenton control room.

The premises had numerous control rooms and as a precaution, if one became inoperable another could still oversee the security of the whole building. The feeds for all the cameras came through every location and all matters of security protocol were sent out from these workstations to departments within the building and also to the outside emergency services when needed.

He swiped open the control room door, where he expected to see his colleague slouched in his chair and goaded, 'Bonjour Gerard.'

'Au revoir Mr. Kadel.'

A gun with a silencer was pointed at his head and the muffled thudding flash was the last thing Kaleem Kadel ever saw and heard.

6

'Okay...,' He took a deep breath and slowly exhaled. '... let's do this partner.'

They carefully pulled the panel back and the blast of the cool air conditioned current hit them like the best feeling in the world. Together they revelled in it, relishing the chilled relief on their sweltering bodies.

Slowly they eased themselves down, one at a time. Dropping delicately into the cubicle and opening its door, they let themselves out into the airy toilet that was in darkness. Despite that, the spaciousness was a much welcome relief after being cooped up in the cramped and stuffy confines of the shaft for over three hours.

They began to limber up and stretch their stiff, sore muscles and limbs for ten minutes before opening their backpacks.

When working at the gallery, Pawel had been issued with two sets of night shift uniforms, one being the spare and he had hung onto these when he finally quit, knowing of course, he would be using them again.

They were now attired in each of the black and white uniform. The large mirrors on each side of the room reflected the whites of the walls, giving a little light to the men's room.

Pawel stifled a laugh and Joseph returned a look that told Pawel to be quiet. His uniform was smaller on him; he could barely do up the buttons on the straining shirt and there was no hope for the top button. The sleeves were an inch short from his wrists and he was constantly pulling the trousers down to no avail, they barely reached his ankles.

'Expecting a flood?' Pawel teased.

Joseph flipped him the finger.

Pawel still smirking, reassured Joseph that it was a minor detail that wouldn't be noticed.

They placed their civilian clothes back up into the shaft which was then pulled closed again. They would be returning here later, part of the plan was to conceal themselves in the shaft once again until opening time in the morning.

The empty backpack was flattened and concealed unnoticeably under Pawel's jumper but Joseph's backpack, with its essential contents, bulged a little. It looked like he had, without warning put some weight on.

With an affirmative nod and an encouraging wink from Pawel, they were as ready as they would ever be. They were now going to leave the safety of the lavatories and head out into jeopardy.

The main door of the toilets was easily unlocked with a copy of the universal building key; a key that was issued to certain personnel for everyday use and unlocked most doors. While Pawel still worked at the gallery, he had easily gotten a copy cut on a lunch break one day and no one was any the wiser. Where they planned to go, it was all they required. There was no need for a swipe which was just as well, as a master swipe would have been very difficult to obtain, if not impossible without arousing suspicion.

The gallery contained nearly three hundred surveillance cameras, sometimes up to ten in a room and many were placed strategically in all the halls, corridors, staircases and recreational areas. By being dressed in shift uniforms and Pawel knowing where certain clusters of cameras were placed, they hoped to avoid much exposure to the control room who would only suppose it was their staff doing their routine rounds.

The CCTV system could only have up to eight cameras on their monitoring screens at a time; there were just too many areas in the gallery. It would be a case of if the staff was paying much attention to those particular spots at that time and that was even if they had the rooms that they, the intruders were passing through on the monitors too. More often than not, they were complacent because there was never any reason to think an outsider was inside the gallery. There had not been an intruder in the building in fifty years! Why would it happen now, was the consensus when more modern and effective security arrangements were now in place? The management genuinely believed the gallery was impenetrable.

With Joseph taking up the rear, Pawel checked left and right down the toilet corridor. The white walls and reflective marble floor gave out a slight illumination in the darkness. No one was seen or heard but it did not ease their trepidation as they began to move forward.

Accustoming their footfalls gradually, they turned right past the empty cloakrooms on either side of them towards a line of black doors.

There were a number of factors Pawel had considered when he had to plan their route and Room 2 could have been unlocked by accessing it from the main staircase for a more straight forward route to their goal but that was too open for exposure. It was deemed too risky to attempt.

Ear to door, Pawel listened. Satisfied, he deftly unlocked one of the doors and they both entered into the Espresso area. He relocked the door behind them.

In the dark, spaces lose their depths, if he hadn't known better, the Espresso Bar seemed endless. It only added to their nervousness and that would only get more pronounced the further they progressed. Tables, chairs, and other fittings filled the area and Pawel cautiously raised his arms up and out in front of him for fear of bumping and tripping over any of these now hazardous obstacles. Even the aesthetic supporting pillars that dotted the space became a hindrance. But he had a fair idea where most hurdles were. He had memorised the place often enough for this stage.

Joseph had to keep touching his partner's back to make sure he was not wandering off. He was practically blind and Pawel was his guide.

Reaching the left hand wall of the area without incident, it became Pawel's course as he hand inched along the wall, guiding them down to the next set of doors.

By touch, he found the lock and slowly inserted the key and turned. Opening the door, they entered the small section of Room 13, where moonlight filtered through the skylight ceiling, irradiating the elevator to their left and the staircase on their right. They could now make out a little more of their surroundings and each other.

'Number thirteen eh!' Joseph made a mocking, frightened gesture with his hands and face.

'Superstitious nonsense!' Pawel rebuffed.

Technically on the gallery guide maps, this hallway did not have a name or number but for the buildings records it was numbered with the so called mythical numerals. Whether it was superstition that restrained the management from disclosing that fact was never really known but it certainly added to the mystique of the spot for visiting tourists.

The emptiness of the rooms seemed to enhance the slightest noise now and as Pawel unlocked and relocked the doors, he was continually conscious of this. The everyday clicks and clunks of the locks were now akin to giant lumbering machines. It was a subjective irrationality though only accentuated by his growing trepidation.

Up the narrow stone staircase they treaded, heads turned upwards on the ever constant lookout. Reaching the landing, they were now on the main gallery floor. Here the dark empty rooms lay out before them. Beckoning, eerily!

Looking left, the eastern most galleries aligned with the Barry Room's axis. Down there in the very end room, the painting of 'Stubbs's Horse' could usually be made out but now all was a blanket of black. Looking right to the west, the Sainsbury Wing omitted a faint inviting glow.

They were in the middle of the vista that ran down the whole length of the gallery. This was the Wilkins part of the building, the oldest and original before they eventually added to it with the extensions of more rooms over its long history. Its interior architecture was typical of the current styles of Victorian times; marbled pillars and skirting's, floors with slate margins, carpet like wallpaper, rich mahogany door cases and grand church like ceilings. It was opulent and grandiose and often the visiting public were more interested and awestruck by the architecture then the paintings themselves.

They turned right into Room 12.

Each room had a motion sensor fitted that would activate the dozens of lights that hung from suspended frames in the room's ceilings. Triggered by movement, they were also energy saving and when the building was empty of most of its staff and no night works were taking place, the sensors and lights would be turned off.

The real concern to them was whether they might meet a member of staff that may be doing routine patrols. Pawel dreaded the possibility that he'd bump into an old colleague, 'Hey Pawel, how are ya? What brings you back? You working again?' As if that person would absentmindedly ask.

'Yeah. Just here to finish the job.' The thought was absurd of course. The staff would undoubtedly know and he tried not to dwell on it.

It was nerve-wrenchingly quiet and the over-whelming feeling of unease gripped them.

So obviously different to when I used to do this for work, Pawel thought. Guess then I became used to it, never paid it much heed after awhile. But of course, it was directly because of what we're attempting to do now, that it's all the more stressful.

In Room 12, the only light came from the LED lights of the ever observing cameras, like piercing, probing alien eyes.

Sound travelled far and clamorously in these echoing and empty spaces. In some rooms, the wooden floorboards creaked and groaned ominously underneath them like booby traps. It felt like the loudest noise in the world that would give them away. However, it also meant they would be forewarned of any approaching staff footsteps and would have the chance to hide.

It helped too, that they wore the only thing which was not standard issue uniform. No heavy heeled shoes or boots but worn in black plimsolls. Their footfalls were almost silent.

As they progressed, they tried to appear as routine as possible in case they happened to show up on any cameras that may be monitored at that time. Trying to avoid erratic and hurried movements or loitering body language that would sure to arouse suspicion in the control room.

Room 11 was a smaller, circular room with three other exits. Moon light descended through its glass roof and lit up the black and white tiled floor like a game board. It made them feel exposed and self conscious. This was no game, Pawel thought, as they moved over the tiles like real life chess pieces and turned left into Room 5.

He was sure he heard Joseph mumbling to himself as they passed through each room, running off each room number with a perceptible sense of progress. He could sympathise, it helped Joseph to relieve the tension a little for himself.

The route had been planned out meticulously months ago and it involved a more circuitous course. What would straight forwardly of only taken half the time, they decided that this was the less difficult and unobserved path. Even while working here, Pawel was regularly making notes, continuously planning and running through all the eventualities. 'Fools don't rush in. This job is more about patience then anything else.' He often reminded himself.

'So far so good.' Pawel mouthed to Joseph who was like a shadow next to him.

He was an encouraging presence and a good man to have with you when you were up against things. His partner's laid back attitude made the enormity of their task a little less daunting and his experience as a burglar was to some degree reassuring.

As their eyes grew accustomed to the darkness, the portraits hanging in the rooms appeared to watch them as they moved past. Painted eyes that followed them, it almost felt that they were security staff as well. Staring and watching vigilantly. Joseph was almost convinced that the portraits would begin to shout, 'Guards, guards. Intruders in the rooms! Come quickly!'

'Giving me the creeps.' whispered Joseph.

They entered Room 6.

Suddenly Pawel froze, abruptly raising his arm out to stop a startled Joseph who bumped into it.

'What?' Joseph wanted to scream.

'Look.' He pointed.

Something on the floor scuttled into a corner of the room.

'A mouse!' He started to breath again. 'God! Thought you heard someone.'

The nocturnal creature was as frightened as them and scurried off again along the edges of the room before disappearing back the way it had come.

'The critter.'

Pawel knew only too well that the sighting of mice was a common occurrence in the gallery. Especially down in the basement of the staff area, the building was practically overrun with the vermin but because of the moment and his nerves, it got the better of him.

'You nearly gave me a heart attack.' Joseph was shaking his head at his partner in respite. He had an urge to push him over. Pawel grinned back sheepishly.

Approaching the next room, they slowed their pace a little.

All was so hushed.

The fact that they had remained undetected so far only emphasised the possible consequences.

The darkness from the room loomed, seeming to suck them in like a foreboding black hole where their future would unravel and end.

Joseph pushed a button on a device that he had taken out of his trouser pocket. It resembled a USB memory stick.

They looked up to observe the small pinpricks of light that appeared to float above them like tiny red stars. That was the confirmation they needed. For they checked each of the seven cameras had red and not the green LED light which normally showed on their units. These cameras should now be under their control. There was no way of knowing for sure of course, they simply trusted that the device did what it was supposed to do. It had been tested often enough.

The expensive piece of hardware would override all the cameras in that room, so the images back in the control rooms displayed an ordinarily empty room, as it was now. No different to when the rooms were usually vacant during closed hours. This was a continuously paused moment, a freeze frame with no live feedback, on a loop.

They would then be able to do their work without the control rooms being aware of them.

The only way security would know the cameras were inoperative, was if a patrol check was due and then they would discover more than disabled cameras.

Reasonably satisfied – he had had experience with this kind of security surveillance before, Joseph placed a hand on Pawel's shoulder, 'Let's go.' He confirmed.

They cautiously entered Room 8.

Being so close to culmination now, their anxieties were akin to hyperactive butterflies in a jar.

They had given themselves a short time slot of fifteen minutes and if all went to plan, forty minutes later they would again be hidden away back in the toilets and security would be none the wiser.

'Can we really get away with it?' Pawel remembered asking Joseph again and again.

'Good luck and bad luck always plays a part.' Joseph often reminded. 'Each and every step of the way, we are taking chances.'

He had been asking himself that question more and more since they got in the building.

7

It did not take long for the man to control the building with one round of bullets in a Sig 22 Mosquito Silencer Pistol.

The Gallery's night shift staff were now all dead. Except him of course! He was the inside man.

Gerard Dubuffe was forty-two and resembled a pro-wrestler. He was imposing and compact and had a face that was a constant sneer, his priggish nose only emphasised this. His eyes stood out like recondite black pearls and most of his head was shaven but for a blonde shoulder length ponytail that grew from the lower back of his head.

He had been a soldier in the French Army and had achieved the highest rank possible in the field with the army's Special Forces 'Spec Ops.' Diligently and honourably serving for twenty years until the army deemed him too old for the frontline. The high risk missions had become less and less and being promoted to a non-combative officer barking orders did not interest him whatsoever. He didn't want to retire from the fray, he had a fight in him still and so he pursued the action. He threw himself into many regular self imposed stints in the French Foreign Legion and went freelance, became a merc; a hired soldier. War was his way of life, and the danger and excitement that kept him going was all he ever needed.

He represented the French Far Right of tonight's outfit.

The eleven months he spent working and waiting in the gallery for this moment was the most torturous time of his life - torture would have been preferable. All so he could fulfil his role as the inside man. Having to put up with the banality of that routine and the morons he worked with nearly drove him insane.

But at last, his time had come.

He had started his shift three hours ago and checking the staff rota established who was due to end their shift, who would be carrying on and who was due in. He had his seven targets.

Approaching the designated time, he checked and rechecked his pistol and went through the plan in his head again and again. He had estimated twenty-five minutes to get to all the posts and eliminate those on duty. All except one were in their working positions and he - Kareem Kadel would be coming into the control room to take over.

Gerard took a beating from the Mauritian last night but it was not the money that had bothered him, it was the losing. Mr. Kadel was always going to be the first to die!

With his first victim dispatched, he began the sprint, leaving the Kenton control room.

As he eliminated each target, he also collected their work radios and any mobile phones that they owned, throwing them into a satchel that he had slung over his shoulder. It was another precautionary step of the plan. The radios of course would stop any internal contact and prevent the staff from warning each other. Also, one of the Colonel's rules was that no soldier could carry any mobiles of any kind. Not only did he not want them getting into the wrong hands but that no calls could be made to the outside world and cause any kind of distractions or interruptions to his men when they should be concentrating on the job at hand.

At one point during his run, where there should have been two members of staff manning that position, there was only one. His silencer demanded an immediate answer from his remaining co-worker, as to where the other was, while at the back of his mind, he had fretted how many more seconds this delay would add to his time. He took pleasure in seeing the vigour drain right out of his face as he gave his petrified reply. He shot him then and raced down the hallway.

His deceased colleagues all believed they were friends. In his eyes they were not even acquaintances, only lackeys.

The slight detour took him around the corner to find his missing target inside the staff toilets. He kicked opened the locked cubicle with ease and sitting on the toilet with her trousers and knickers down around her ankles, was the missing co-worker, playing with her mobile phone.

The look of absolute astonishment did not get a chance to change to horror as the bullet smashed into her head via the bridge of her nose. Splitting the glasses she wore completely in half.

Glancing at his watch, Gerard noticed he was behind in his schedule by about two minutes. Cursing, he sprinted off again. Faster.

He had no more setbacks after that. One by one, he clinically disposed of the rest of the shift staff and was now in the back gate office. He had checked his watch each time a kill was done, making sure he was still on track. He had wanted to complete it within the time he had set himself, relishing the challenge. The thrill of it had pumped his adrenaline levels to exhilarating bursts. Breathing profusely, he saw he had regained his original time and completed the task with over five minutes to spare. He had done it in just under twenty minutes.

While revelling in self satisfaction of his feat, the alarm on his watch began to bleep. The squad would be now approaching the building from the Haymarket backstreets, he turned the alarm off.

'Horaires d' ouverture!' Gerard triumphed.

He pushed a button on the console and the two massive doors of the back gate slowly rolled apart.

The road at the rear of the building was not a busy one, a one way street used primarily for the gallery's traffic. A few members of the public walking by had not paid much attention to the gate opening at this unusual time. If anyone had given it much thought, it would only appear as regular movement for a tradesman entrance, even at this late hour.

Two silent ambulances swiftly sped up the street and entered through the opened gate.

The public had paid no heed. Why should they? Gerard assumed, as he watched the monitors that the CCTV outside observed. He pressed the button to close the gate again.

Turning and manoeuvring with precision into the yard space, the ambulances then reversed up to the loading bay shutter. Even as the last vehicle turned off its engine, the back gate had closed. The huge two and a half feet thick steel bomb proof doors sealed shut and the numerous reinforced locks and bolts automatically slotted into place.

Satisfied, Gerard then pushed the button for the loading bay shutter to open.

Two dozen personnel poured out of the two ambulances. Stern and determined countenances lined their faces. They rolled out with them four black Aprilia SXV 125 motorbikes, two from each vehicle.

Gerard grinned at seeing the bikes. It was his idea to have 'Biker Raiders' - as he liked to term them - for this part of the operation. He had a love for bikes and knew these machines inside out. Light and fast with devised manoeuvrability and handling and fitted with muffled exhausts, they were perfect for moving around the wide open spaces of the gallery's rooms.

Most of the men assembling in the loading bay area were battle dressed and equipped like Special Ops government forces. Others were stripped down to the basics and more akin to guns for hire. On some members exposed limbs were adored various tattoos, including Far Right symbols and even the illegal Swastika. Utilities belts and assortments of weapons in slings, holsters or just tucked behind belts. Standard Israeli IMI Uzi's were issued to all. HK and various MP submachine guns, numerous Mausers, Sauers, Walther PPS pistols and a variety of Jerichhos, Berettas and Steyrs guns were on show. One member even had a SPAS-12 shotgun. Bowie and tactical bayonet knives were equipped too. Small black rectangular devices could also be seen clipped to their ears; these were two-way radios.

Backpacks, hold alls, large silver briefcases and even portable compressors were unloaded from the backs of the ambulances that contained all of the varied tools and equipment for the intricacies of the whole operation.

The majority of the men that had been recruited were Army Corps Engineers from different military backgrounds from around the world but with one thing in common; Far Right and Fascist beliefs. Specifically chosen men from their home grown National Parties; The Homeland Faithful German Youth and the Nationalist Front which was significantly active in England too. From the U.S.A; the National Socialist Order of America and its respected counterparts, the best that represented this cause were here. Even the illegal minorities of Neo-Nazis White Supremacists and the still thriving Ku Klutz Clan – though prohibited and in most places outlawed - all were growing measurably as they operated, recruited and organized underground activities. Fascism was far from defeated.

On the monitors, Gerard watched the last man to leave one of the ambulances.

This is who they were waiting for, the man in charge of this whole operation, Colonel Jan Lochner. To them he was the epitome of the perfect soldier. A leader and a fighter!

He was dressed in an opened wool tunic uniform jacket of blue-ish grey with decorative epaulets on the shoulders, black combat pants and his familiar trademark black German Army high length, steel cap boots. He looked enviably good for his age, Gerard had always admired. Though slimmer and leaner then himself there was no mistaking the strength and fitness of the man. Often his foes made the mistake and misjudged his capabilities to their cost and his demeanour evoked unease and panic into the minds of most. Gerard often joked with the Colonel that he was just that much better than him, only because he chose to command.

With a nod of the Colonel's head, the Biker Raider's engines roared into life, the glare of the headlamps momentarily blinding as they flashed on.

Initially they would double up on the bikes, to get as many men to their positions as quickly as possible. To get all the equipment to the designated locations while along the way, opening all the doors on the main gallery floor for uninterrupted access, as they roamed around the building. Also to take out any possible remaining staff that Gerard may have missed in his sweep, despite his insistence no one else would be left alive.

Those on foot began to utilise the loading bay elevator inside the building, to transport all the heavier equipment up onto the main floor. The rest dispersed to specific locations, carrying what they could. In all – including himself and the Colonel – they were a squad of twenty-four.

Despite the exhausts being fitted with mufflers, the combined noise of all the motorbikes setting off was a thundering rumble akin to the start of a speed race. The reverberations excited Gerard; to him it was very much like the machines of war starting their assault.

With the soldiers dispatched into the building, the Colonel quick turned and made his way over to his number two in the control room for an update and of course, the meet and greet. They had not seen each other since Gerard had infiltrated himself into the job. It had been months. To Gerard, it had felt like years.

He had met the renowned man on one of their other ventures in their associated fields and both had developed an immediate and admirable respect for each other. From what they had previously heard of each others exploits was proven on that day and that mission when French and German forces successfully combined to take out an al-Qaeda stronghold in Kahtaniya, Iraq.

The Colonel was already well known and respected throughout Europe and America and he had a reputation as a very capable leader and a cunning strategist of soldiers, who in turn admired him to the point of idolisation. After the first few days skirmishes, the Colonel had approached Gerard during meal time to simply say 'The man without fear,' slapping him on his back as he left. Later, with the mission completed and both of them about to go their separate ways, the Colonel had again approached him and said, 'You may be Gallic born but you have the 'geist' of a German,' laughing as he walked away.

Gerard was the Colonel's second in command that day and now, he was again. That set up had always suited him. He followed orders and executed them well, it took a certain kind of bastard to be a leader.

In the control room they met.

'Gerard.' The Colonel greeted him with esteem.

'Lochner.' He had always called him that.

They shook hands firmly, testing each others strength and grip. It was a ritual that they always played with each other, whenever they met.

The Colonel looked around the control room; barely acknowledging the dead body of a member of a staff in the rear of the room. His eyes passed over the various TV monitors. 'Any problems?' he asked.

'None whatsoever. All staff eliminated and no alarms raised. The building is ours.' He answered matter of factly.

The Colonel had complete reliance in Gerard's abilities. There were no shortcomings with this soldier; the man had never failed an order.

All was going as planned and he was satisfied.

'You certainly did your time for this mission.'

'Time!' Gerard exclaimed. 'Merdé, it was a sentence!'

The Colonel nodded his head empathically. 'I'll have to give you a medal.'

'Pah!' he scoffed. 'Give me some action.'

'That will come. I guarantee it.'

He reached into his jacket and pulled out a Corona Gorda Honduran.

'Good work Gerard…' and throws him the cigar. 'Take a break.'

Catching it, Gerard said 'Ah! One of your cigars. I'm privileged.' He nodded appreciatively. 'I'll smoke this Lochner but I'm still on duty.'

As the Colonel began to walk out, he comradely slapped Gerard on his back, smiling at the characteristic reply, 'See you later, kamerad.'

Gerard smiled; his famous teeth sparkled like porcelain. He lit the cigar, propped his feet up on the console and blew smoke satisfactorily at the screens.

'Viel glück.' He called back to the departing Colonel.

8

It was a room fitting for the splendour of the Renaissance and a truly remarkable collection all on its own. Various iconic works of art from Michaelangelo and Bronzino decorated the walls and now they both stood before their goal; Raffaello Sanzio - more famously known as Raphael and his masterpiece 'Madonna of the Pinks.'
Its condition was still as excellent as the day it was first painted with its exquisite lines, distinctions of light, dark and its vibrant colours. Acquired in 2004 with the help of a public appeal, it was valued at an estimated £40 million then. Joseph speculated on what the public would say now, that they were going to steal it. On today's market, it could be worth double. At least!
It still had its controversy, a painting that influenced countless fabrications. Completed in 1507, it would go on to be his most renowned work. Some of the art establishment had denounced it as a fake throughout the years but the Gallery's experts insisted that this painting could not be a forgery. State of the art infrared reflectography revealed detailed drawings of what was characteristic of Raphael's sketching style and its near perfect condition of oil on yew was untouched. Nevertheless something so renowned for its grandness, people were often surprised at its humble size. Perfect for this operation.
Had Mr. Golyadkin, who was prepared to pay a lot of money to steal it, realised that? Did the size influence his decision?

Probably not, Pawel thought but it was a sought after piece that the gallery wouldn't sell for all the money in the world and what Mr. G wanted, he was sure Mr. G got.

Pawel pulled out two pairs of latex gloves. Handing a pair to Joseph, they pulled them on like surgeons readying for an operation. He then took out a penlight torch and turning it on, he gave his partner light to perform his work. Joseph would do most of the precision handling, as he had the electrician's expert hands and the burglar's deft fingers.

Joseph stepped over the roped barrier that ran around the room; a foot and a half above the floor and two and a half feet from the wall.

The painting was alarmed, as were all of the pieces in the gallery and from his pocket, Joseph took out a tiny protective plastic case which contained what looked like a mobile phone sim card. It was in fact a signal jammer, which once placed on the wall close to the painting, would locate the security microchip situated on the back of the painting's frame.

Wireless alarm systems which were common in most buildings worked via radio signals, which were vulnerable to interference through jammers. This alarm was not only used to alert removal but also motion detection. By overriding the alarm's security code and disabling the system, it would then run through a set of permutations and eventually find the alert codes and cleverly supersede them. Subsequently replacing it with its own set of digits and more importantly invalidating the alarm. It was a little similar to nullifying your own alarm system at home when it accidently malfunctioned and rings for no reason. So advanced was this minute piece of technology that at most it would only take ten minutes to locate the code. It could only be used once because of its immense capabilities; the capacity of a hundred PC's and a battery life that could only sustain so much of its advanced abilities before it expelled all of its power.

Removing a strip covering on the back of the device, it exposed a light gluey substance. Joseph pressed it onto the wall next to the frame, where it would remain fixed until it could then be easily removed afterwards.

It had put them back twenty-five thousand pounds this piece of hardware, a considerable amount of money for something that looked like a minuscule piece of plastic. The camera-immobiliser cost another eight thousand pounds and all these expenses were their investment, including all the other necessary equipment and tools for the job. All Mr. G had provided was the contacts for the illegal black-market gadgets and a verbal agreement to pay for the job on delivery of the painting.

It would be a genuine act of intention demanded by their employer, if they could prove they were serious about this plan and prepared to put their own money up front. Pawel and Joseph were using most of their own combined savings as stake and if successful, their return would be millions.

'More waiting.' Pawel was apprehensive as they both watched the rapidly changing digits on the device's small screen.

His hand that held the penlight was shaking. The illuminating beam moving erratically and Joseph noticing this, did not say a word. He understood the anxiety.

Never once did they mention to each other what would happen if they did get caught. It seemed there was an unspoken rule between them not to talk about it and if by doing so, it would jinx everything they had worked so hard for.

The impending sense of ill-fate that something could still go wrong after all this time was becoming tangible. The odds screamed at them, telling them that their good fortune up until now would only last for so long.

Joseph had a compelling urge to whistle to see if the room's silence would echo their predictable existence. It was a need to just do something that would make him feel all was not quite out of their control. That he could break up the unease which was taking hold and virtually suffocating his optimism.

Creeping over him like the onset of a fever, Pawel broke out in a cold sweat that was characteristic of him whenever he was put in an uncomfortable circumstance. Why do we do this to ourselves? He criticized.

He also heard Joseph's often said words again and again in his mind, prompting and apprising him about luck and circumstance and how…..

There was a beep.

They looked at each other expectantly.

Joseph checked his watch. It had taken under seven minutes.

Now the moment of truth, Pawel contemplated. Are we going to end up in prison, locked up for a very long time or will we be able to live comfortably for the rest of our lives?

From the backpack, Pawel took out a roll of bubble wrap and unrolled it on the floor. He also retrieved a mini cordless rechargeable screw driver and drill and two specific drill pieces.

The screws which hinged the painting's frame to the wall had heads that had been deliberately filed down to flush with the wall. There were no grooves and so making the removal of those screws much more difficult, another deterrent to any opportunists during opening hours.

The whirr of the drill was almost soundless as Joseph painstakingly worked it into each of the screw heads and satisfied with the motion, began to create small grooves into each.
All Pawel could do was watch and wait. Admire his friend's adeptness and efficiency as he worked quickly, as if it were an everyday job for him.
Then he thought he heard something.
He put a finger to his lips and Joseph noticing this, paused.
They eyed each other alarmingly, seeing the concern in each other's faces.
After an agonising long few minutes, nothing was heard but the beating of their own frenzied hearts.
'What was it?' Joseph asked quietly.
'Not sure. Distant. Maybe from outside.' Pawel whispered back. Often noises from outside had a tendency to gravitate into the building, especially during the late and early hours. He experienced it often when he had previously worked the night shift. Then again it could well be the old building itself.
Joseph raised the drill, looking at Pawel for confirmation to continue. He nodded and Joseph resumed his work. The muted whirring began once again.
Pawel was beginning to think he imagined the sound and put it down to his nerves.
The drill stopped again shortly afterwards and Joseph began to delicately blow away the excess shavings out of the newly formed grooves. Satisfied, he then changed the drill piece for a screw driver head and rotating the direction of the drill, he began to slowly unscrew the screws which hinged the painting's frame to the wall. With each soft purr of the drill, each screw was turned loose which in turn, Pawel caught and deposited into his pockets. Nothing would be left

behind. No immediate clues when the painting was eventually discovered missing.

With the penlight now being held in his mouth and still illuminating the area, Pawel held the frame with both hands for fear of the painting dropping, as each hinge loosened from his partner's labouring.

With Joseph finished unscrewing, he placed the drill back into his backpack and then joined Pawel in gripping and holding onto the frame on both sides and together they pulled. Gently at first and then with a little more jerking, it came off its brackets with a brittle sticky sound, exposing a pale surface on the untouched wall where it had been hanging for many years.

Early antique frames were made and produced with hand-carved, intricate and embellished inlays, sometimes as exquisite and adored as the paintings themselves. This particular frame was not the original but it was still over a hundred years old. The poplar wood was splitting in a few places; its edges worn and darkened, yet it still gave the frame a distinctive old worldly feel with its lacklustre golden stain like varnish. Some said it was a deliberate effect, so as not to draw your attention away from the beauty of the painting itself.

For added protection, a sheet of glass sat between canvas and frame and because of its moderate size, Pawel and Joseph deemed it was best that the painting should remain in the frame, so as not to waste precious time taking it apart. It would fit securely into the spare backpack which Pawel took out from underneath his jumper. It had been carefully chosen and measured months ago.

Throughout all of the operation, not a word was said between them. There was a mutual and respected silence as they both executed their practised tasks. Leading right up to the day before, they had put in hundreds of hours of rehearsals and run-throughs to get all aspects of the robbery as natural to them as an everyday chore. They still had two minutes remaining of the allocated fifteen minutes they had given themselves.

In spite of that, they were unsure if they were successful. But no alarms blared and there was no stampede of rushing feet or urgent commotion. Not yet anyway!

They quickly gathered their tools, placing them back into the backpack. Once again, both backpacks would be concealed under their stretched and baggy jumpers. Joseph would carry the equipment and Pawel, the painting.

Joseph also remembered to pull the signal jammer and now defunct chip from the wall. He also gathered most of the screw shavings on the floor, discarding them into the backpack and blowing, scattering the remainder as far and apart as he could.

He was so in tuned, Pawel admired. He had forgotten about the smaller details of the shavings.

As a rule, if a painting was not in its room and place at any given time, a simple notification card was inserted with the information plaque, informing the public that the painting had gone to conservation for examination or cleaning. It was not uncommon for this to happen, much to the chagrin of visitors to the gallery, eager on seeing a favourite painting, only to find it had been removed. Even most members of the daytime staff wouldn't look twice at the empty space. They were used to vacant spaces on the walls and seeing these cards frequently. They would be none the wiser.

Again it was something Pawel was able to easily get hold of before ending his employment with the gallery and he had already filled in the white card with a tick in the

'Examinations' box. He placed it with the information plaque.

Pawel had considered how long it would be before it was discovered, that the card was not telling the truth. It was this, they were counting on. Would it really be before opening time? He didn't think so. It could possibly be hours or even the afternoon. They were hoping for any luck they could get. With the prized possession in their hands, the two men were ready and eager to head back to their clandestine hole. To retread their earlier route back to the public toilets and remain there until opening time the following morning. Only then did they have the opportunity to escape when the gallery was re-opened on the busiest day of the week.

Their trepidation was growing even more, now that they had the painting in their hands. So close and yet so far to go, Pawel bemoaned to himself.

Joseph groaned, 'More waiting to endure.' He agitated about going into hiding again. He never had to steal stuff like this before. He would usually be in, out and gone before the dust settled. It was this part of the job that made him nervous. He just wanted to run with their loot.

Pawel was just as fidgety and he did not want to worry his friend anymore with his doubts too. He took some comfort in knowing that their hiding place would offer them some reprieve from their perturbations until the next morning. In there, they could at least relax a little.

'In a few days time brother, there will be no more waiting ever again. People will wait on you.' Pawel quietly reassured with a squeeze on his friend's shoulder. It was said as much for himself as well as for Joseph.

Once more, they gave the area a check over. Making sure that nothing was left behind or out of place.

Outside of the room, Joseph reached into his trouser pocket and pushed the button on the camera-immobiliser. Looking back up into Room 8, he saw the red LED lights up in the ceiling change back to green. Their trust in the gadget had paid off. As far as they were concerned, it had worked. No one had come to apprehend them.

Feeling somewhat upbeat, they began to make their way back to their original hideaway.

As they passed through Room 6, they began to hear a distant buzzing noise. An odd, out of place sound, not at all associated with the building.

Pawel had never heard anything like it while he worked here.

Joseph whispered, 'Alarm?' He could not shake the feeling that they had been discovered.

Pawel shook his head firmly, 'No.' He knew what that would sound like!

It grew louder, getting nearer and nearer more rapidly. Fear inducing it became; a monstrous reverberating sound coming through the empty tomb like rooms.

Before they could even decide what to do, it was upon them. Its origin revealed. A speeding motorbike exploded into the room!

Not only was the din of the bike's engine a terror-stricken assault on the ears after the silence but the light from the bike's headlamp blinded them, stinging their nocturnal eyes. It lit up the room with a discharge of bright intensity. Both the light and noise was like a bomb to their senses.

The rider braked; its rubber tyres squealing unpleasantly on the wooden floors as the bike turned in an arc.

They were frozen from this aberration. It just did not seem real. They tried to comprehend; a motorbike in the gallery's rooms!

Their heads turned as it moved past them and then something flashed. The rider had raised his left arm and in his hand was a gun.

There was something shocking about the bright patch on the front of the rider's black helmet that Pawel fleetingly glimpsed before the Uzi gun flashed again, its staccato heard this time above the riotous bike engine. Before he could register what it was, the bullets felled the two men.

The biker burned rubber again turning 360°. Its headlamp strobing around the room's walls, highlighting the paintings briefly – they appeared to observe the scene like a hall of pious ghosts.

As the biker headed back the way it came, it left circular skid marks that tarred the polished wooden floorboards.

Once again he let off a volley of gunfire to the fallen men, spitting up splinters around them.

The phantom biker braked sharply in the next room to eject an empty Uzi cartridge and it clattered to the floor. He reloaded with another fresh clip from his lower combat trouser pocket while peering through his helmet's black visor back into Room 6.

The bodies were not moving.

Satisfied, the biker yelled to the room, 'Dead. Woooo!' he let out a victorious yell. 'Did anyone see-ee that move? Yaaa!'

He revved the bike's noisy engine again and again, a statement of his exhilaration. Smug with himself, he sped off.

9

In the lights and glare of a bustling Friday night, the exterior façade of the building was lit up magnificently and stately. People went about their evening entertainment and were completely unaware that the world famous National Gallery in Trafalgar Square was now under the control of a group of uninvited militarists.

Since leaving his second in command - Gerard in the control room, the Colonel and his two soldiers had taken a reconnaissance around the external rear of the gallery within its premises. He was biding a little time while his team got to their positions and completed individual tasks throughout the building. Strolling up and down, his two men followed behind, alert like presidential bodyguards. They were his lieutenants and expert backup. If anything did happen to him, they could at least continue the mission. Not that he needed protecting, he could look after himself but he also conceded that the 'Phoenix Project' had too much to lose to completely rely on him. His lieutenants had their orders too. They were watching him as much as they were watching out for him.

Smoking his favourite cigar, he was in a reflective mood. This is it! We have been waiting in a sense over 60 years for this. The chains of events set in motion at the end of the Second World War have finally come into play and this site, the gallery itself that represented the resilience of the

Londoners during the war and the Blitz would represent 'aufstands.' The insurgency!

He had visited this iconic landmark back in his twenties, at a time when both his country and Britain were still establishing relations long after the war. Unknown to him at the time that beneath his feet and this building would be something that would bring him back here in the future to fulfil his destiny, as the old man had melodramatically put it in his letter.

Hitler himself had loved fine art and wherever his Army subjugated, European paintings became part of the haul of money and gold as well. He had even planned his dream museum to house all the stolen art. Ironic, considering where we were now!

Here, right in the capital would be the start of a new Europe, a new reign. Maybe even this building itself which had come to represent so much since the war ended could become their base of operations.

They reached the end of the passageway at a doorway he needed to get through and aptly timed, he heard the synchronized sound that would echo all over the building. The swipe units on all doors beeped.

'Efficient.' Jan remarked, nodding approvingly at his two lieutenants.

His radio then crackled in his ears.

'Phoenix Four to Phoenix One....'

'Go ahead.' He replied.

'Swipe system all go.'

'Can see. Good timing Phoenix Four.'

'Thank you sir. Phoenix Four out.'

The main switch for the swipe system had been turned off by one of his men who had made it to one of the control rooms. It was simply a matter of pushing one button. No codes or computer passwords had been needed. The plans were moving along much more briskly than even he could have wanted. He was impressed with the timings of his men and their efficiency, testament to their overall talents.

No doubt the next stage was already underway; to have all the doorways, gates and shutters that would normally be used, locked in place – most already were at this time of the night. Particular entrances and exits would be barred and blocked, deliberately damaged or destroyed, simply made impassable. In some places, booby traps were even rigged. No one would get in or out and if attempts were made, it would cost them their lives.

Internal CCTV was immobilized, there would be no record of them and their identities because once the authorities had got back into the building, the camera footage would undoubtedly be scrutinised. External CCTV they kept running, it was crucial that they could monitor what was happening outside the building.

Every specific of the plan was working and he did not anticipate any complications. If they transpired, he would deal with them there and then. He was not inexperienced to know that the unexpected could arise no matter how much meticulous planning was made. You had to be prepared for the unforeseen. Many contingencies had been drilled and rehearsed into each one of his men. Including himself!

Jan and his two lieutenants passed through the now unlocked swipe door into a corridor where all the relevant offices and departments worked from.

The lights came on at that point, illuminating the briefly darkened corridors. They had not been triggered by the sensors as they usually were but again, one of his men had located the office which controlled all of the building's lighting. The system was a universal one used by many premises and properties and easily navigated if you knew the system. This soldier had done his homework. In specific rooms, hallways and corridors around the gallery, lights were now flickering on and illuminating up their planned routes in areas that they would utilise.

Satisfied, Jan spoke into his radio headpiece, 'Phoenix Five, this is Phoenix One. You have given us light.'

'Phoenix Five received.' came the reply.

All areas that were essential were now lit up and unlocked for easy access and manoeuvrability apart from the most secure areas which still required a master key.

All but one bunch of keys were found in the two control rooms. The one remaining set of keys belonged to the Head of Security and it was here, outside this office that Jan and his lieutenants had arrived.

10

William 'Will' Booker was having his first cigarette of the day.
Normally he wouldn't smoke at work - it was his way of cutting down but today he was past his clocking off time and he craved one now. He had been waiting to finish work and start his long weekend ever since he got out of bed this morning.
He had started his shift at eight and should have been home by now but his boss had asked him to stay on for a few more hours until a few late comers had made it in for their shifts.
Fourteen hours so far and he was yearning and yawning to go home. He didn't mind staying on a little longer; a bit of easy overtime and he would be off then for four days. He was looking forward to it and his body was already starting to wind down.
He was going to give it another hour.
He was excited about his plans for his time off and it would begin with collecting a very special package. A new piece of equipment that would improve his home made dairy product; a cheese vat agitator and frame used for the separation of milk into solid curds and liquid whey. Being able to produce his own was an immensely satisfying hobby and he had plans for an orange and apple flavoured cheese which he was sure was an untried novelty. He loved the creamy, strong textures and flavours that melted in your mouth, there was nothing like in the world. Yet people have

often been put off by cheese's unpalatability, saying it gave off pungent, smelly and mouldy odours. He couldn't understand that. For him, it was pure delight!

All he wanted to do now was go home and make cheese.

His eyes were a marine green and his mixture of winsome black and grey tousled, shoulder length hair and shaggy beard was a reflection of his letting go since his days of regulations and duty - scissors and blade had become almost redundant. He was what he always called himself; an average guy with average looks and average height. No one special, just an average Joe.

He was an ex-serviceman and one of the fortunate few to have had many uneventful tours. Fortunately, he never had to kill any of the enemy and he was proud of that fact. When the Gulf War ended, he saw it as an opportunity to get out, rather then be called up for another one. He knew his luck would run out sooner or later and he did not want to end up as another fatal statistic for a country that was fighting the wrong wars. It was not what he joined the Army for and he had become disillusioned by it all. That was 22 years, 1 month and 29 days ago. You don't forget things like that.

The normality of everyday jobs that followed, all involved security work and mainly at night, which he preferred. When there were fewer personalities to put up with. Many people would be surprised at this inclination because he came across easy going and affable but he opted for his own company to anyone else's most of the time.

This present job which he had been at for the last five months was simple and unstressed and the hours suited him perfectly. He had no complaints; anything else was a doddle after years on the frontline.

He was happily divorced and it had been 20 years, 5 months and 16 days ago. You don't forget things like that and it was the best thing that ever happened to him. He had been married to a woman who was a teenager in mind; scatty and unimaginably naïve but boy, was she a looker. It was the only thing that attracted him to her in the first place. He was a young and cocksure soldier and the whirlwind romance and marriage was just a blindless whim, lasting only two more years after he quit the Army. By then they were already bored of each other, nothing in common other then the marriage certificate.

As he finished his rollup, he reminisced at where life had got him so far. They were not always his choices but things still turned out okay. He often supposed; they were blessings in disguises.

Back to work, he told himself. He took the staircase down to re-enter the building and went to swipe but noticed the light on the unit. 'That's not right.'

Stepping through the unlocked door and firmly closing it after him, the swipe system remained green. He tried swiping again and again, opening and closing the door but nothing changed. It remained unsecure.

Still puzzled, he radioed the control room.

There was no reply.

He called three more times and knew that that was enough. Something was up.

He was about to head back outside and upstairs to the smoker's yard when he heard a crash from the kitchen area further down the corridor. Curious, he set off in that direction.

Approaching the kitchen, he stiffened at what sounded like storage closets being opened, contents spilled and doors being slammed.

Cautiously peering around the doorway, he was unnerved to see splashes of red on the floor. Further scrutiny and he could see the body of one of his colleagues flat out on his back, unmoving on the floor in a pool of blood.

He didn't like the fact that his heart started to beat rapidly.

Someone wandered into view - his back to Will and stuffing his face with food.

He didn't recognize him. He was no member of staff.

The man's apparel was of a soldier. He knew one when he saw one, he had seen enough in his time as an ex-service man. There was nothing distinguishing about the uniform but there was the familiar black attire of a bullet proof vest jacket with straps, belts and pockets of equipment on him, bulking his already considerable physique out formidably. A packed holster and the handle of a combat knife protruded from a sheath strapped to his leg and he noticed a Uzi sub-machine gun resting on the kitchen counter.

For some reason, the man suddenly turned around and spotting Will, he scrambled for his weapon on the counter.

Will lunged for him instinctively, had no choice. His background experience taught him that; act before you have to react!

Bending over forwardly, head first; he aimed for the man's chest. Ramming into him, the momentum carried the soldier backwards as Will's arms came up, pushing him further back. With his head in the man's stomach and his legs and feet pushing from the floor, it gave him the extra push.

Will only stopped when the goon smashed into the back wall, his head smacking against the concrete with a loud crack. The soldier slumped to the floor unconsciously, his Uzi clattering beside him.

He was staring down at the man in stupefaction - some food caked the corners of his mouth - while trying to control his rapidly thumping heart.

He heard distance voices approaching.

The noise of the scuffle had alerted two more soldiers. As they entered the kitchen, they promptly took in the scene and him. They were dressed similarly to the first guy and immediately went for their guns.

Will ducked down hastily behind the kitchen work top as the whizzing of bullets from both the goon's guns punctured the metallic walling behind him in zinging pops.

He could hear them as they began to manoeuvre around the work tops, trying to surround him by taking separate ends of the counter. The work top was a free standing unit without any backing, it meant items stored beneath and on its shelves were open on each side for equipment and stocks to be placed and pulled.

Furtively shuffling his way along the tiled floor, Will moved towards one end of the counter and through the openings underneath, he could see the legs of one of the soldiers edging his way around.

When the soldier was exactly opposite to him and utilising one of the metal containers on the shelf, Will shoved it violently, slamming it into the knees of the soldier. He yelled as its sharp edges impacted his knee caps, bending him over in pain.

Will instantly reached up and over the counter top to the other side and grabbing the hunched over and groaning goon's head with both hands; he pulled it down onto the surface of the counter in a smashing blow. The man slumped to the floor apparently knocked out, his nose a bleeding mush as Will quickly ducked down again for cover.

He was in the others soldier's gun sight and a blaze of bullets trailed the table top, running off the edge where Will could feel the heat of them rush above his head. He was convinced that they had singed his hair.

The soldier was keeping a distance as he fired another wasted round overhead where Will cowered.

'Hey! Why are you shooting at me?' Will shouted and then ever so silently shuffled along.

The reply was another deadly Uzi blast where Will had just moved from. The goon had fell for it!

Will was looking for another distraction or weapon that the counter shelves could offer.

Pots, pans, plastic and metal containers were then hurled over into the soldier's direction when Will then spotted the nose of an Uzi on the floor. It must have belonged to one of the unconscious goons.

Clearing the space and while still hurling kitchen equipment, he snatched it. He then slid along the tiled floor and popping his head up, he saw his only chance as the goon had lowered his weapon to fend off the barrage of objects thrown his way.

Will stood up, 'Drop the gun.' He beseeched. Adding a 'Please.'

The soldier raised his weapon and Will yelled 'No!' as he unleashed a round.

The impact of the bullets slammed into the man's chest, hurtling and crashing him through the second set of closed kitchen doors and out into the hallway where he smashed to a stop against its wall. Smears of blood trailed his body as it slid down the wall. He then slumped and sat with his head on his chest.

Will shook his head ruefully, 'I did say please.'

He tossed the gun away feeling appalled.

The actualisation that he had killed someone began to make him feel lightheaded and he had to lean on the counter as waves of nausea overwhelmed him. He felt hideous!

I go through three tours without having to kill a single enemy and all of a sudden from out of nowhere, this goon turns up. Had no choice! It was him or me.
He licked his lips, his mouth was unusually dry.
He went to the sink and began running cold water and drank thirstily. Splashing water on his face, he vomited.
Rinsing his mouth out, he brooded. I've travelled thousands of miles to a foreign country prepared to kill and nothing. Come home to leave that godforsaken business all behind and this happens. It's all screwed up! We all had the training on how to deal with it when it happened and now here at work, as far away from all the horrors of war, I'm beginning to know what it feels like.
He stood leaning over the sink, continuing to spit out the foul taste in his mouth and letting the cold water drip off his ashen face.
'I should be at home making cheese.' He said to himself.
He stared numbly at the vague shadow he cast in the dirty sink.

11

Jan was taking no chances, not that he thought he had to. Like any trained soldier, it was the precautions you always adhered to.

The profile he had received of the Head of Security was that he was a man with not a lot of responsibilities, regardless of his title. Gerard had informed him, that the Head was only a face people could associate with when the shit hit the fan, someone who could take the blame and who better then someone who couldn't care less. He had other people that dealt with the predicaments and decisions that came with the job.

The door to the office may or may not be locked but Jan wanted the element of surprise, an assaultive upper hand that would immediately put the fear into the mind of the man.

He pulled out his very own weapon, an unusual metallic brown coloured HK USP Match and fired two shots into the lock and kicked the door open.

Classical music blared from a radio in the corner of a small, antiqued furnished room.

A man and a woman were stood together in an embrace. Their groping hands froze and their heads turned in startlement.

The volume of the music must have blocked out any outside noise, so blaring was it. No wonder they were unaware as to what was happening in the rest of the building. In their tryst, they were totally oblivious.

Jan turned the sound off with another bullet from his HK Match and the wireless blasted into a thousand pieces.

The man looked aghast at his radio and oddly then screamed 'Get out!' as if Jan was a member of staff that had not knocked first.

Jan smirked at the absurdity of the reaction. Did this man not realise what was happening here?

The room felt crowded. His two imposing lieutenants stood either side of him, weapons ready as their eyes scrutinised the surroundings. One had a token SPAS-12 shotgun.

'Look at what we've found burning the midnight oil. It's the National Gallery's Head of Security, Malcolm Jameson Powell. With a play thing too,' referring to the young lady in a partially undressed state.

The two lieutenants grinned at each other perversely.

Jan waved his gun at her irritably, 'Get dressed. But not you Powell.' The gun was now pointed at him and his face looked like he had just swallowed something that he disagreed with.

Jan was going to use this to his advantage. Leaving Powell with his trousers around his ankles would keep him feeling vulnerable.

'Call this work? Hope you don't expect to get paid for this nocturnal activity Malcolm. It won't be overtime this playtime?'

It was obvious the Head of Security was trying to get his lecherous way with the woman.

'Are you not aware Mr. Powell that the domicile you are in charge of, is under attack?'

He did not seem to appear embarrassed by being caught in flagrante; in fact, he came across completely blasé.

He looked like he had been painted by Hogarth. He had uncombed short grey curling hair with a balding circle on the top of his head. His round face gave a constant impression of distress but that was far from the truth, it was just plain impudence. He wore small round unfashionable spectacles and his eyes were a watery grey. He was always attired in the most awful jumpers that he wore over even more garishly coloured ties. Unfitting to his role, it did nothing for his respect from others. There was always something said for appearances!

Powell had left the Police Force after thirty years, disappointed that he had not reached the rank of Inspector. Even with his family's wealth and political influence, he still got no further then being a pen pusher in Operational Supports.

'Why isn't my son a sergeant by now?' His Ex-Barrister father demanded from the Chief Superintendent, at the time when Powell frequently bemoaned the fact he was not getting any promotions.

The Chief replied matter of factually that his son's 'Pompous and holier then thou attitude was not suitable for leadership in the force. His position now, behind a desk, is the most any of us can bloody well put up with.'

So in his early fifties, he applied for the extremely well paid role of Head of Security at the National Gallery and with the embellishment of a family friend who knew someone who knew someone, landed the most undemanding job in the world.

He was still behaving as if someone had interrupted one of his meetings. 'What's going on here? Powell hollered annoyingly. 'What do you want?'

The profile of this man fitted perfectly, Jan could plainly see that. Obnoxious and demanding.

'We are here to collect something we deposited in this building many years ago.' Jan taunted, 'Were you not informed Mr. Powell?'
Puzzlement and annoyance confused his face. 'I don't understand? A painting?'
'Nooo! Nothing as trivial as that.'
'Who are you?' He was becoming nervous. 'How did you get into the building?'
'I got in because you have no staff on duty.'
'Impossible!' he blathered uneasily.
Was it true? He began to fret. Had they gotten control of the gallery? The fact that these men were here seemed to validate that. But his stubbornness refused to believe it.
Jan continued, 'And while I am here, I'd thought I'd pass by and pay you, the Head of Security, a social visit.'
The woman now dressed, edged away to the side of the room. Her eyes were big and frightened. This young and very attractive woman should not be here, Jan regarded. It could be very unfortunate for her.
The two soldiers continued to eye her lasciviously.
'Why?' Powell shuffled about uncomfortably.
Jan pointed a long finger at him.
'Me?' he feebly answered. 'Why me?'
As soon as he said it, he knew the answer and his face drained of all colour.
There could be only one reason why he needed me, the only real responsibility that I ever had to consider. The rest of my obligations, I never cared about and this was something I very rarely thought of despite being warned from the very beginning of this employment. There had always been the slightest possibility that it could occur and he was beginning to feel sick in his stomach now as he was convinced, that this was it. Why did it have to happen on my watch?

Especially too, as I was just about to get my end away with my secretary after all this time. For months the urges and advances had built up and to be denied the satisfaction and release now was not fair. Ruined by these soldiers. Why me dammit! He felt utterly disappointed and terrified.

Jan mocked, 'You look like a child who has had all his candy taken away from him.'

His two lieutenants simpered at the remark.

Powell started to say something when Jan interrupted, 'Your words will make no difference to what will now take place.' He glared him down meaningfully.

Powell felt like a schoolboy in the Headmaster's Office.

'Now, you are the Head of Security and you have the means to get me in to the vault. Please……' He took a step towards him, 'Or I will start putting some bullets in your cute play thing.' He waved his gun casually in her direction.

Despite this threat on her safety, the secretary did not appear any more alarmed. If anything, her look was now a measured concern.

She stood tall at just under six feet; her figure was slender in a knee length black skirt with long shapely black stocking legs. She wore a white pleated blouse unbuttoned slightly that revealed a glimpse of a generous cleavage in her red bra underneath. Her skin was olive toned and her lustrous black tumbling curls of hair fell beyond her shoulders. On her attractive angular face sensuous lips were highlighted in bold cherry and her hazelnut eyes were a little larger then normal, giving them an innocent quality and a school girl naivety.

Powell reacted the only way he knew how and forthwith portrayed his pathetic and feeble colours. 'Shoot her. I don't care.'

'You bastard!' She screamed and lunging for the desk, she picked up a glass paperweight. Intending to throw it at him, one of the soldiers stepped forward, grabbed her arm and shook it forcibly until the paperweight dropped out of her hand onto the carpeted floor.

'At first I wondered what this woman saw in you Powell, but I now see her motives…' Jan gave her what seemed an esteemed smile. '…Why can you not? In your line of work, you should have more foresight.'

'That's right.' She spat. 'I've been using you to further my career. My body for favours. All the attention and gifts, they were just perks of the job. I put up with your feeble attempts at foreplay and it was all pathetic! You are a terrible excuse of a man and a self centred arsehole.'

The two soldiers briefly tensed, fingering the triggers on their weapons at this unexpected outburst. Jan was moved at this unexpected side to her. She had bite!

'Been wanting to tell you those things since day one, you stuck up prat!' She continued fervidly.

He had to take control of the situation now, it was becoming a domestic. He decided to put a bullet in Powell's leg instead.

Screaming, Powell managed to stumble into a chair despite the encumbrance of still having his trousers around his ankles. Blood could be seen spreading out through his hands that clutched the wound in his right thigh. His shocked eyes filled with some tears and his bottom lip began to tremble.

He could quite easily of shot the secretary but Jan couldn't be sure it would provoke Powell to comply, but because this woman showed more 'gehänge' then Powell, he changed his mind. It was not an act of pity or submission. He knew there and then, he had Powell and the pretty lady need not suffer for his cowardice.

The two lieutenants, who had not once uttered a single word, stared down at Powell unsympathetically. His secretary showed no pity whatsoever.

'Now, Powell. Is your petty job and feisty lady, who clearly has more balls then you have spunk, really worth it?'

Begging now, he pleaded, 'Please don't kill me. I'll show you. Please. Please let me go after…'

'Now you see.' Jan exclaimed vigorously. 'Why do they always want the violence before they co-operate? Never doubt a man with a gun……' He turned his HK Match in hands, emphasizing as he gazed down at it. '…He has it for a reason, you know!'

12

'Nothing!' He said to himself as he put the phone back on the wall.

He had tried half a dozen different numbers and locations throughout the building and not one of them answered. They only rang more and more eerily.

He left the turmoil of the kitchen then, where all he smelt was the cordite of blood and even now, he could taste it in his mouth. It lingered unpleasantly.

Making his way down the empty corridors towards the Group Office and ever mindful of any other goons that might be lurking about, he was trying to understand what the hell was happening. Was it terrorists? Was that possible? He remembered a memo that was circulated years ago, reminding all staff that the building was on alert. The ongoing threat since 9/11 had never ceased.

These men were equipped and behaved like soldiers, that was obvious but what were they doing in an art gallery? Were they really here to steal paintings? And if it were terrorists, what was their motive? It was not some simple political protest; they were armed and seemed too organised for that. There were many groups and factions that all had different agendas these days and they came in their dozens with their holier than thou causes.

In the Group Office, he tried various internal numbers but still they rang and rang and when he attempted to get an outside connection to the police, there was no dial tone, it was disconnected. Figures, he sighed. It was at times like these that a mobile phone was indispensible. The one he had was sitting at home in his drawer like the rest of his clutter. Very rarely used it. It was given to him as a present and he spent more time charging the bloody thing then using it.

The thought gave him an idea and it would not be pleasant.

He briskly walked back to the kitchen and anticipating the overwhelming smell and sight of blood again, he approached his dead colleague's body. It was a repulsive mess. Blood was still oozing from the body and it seemed to permeate everything.

Poor Larry! Will mourned. This should never have happened for just doing his job.

With as little handling and turning of his colleague's body as possible, Will could not find his co-worker's mobile phone. He knew he had one, he was always on it.

Larry's vacant face stared up at him and Will actually asked him 'Where is your phone Larry…?' He looked up at the soldiers that he had fought with earlier and said, 'With them?'

He searched their pockets and found that they were without phones too. Well there goes that idea, he conceded.

Turning his back on the bodies, he was at a loss at what to do next and then all of a sudden, he made up his mind.

He walked back down to the fire exit door that he had passed through earlier, heading for the rear of the building. There would be someone on duty there and he had convinced himself that they had locked themselves in when the trouble had started. If the phone lines were still down, then he could at least find out from his colleagues what was going on via the security cameras.

One more time, he checked the swipe system, it still glowed green and he vainly tried the radio again. Silent.

Back outside in the crisp air which was welcome after the stench of blood, guts and vomit, he was taking two steps at a time up the outside staircase to ground level and the smoker's yard.

As he reached the top, a volley of bullets exploded around him like firecrackers.

He ducked back in panic and stumbled backwards down the concrete staircase. Twisting and turning awkwardly but somehow remaining upright on his feet until the bottom of the staircase where he finally lost his balance and landed on his bum. Unscathed.

'More of 'em,' he groaned as he picked himself up, rubbing his sore backside.

He couldn't believe how he tumbled down the stone steps without breaking a bone or two. More crucially, lucky that none of the bullets had caught him.

He brushed himself down and seeing no goon at the top of the staircase about to shoot him, he cautiously crept back up. Surveying the area above him as it all slowly came into view, he peeked over the low concrete parapet that bordered one side of the staircase.

Another barrage of bullets came screeching and ricocheting off the metal railing above him.

Ducking, then immediately popping his head up, he was able to spot where the attack was coming from. He saw the man up in the gangway that ran around the top of the external part of the building, just below the roof level.

He took a few steps back down for cover and contemplated his next move.

Top of the stairs to Will's right was an arch he needed to get through to continue but he was hemmed in. He was reluctant to take a running chance with this trigger happy goon. He'd put bullets in my back before I'd reach the arch. Cut me down!

Once again, he was back downstairs in the staff area. From here, there were a few more ways to get back up to ground level and bypass the smoker's yard but after twenty minutes, he found there wasn't. All the routes that led to the rear area were blocked; even the adjacent arch to the left had a route down that was cut off from below. He was frustrated by these barricades he could not pass. He couldn't understand how they were obstructed despite the electronic locks of the swipes showing green. His bunch of keys did not open all the doors and the ones that should, their locks had been jammed and this puzzled him.

Then he thought of something.

He went back to the kitchen and picked up one of the soldiers' guns. He was hoping that it might give him some cover, which would enable him to get through the arch.

He was now back where he had started on the staircase and the goon was still up there, as another round of bullets erupted above his head. Ducking down for cover again, he remarked to himself that this goon was certainly watching this space!

Taking a few deep breaths, Will grudgingly readied himself, making sure the Uzi was loaded and ready to fire. Old habits die hard, he muttered to himself.

Lifting the weapon above his head and over the concrete parapet cover, Will let off a round in the direction of the goon up in the rafters and then sprinted to the top of the staircase.

He was completely taken by surprise as Will intended. The soldier did not expect him to be armed and had to dodge to avoid the volley of bullets. Yet he recovered quickly to let loose a round from his Uzi.

The bullets dogged behind Will's running feet, spitting up the concrete ground and with his body still turned around and trying to keep his covering fire on the soldier, he panicked and slipped.

His arc of fire dropped beneath the rafters, bullets chewing a downward line into the brickwork of the building and then struck an open crate containing cylinders. Measuring at 5ft, they stood stored and chained together in one corner of the yard. Six of these high pressured gas cylinders contained propane which were used by the maintenance and scientific departments and had been left here temporarily.

The result was explosive. The bullets had punctured the metal casings of one, its gas contents ignited and the eruption which followed was deafening.

The fireball shot upwards and through the overhead rafters, catching and burning the unfortunate soldier. He fell with a horrible scream and crashed through the glass roof of the smoker's shelter and onto the concrete ground.

The charred and smoking body was dead.

As the black smoke cleared, Will picked himself up from the ground.

Debris had rained all over the area and the yard looked like a bomb had hit it. Glass, metal, wood and plastic littered the place. The gas bottles were torn apart, their still searing edges twisted and curled like macabre fingers. Most of the windows of the surrounding offices had been blown out too.

He knew he had gotten off lightly. His distance had saved him from the worst. The blast had thrown him to the ground; his raw and grated hands had taken his weight. Though his jumper and shirt on his back smoked a little, they had protected him from the searing heat of the explosion.

He kicked away the Uzi he had used in disgust. 'Just can't seem to avoid death now.' He said sullenly. 'Killing is my new profession!'

Further up the arch corridor and around the corner, he heard the sound of running steps approaching. That explosion was certain to attract attention. More goons no doubt!

Will quickly side stepped up against the left side of the arch wall as the sound of boots came closer. He was desperately thinking of what he could actually do.

Another person came into view, slowed down and surveyed the scene of destruction, unaware of Will behind him, flattening himself against the wall.

The soldier was a few feet in front of him and slightly to the left and Will decided he couldn't take any chances, he would be discovered before long. His ex-military experience kicked in. Even now after all this time away from battle, you don't forget things like that and instinctively he acted.

He lunged forward and catching the soldier on his right shoulder side, pushed him.

The man was about to radio in but was caught completely by surprise and flung sideways. Lifting a few feet off the ground, he propelled down the staircase that Will had used earlier. Tumbling down the concrete steps like a drunk, his limbs and body twisted uncontrollably, unavailing trying to grab anything that would stop his fall. The Uzi on its strap cluttered on each roll until the soldier hit the bottom, curled up, upside down and tangled against the corner wall.

Will stood at the top of the staircase looking down, watching the goon closely. He was groaning in frustration and pain, staring up at Will with angry eyes. He was trying to reach his Uzi that was caught up behind his back.

Will knew this soldier would eventually get his weapon free and once again his old instincts took over. He bounded down the staircase.

He did not know if the goon had broken any bones or whether he could walk after a fall like that but Will could not take any chances. The man would continue to hound him until he was dead.

With a foot on the man's chest, Will was able to pull the weapon out from behind the goon's back and over his head. He also pulled a Bowie knife from the sheath strapped to the soldier's leg and proceeded to cut the Uzi's strap into four lengths.

Still pushing down on his chest but now with his forceful knee, Will began to tie the goon's hands together with the make shift rope and then tie the other end to a pipe that ran down the wall behind him. The man tussled at each tight knot and growled at Will as he finished tying his feet together.

He pulled off the radio ear piece and crushed it beneath his other heel and also repeatedly stamped upon the Uzi until it was unusable. The knife he dropped into a drain.

He checked the goon for a mobile phone too but again, none. No one had a mobile, Will exasperated and he was now certain that these soldiers must have taken them from the staff and that they themselves were not allowed to carry them. It did not surprise him. This evidently was a military operation taking place in the building and experience backed this surmise because the army always insisted no soldier possessed a mobile, it was standard protocol on any mission.

Whether it was the goon's persistent struggling and cursing or the insanity of the entire night's situation but something got to him and with a wave of anger welling up inside him, Will punched the man a cracking blow to the face.

It knocked the soldier unconscious.
'Shut up!' Will sneered.

13

He groaned inwardly, gritting his teeth.
He was not sure how long he was unconscious but he was alive. The pain was testament to that. His low left side torso was searing and his upper right hip ached. It brought back the memory of what had occurred and it was real.
Pawel felt groggy and his head a little stuporous. He felt like he had just woken from an operation.
He recalled a gradually germinating noise that sounded like some growling advancing beast and blinding lights that stung his eyes which had been so accustomed to the darkness.
It seemed like a dream; a motorbike tearing through the gallery rooms and then the astonishment at the blast of a gun.
He lay there for awhile, eyes open and trying not to move or make a sound despite the agony. He was conscious the assailant may still be around; even though he was sure the room was empty. It was behind him and the doorway into the other room that he couldn't see. He didn't dare move just yet, but listened out while feigning death.
It was only then he noticed that the lights in the room were now on. His eyeline peered into the neighbouring room and down through Rooms 6 to 2 as well. Someone had turned them on, perhaps all of the rooms. Why?

And then he recalled Joseph. He was annoyed with himself that he hadn't remembered sooner and could only put it down to shock.

Turning his head, he saw there was no assassin lurking about and his eyes darted over to where his partner lay and noticed he wasn't moving.

'Joseph.' he whispered desperately.

Nothing!

He called again quietly and still there was no response.

A dread took hold and he refused to believe the worst. He had to move and attend to his friend. He slowly rolled over to his side, grimacing with agonizing pain and pulled himself up to a sitting position. The room was clear but his head began to spin.

He had to be restrained despite his urgency to examine Joseph. He needed to check himself.

He had burn marks to his jumper on his inside right. Lifting it, he scrutinized the backpack on his front and realized he had been lucky to fall onto his back. Probably instinctive that, he concluded. Don't think the paintings damaged but pressing problems first.

The burns had passed through his shirt too. Examining his flesh, he found two scorched marks on his skin. There was also a tear to the clothing of his upper trouser leg with dried blood stains and pulling aside the rip, saw a fingernail sized piece of flesh had been lacerated, the bleeding had stopped. With a mixture of relief and pain, he was still more concerned with Joseph.

He dragged himself over the floor to his partner, wincing with every move.

His friend was lying in a pool of blood; there was alot of it and the smell was nauseating.

A line of bullet holes were clearly visible through his clothing. Blood was still moist around the edges where the bullets had entered into Joseph's chest and neck.
He checked Joseph's pulse longer then necessary. Nothing.
'Oh Jezu!' His partner was not as lucky as him.
It felt like a vacuum was engulfing him, hollowing out his heart like the empty feeling that was at the pit of his stomach. He resisted the urge to vomit.
He was paralysed and remained crouched over his friend's inert body. His trembling hand rested on Joseph's head and he wanted to cry but no tears came.
Any thoughts of deliberation were absent at present.
Pawel closed Joseph's vacant eyes that still stared out at the last person he ever saw - the man that had murdered him. He wondered what the last thought going through Joseph's mind was at that final moment. Despair? Consternation? Because it happened so quickly, Joseph's 'devil may care' attitude was probably too laid back to comprehend. He was most likely asking himself when he could have his next smoke.
A sudden surge of realisation that he was alone overwhelmed him. He felt guilty for the emotion. Yet despite this loss, a fundamental part of him told himself, he had to focus. Fight the numbness that could overwhelm him and prevent him from moving on. He had to remain alert. Alive!
He had to turn away then, not at all being comfortable about leaving his friend like this. Time enough to grieve later, he rued. Now was not the time or place.
He made a sign of the cross and said a silent prayer.
Never thought this would happen. The worst was, we wasted our lives locked up in prison.
He painfully stood up, flinching from his wounds that were now being moved and stretched.

The weight in the backpack tugged at him. It felt like a burden now, a wasteful encumbrance.

To have overcome the security and alarms and finally possess the painting, didn't feel so euphoric now. The accomplishment was a tragic failure.

He half-heartingly ran his fingers over the material, checking for any damage. The painting seemed in one piece. For an agonisingly long moment, he seriously considered leaving the painting behind. Give up and turn himself in yet the resignation and grief pulled at him contradictorily because Joseph's death would have been for nothing. Joe would have said that. Could hear him, telling him to continue, giving him the kick he needed. 'You got it now Pawel, see how far you can take it. Finish the job!'

He hurriedly tended to the wound in his thigh by tearing off a piece of his shirt and tying a tourniquet for it. The grazes would be okay for now.

His deliberations returned to that moment. What the hell was that all about? A gunman on a motorbike running amok! He still couldn't quite comprehend it! Were there more? Have we got other burglars in the building? It was all questions and he just couldn't understand it. Of all the nights! He continued to shake his head.

It reminded him of what Joseph had said about good and bad luck possibly occurring in many stages of the plan. Joseph was so right and the bad cost him.

Where the hell is security? He angrily asked himself. Or was that the new security protocol in place already?' He stupidly joked. Armed staff on motorbikes with machine guns!

It wasn't funny and he quickly dismissed it. Disgruntled with himself and his inappropriate notions. My friend has been coldly murdered without any kind of warning or a chance to surrender. How gutless was that?

He couldn't even call the police. How would he explain their unauthorized presence in the gallery? Anyway, they had chosen not to bring mobiles into the job.

The urgent feeling now was to get the hell out of here, that the biker could come back.

What can I remember of him? It happened so quickly. A guy on a bike with a helmet on, the visor down. He was all in black like Death himself personified on a steel horse.

Then he recalled something painted on his helmet. Couldn't quite recollect what is was but something white on black. It was the only other dissimilarity in all that ebony.

If the biker is a burglar, there's no way that he could run around this place on his own? Where was the existing night staff? Should they have not already raised the alarms by now? What the hell was going on?

He heard the ominous bikes clamour, distant, far off somewhere and fear propelled him.

Get out of here! He silently yelled.

He had no other choice but to head back, retrace their earlier path. Stick to the original plan and try to avoid that biker until he got to the toilets. At least if he got back to safety, to their previous hideout, he could think things through a lot clearer and then decide what to do.

He gave a final rueful look at the body of his ex-partner. With a heavy heart, he whispered, 'Do Widzenia Joseph.'

Then he heard a faint voice coming from the direction of Rooms 8 and 9.

He froze with apprehension.

Then again the same voice, clearer this time. 'Yes. Affirmative. Ready and standing by.'

14

They were both Americans and built like lumberjacks. Their muscular and tanned arms were on rippling show and their attire was khaki t-shirts, combats pants, as well as the usual array of weapons hanging off them. One of them was slapping a crow bar into his palm again and again, the other wore a weather beaten 'Indiana State Fair' cap.

As part of a six man team - the demolition crew as they were designated - it was their responsibility to rig explosives in various points around the building and make exits and entries impassable. The majority of doorways were put out of use by the bending and breaking of levers and locks. Vandalising them beyond use; the crow bar made easy work of this. The other measure was having some of the more important and crucial exits and entrances that led out of the premises, booby trapped with explosives.

Their part completed, the two yanks were now here to relieve Gerard. To take his place and remain at the back gate. Guarding it throughout the remainder of the operation should any problems arise?

They filled the control room like two huge bears. They rarely spoke, even to each other but seemed to understand each other with grunts and smirks. They had been inseparable ever since they met in the first brief for this mission. Latched onto each other like school chums and were never seen apart. The nickname going around the ranks for them was the 'Yankee Tweedledum and Tweedledee.'

'Destroy those radios and phones.' Gerard pointed to the satchel that was left on the control panel, 'Nothing working. Understand?'
They nodded in synch and looking into the satchel, they grunted at each other, nonplussed with the French man's haul.
He was glad to leave the stuffy, putrid confines of the back gate control room. The smell of the dead body was already becoming overbearing and it was beginning to make him feel nauseous.
'I'd advise you to get rid of that body somewhere. Leave open the windows and doors too.' He told the two men.
They both turned their heads to see the body and together they turned their noses up at it.

He stayed outside for awhile, taking in some fresh air and trying to clear his head.
Needing to urinate and out of sight of the men in the control room, he relieved himself behind an ambulance. It was when zipping up his fly; he heard a sound around the corner. It was probably nothing but it had to be checked.
Earlier, a bang was heard in the direction of the smoker's yard and over the radio one of them had said he would check it out. Like many of them no doubt had thought, had the next stage of the operation already started earlier then expected? It was not that surprising considering their efficiency.
Turning the corner, he looked down the walkway that would turn again and lead to the smoker's yard and saw nothing out of place. A line of bins lined one side and he wondered whether it was the mice that usually foraged around here that had caused the noise.
Dismissing it and about to continue on, he heard the sound again. A dull clang but it now came from above him. On his

left, his eyes were drawn to the emergency staircase that ran from ground level to the roof on the exterior of the building. He spotted movement near the top through the silver mesh that made up the design of the metal spiral staircase.

No one was meant to be up there, not even a member of their team.

So he unhooked his weapon and began firing.

15

His back to the wall, he had been contemplating where he could possibly try next to get to the Sainsbury Wing.
The huge black security gates were closed, as they would be at this time of the night and his hope of finding other members of staff at the rear control room had been dashed, as he had spotted two strangers through the large windows of the security office. They had been sitting with their booted feet propped up on the control panel counter and appeared to be in a jovial debate, paying no attention to the monitors at all. These goons were more casually dressed then the other soldiers but were much bigger men; almost behemoths and no less dangerous, no doubt. After the last encounter, he was much more wary.
He had wondered if more of these men had gotten as far as the Sainsbury Wing and where was the staff? What has happened to my colleagues? Receiving no replies on the radio had not been encouraging. He imagined them tied and locked up in some room until these terrorists - if that was what they were - got what they wanted? A part of him had a horrible notion that they may all have been murdered. The ruthlessness of the earlier soldiers he encountered, led him to partly suspect that and he tried to shake the conviction.
Two ambulances were parked in the loading bay which he thought was odd. Their rear doors were open and inside he could just make out that they were empty. Much of the usual equipment that should be in the back of an ambulance was

missing, these had been stripped out. He theorised whether they would be filling them up soon with the gallery's valuable paintings? Or was it the thought of what they had taken out of them that worried him? Nevertheless, he was convinced these ambulances were part of some ruse.

There were two other possible ways back into the building from this area. One was a standard door that would lead to the Scientific Department – even if it wasn't barred or obstructed like so many others he had come across, he didn't have the key on his bunch to unlock it. It made no difference anyway because from where he stood, he could discern the device fixed to the door and realised with loathing that it was explosives. It unnerved him!

His earlier instincts about not persisting too much with the pushing and pulling of trying to get these obstructive exits open, had saved him. If anyone inside had tried to escape the building and opened that door, they would be blown to kingdom come. Once again his previous army experience and intuition had kept him alive. You don't forget things like that, he reminded himself yet again.

It was becoming more and more dangerous by the moment. What were these crazy goons up to?

The other way into the building was via the loading bay, the corridors through there gave many options to proceed but that hope was short-lived as he spotted someone walking out from inside. Tucking himself against the wall and out of sight, he watched the soldier. He seemed to be patrolling and guarding this area.

'How many more of them were there?' he speculated. 'They're probably swarming all over the place.'

That route too, would be risky to attempt and anyway, it was also in the eye line of the goons in the back gate office. Bound to be sighted!

So here he was around the corner in an area between the back gate and the smoker's yard, looking up at a fire escape staircase.

'Up and over...?' Will proposed to himself.

He began climbing the fire escape staircase as quietly as he could, 'Where there's a Will, there's a way.'

He was almost begging to fate that these terrorists had not barricaded the roof doors. He guessed it was unlikely and believed his chances were good. From there, he would be able to use his set of keys that would give him access back down to the second floor, by bypassing through the skylight corridors above the rooms and then down the staff staircase to the Sainsbury's Wing control room.

Approaching the last steps at the top of the metal staircase, the silence was torn asunder by a screeching blast. Instantly, he started sprinting up the remaining steps.

With a few feet to go and his boots clanging with his ascent, he didn't dare look down, just kept going.

Ricochets sparks of bullets whirled alarmingly close. He was convinced he could feel the searing heat of them until he finally made it to the rooftop and its cover unharmed.

Catching his breath and remarking that that's all he had been doing of late, he took a guarded peek over the roof edge. There on the ground, in the dark, he could make out another goon.

Will quickly pulled his head back as the soldier let off another volley, its weapon spitting in a lethal shower of lightening flashes.

Heart beating frantically, he knew he had to get to that exit point on the other side of the roof.

He then heard the clanging of pursuing movement on the staircase below him. He did not wait any longer.

He willed the access he was heading for to be passable, otherwise he was trapped and exposed up here on the roof of the National Gallery.

The London night was lucid. Stars were making a rare appearance through the usual smog filled sky and the weather was dry and crisp. The bustle of an energetic West End played out its Friday evening and its infinite neon coloured bulbs twinkled like a haphazard trail of Christmas lights. He could hear the hubbub of the square below, just as busy as it always was with crowds of tourists and weekenders. Often he quipped that Trafalgar Square was the capital of the world. Everybody from all parts of the globe came here, day and night.

Whenever he was up here on the odd stint, he always felt like he was on top of the world looking down upon this great city spread out all around him. He relished the space and the wind on his face. Each time he had found it exhilarating but there was no time to enjoy it now.

As he traversed across the criss-cross gangways of pipes and cabling and the vast array of generators, he was convinced he could lose his pursuer. He had the advantage of knowing his way around, the goon would not.

Reaching the hut like structure that housed the maintenance ladder down into the building, Will was able to unlock the door with his keys.

'Yes!' He silently yelled to himself and as he entered, he took a quick glance back. To his relief, he noticed the goon had not reached the roof yet.

Inside, he closed the door and relocked it.

Resting his back against it, he let out another long and exhaustive sigh.

Been doing a lot of those too, Will murmured.

16

Adjacent to the Sainsbury Wing was the neighbouring Human Resources' St. Vincent's house and situated in this building's lowest level, the uncompromising Colonel, his taciturn lieutenants, the injured and insufferable Malcolm James Powell and the hostage secretary, all stood before the immense grey vault doors.

It had been an aching and difficult walk for Powell along the one hundred and twenty metre underground tunnel that secretly connected both buildings. His gun shot wound had been partially bandaged up with a torn piece of his own unfashionable jumper to stem the bleeding but it did nothing for the pain that was shooting up and down his leg.

The Colonel had promised him that as soon as he gave him access to the vault, he would get medical treatment. Powell agonised miserably, he did not know how long he could hold out for.

The Colonel looked down on him with annoyance, like he was a piece of dirt stuck to his boot and after Powell's cowardly outburst earlier, what little respect he had for the man was now non-existent. If he hadn't needed the spineless worm, he would have put him out of his and their misery there and then, with a bullet to the head. No one would miss him!

The Colonel's soldiers had still not said a word and the woman was very conscious of their sidelong glances at her body, as they encouraged Powell on with pushes and prods from their weapons. Even from behind, she felt their continuing gawps. She could deal with that, men always ogled her and she did not at all feel threatened. If anything, she was going to let them continue, it could be to her advantage later. Her name at present was Hannah Ellis.

It was not common knowledge that the gallery had a vault and even less was known of what it actually contained. Of course, it had its rumours; some had suggested that it housed the very first gallery guard's uniform from the 1830's. Others even believed the real Crown Jewels resided down here and the ones on display in the Tower of London were only replicas. Still whatever rarities were locked up inside, it was only accessible to a few members of the highest clearance security staff.

Surrounded by hundreds of tonnes of reinforced concrete, its 3ft deep walls, ceiling and floors were also embedded with 4inch steel wire mesh and its heavy duty 5ft steel doors were formidably imposing. It was fire, flood, bomb and earthquake proof.

They all stared at it as if it was some alien artefact.

The Colonel broke the silence, 'Get these doors open Powell.'

Powell wanted nothing more than to get this over with; to curl up and be left alone. In his self pity, he was convinced he was bleeding to death and the promise of getting to a hospital seemed far away.

'Would you like me to hurry you up?' The Colonel patted his gun in its holster.

One of the lieutenants prodded Powell in the back with his Uzi. No one was coming to rescue him, he despaired.

Attached to his belt was a key chain that had a large bunch of keys. They all looked the same through the discomfit and light-headedness he was experiencing. Despite that, he picked out the relevant ones.

The two locks on the main door required individual keys and at first they would not turn. Initially reluctant to rotate because of infrequent use, they eventually shifted in their idle sockets until each hefty duty lock released.

Already Powell felt robbed of all his energy. The gun shot wound was sapping what strength he had left in him.

Next, two broad steel levers connected to each lock had to be pulled down and Powell did so by using the weight of his body, lolling weakly over each. They fell with a resounding clank.

Pausing for a drawn out moment, he was then able to pull one of the double doors open. Lumbering under its own immense weight, it swung out slowly. It took more effort from him as he was becoming more exhausted.

The sheer thickness of the doors could now be regarded along with the retracted bolts that formed part of the lever system. Another set of huge doors identical to the former presented themselves. On one of them was a small electronic panel at head height.

Powell was now breathing quite heavily as he leaned against this second set of doors.

'Start talking.' The Colonel instructed.

One of the soldiers came forward, closely watching Powell's movements. The other remained at the back of the group, admiring the secretary's rear.

Powell slanted towards the panel and stated his full name, followed by a set of six numbers.

The electronic panel buzzed into life with an intelligible feminine robotic voice, 'Not recognised.'

He slumped against the door, looking defeated. His breathing had become more laboured and panic stricken. He was also wincing with pain as he spoke and it was this that was having an effect on his voice.

'Control yourself Powell.' The Colonel prompted.

He felt that if he dropped dead now, he would be content but his body obeyed with an independent will of its own. He lifted his head and again spoke into the panel, propped against it like a drunk.

Again the same automaton voice replied, 'Not recognised.' But this time followed it with the warning, 'Failure to register once again will lock down system. Outside authorities will be subsequently notified.'

Powell was becoming delirious and his legs were ready to give out beneath him. He just wanted to lie down. Pull some imaginary blanket over himself.

The Colonel pointed at his soldier, 'Help him stand up.' he ordered.

The lieutenant approached Powell and pulled him up violently from under his arms and shook him too, to awaken him from his stupor. The Head of Security weighed nothing, the lieutenant discovered. Limp as a rag doll!

'Deep breaths, Powell. Relax.' The Colonel had to give him some encouragement before he passed out or completely ruined the last chance of gaining entry into the vault.

Knowing this was the only way he was going to be able to finally rest, Powell coughed, cleared his throat, shook his head and with a few deep breaths, once again spoke into the intercom with renewed urgency and pronouncement.

'Verified.' The panel acknowledged.

The large doors clicked inside and automatically began to slowly open. Trapped air escaped with an awakening sigh. It smelt of metallic and stale dust.

Powell's sigh expelled all the energy he had left in him and therefore melted into the soldier's grip. The lieutenant proceeded to let him drop and Powell fell to the floor where he lay in his own self pity.

The doors were as thick as the outer doors as they finally coasted to a stop and the lights inside the vault flickered on.

The Colonel immediately stepped over the collapsed Powell like he was roadkill and entered the vault.

Surprisingly it was spacious, measuring 34x29ft. Its floor was polished obsidian marble that reflected everything like still water. A metal table stood in the middle of the room and leaning against the steel grey walls were wooden crates of varying sizes. They would contain paintings awaiting shipment after a recent exhibition or valuable and precious pieces that would never be hung in public. Also items and artefacts stored by cautious private owners for insurance reasons.

Set in the far wall was row upon row of numbered safe deposit boxes, each with its own digital display that needed a numerical code to unlock their secrets.

The Colonel pointed at one marked *55* with concealed anticipation. 'This is it, Hendrik. Get it open.'

Whereupon one of his lieutenants pulled a crowbar from one of the deep pockets on his combat pants and proceeded to wedge it into the metal box, working it by pushing it forward and backwards with brute force. Twisting and buckling the malleable metal in between its edges and slowly but surely forcing apart a groove behind its panel.

The other lieutenant waited outside, paying more attention to the female hostage than Powell who was whimpering unintelligibly to himself. He was not even bothered when Hannah moved over slightly to observe what was going on in the vault. As far as he was concerned, this beautiful creature could continue being curious and moving her delectable form.

When the Colonel learned he would be paying a visit to the National Gallery, he had enquired to a few associates in intelligence of what he should expect. It was the usual related information but one source mentioned the vault. Intrigued, he had delved deeper and eventually received credible information that there was a significant and valuable object in the highly sealed repository. Despite it being a deviation from the overall plan, he could not but help himself while he was here; a little something special that the 'Phoenix Project' did not need to know of.

The soldier reached into the pried opening and pulled out the tray like box. Placing it on the table, he made light work of opening its lid.

All eyes were inquisitively on it as he lifted out the box's contents and carefully handed it over to his superior.

A glow reflected in the Colonel's intent face. 'Ah! The spoils of war…'

Everyone watching noticed the spectacular stone twinkle in his eyes as he handled it.

The Cora Sun-Drop Diamond was the largest yellow pear brilliant diamond known to the world. Weighing in at 110.3 carat, it was valued at $11 million. Discovered in South Africa, tests showed it had formed 1 to 3 billion years ago. It took its manufacturing company six months to cut it to its completed pear shape and it had been stored in the National Gallery's vaults awaiting auction.

Momentarily, Powell forgot his suffering and eyed the diamond. He would never have guessed that one of the world's most renowned jewels was in his care.

The concern that he could well be in a lot of trouble for opening the vault had passed quickly. He had no choice but to do what he did with a gun to his head. Who wouldn't? He did not sign up for this treatment. The moment he had been shot, the responsibility was no longer his. The authorities would understand that. Now all he wanted was that this Colonel, this terrorist, kept his promise and got him medical assistance.

Hannah's hazelnut eyes remained mesmerised on seeing the stone and the Colonel saw this. He took it as a simple infatuation from a woman for a girl's best friend.

He said to her, 'Would this not be a splendid gift for a woman like you?' He smirked at her as he held it up to the light, turning it in his fingers, admiring it.

'If only you knew?' she told herself. But it sure was beautiful with a light source all of its own. So radiant and shimmering with its intense yellow, it was the fifth rarest colour for a diamond. All the talk and all the pictures would never do it impartiality. It was the most beautiful thing she ever laid eyes upon.

Hannah watched the Colonel pocket the Cora Sun-Drop into his jacket and said, 'Back to the real job at hand. Fun is over!'

Leaving the vault and once again stepping over the Head of Security still curled up on the floor, the Colonel gazed down on him distastefully and ordered, 'Throw him in the vault!'

He could not understand weakness and had no time for men unable to control their emotions. Very much like Powell displayed earlier, when he interrupted him in his office. Men should always be silently strong willed. Keep their mouths shut and make their points by their actions. If not, then they should be led by example and if they could not do that, then they may as well be put out of action.

As his soldier moved in to pick him up, Powell began to scream. 'No! NO! You promised me. You said you would help me. Get me some medical…..'

The soldier handled him like a sandbag and threw him into the vault.

He yelped as he landed awkwardly on the marble floor, 'Ah! Ohhh! Oooohh....! He was beginning to cry. Babbling like a child. '.....said you would give me medical assistance.'

Christ, he was pathetic, Hannah said to herself.

The Colonel pushed the button on the electronic panel that started the interior vault doors to slowly close again.

Powell tried to get up but howled even louder with pain and collapsed again, clutching his right foot which had twisted horribly. He managed to pull and slide his body along the polished floor. His aching, throbbing ankle made him forget the discomfort further up his right leg and the bullet wound. Yet his whole leg was becoming numb and useless.

He was now at the closing doors and leaning on one arm, his other was stretched out in desperation, appealing to everyone present to pull him out of the vault.

The Colonel lifted his boot and placing it upon Powell's left shoulder, pushed him firmly, whereupon he fell backwards, splayed on his bottom.

He was squealing the same word over and over again, 'No, no, no, no.....'

'Don't worry.' The Colonel calmly said. 'I'm sure you'll be found.' In cold blood he added, 'Eventually.'

The doors were only inches apart and the Colonel, his two lieutenants and Hannah could see his face contorted, pained and wide eyed with the realisation of his plight.

Hannah was the only one who almost began to feel any kind of sympathy.

'You lied.' Powell screamed dismally and desperately through the closing gap.

'I'm a revolutionist. Sometimes we lie to get what we want.' The Colonel stated.

And then the thick steel doors sealed completely shut, cutting out Powell's piercing scream.

17

He stepped off the fixed ladder that descended from the connecting shaft of the roof above.

His presence triggered the sensors which in turn flashed the overhead lights on, illuminating the loft like space. Initially it made him jump, until he remembered the automated system.

These maintenance corridors ran above all the rooms in the Sainsbury Wing. Covering a lot of ground, they often appeared a completely different and separate complex. One side incorporated much of the numerous piping and cabling that handled the running of the building and the opposite wall had floor to ceiling frosted windows which overlooked the gallery's public rooms below; it was an aesthetic touch that gave the impression the rooms were much more spacious and airy. The walkway itself resembled the bowels of a futuristic spaceship in pristine white. The heating, air conditioning pipes and electrical units gave out a constant ship like engine noise that became headache inducing after a while. It was a stark contrast to the stillness of the rooms below.

He set off briskly for the far end of the corridors where he hoped to gain access to the shaft ladder that would lead him down to the staff stairwell. Again to his relief, it was not obstructed, only locked and the keys on his set rectified that. He began to feel he was getting somewhere.

Pulling open the door, a sudden weight fell against him from behind, slamming him into the opening door and closing it again with him pressed up against it.

It knocked the wind out of him and he wasn't sure whether his nose broke as it smacked against the solid metal door.

'GOT YOU!' A voice behind him growled and an arm wrapped around his neck.

The voice sounded familiar but it was hard to be sure with the racket in the roof space. It was why he failed to hear this person approaching him from behind.

He was still reeling from the collision and the arm was tightening around his throat, making it difficult to breathe. He would black out shortly unless he did something.

He raised a leg, planting his foot squarely on the door in front of him and tried to push back but his assailant was strong.

Knowing this the goon taunted in his ear, 'You're a weakling Booker.'

He knew that voice!

'Gerard!' he managed to get out of his choking throat.

'Le seul et unique!' The voice boasted.

The confirmation angrily urged him on and planting his other leg and foot on the door, he pushed again, groaning and grimacing with newly found strength.

They both toppled backwards, crashing to the gangway. Gerard's back took the pain of their weight but still an arm clamped, crushing Will's airways, refusing to let go.

Will swung his head back, head-butting Gerard squarely in the face.

The blow loosened the suffocating stranglehold and Will took advantage of this to elbow him in the ribs. Pulling himself up onto his feet, he spun around to face his tormentor.

Gerard got up laughing. Unfazed.

He towered above Will by half a foot, his shaven and ponytailed head brushing the ceiling of the roof space.

Will tried to regain regular breathing as they eyed each other in a kind of stand off.

Gerard was grinning with his thousand pound sparkling dentures. Often Will was tempted to knock a few of those pearly whites out of his mouth. It wasn't the teeth that he had a problem with; it was that they happened to belong to an arsehole and what better way to hurt this unlikeable piece of Gaul then to smash what he was so vain about. Just a well aimed punch to those set of false gnashers. That would wound his pride.

They had to talk louder above the engine like throb that filled the area.

'Thought it was you, Booker! Recognized that shaggy-dog face of yours.' He sneered. 'How did I miss you in my rounds?'

'When I was smoking maybe?' Will obligingly sneered back.

'You weren't meant to be working.'

'Sorry to disappoint but the boss asked me to stay longer.'

Gerard grinned that cheesy grin again, 'Oh, I'm not disappointed. Finally get to beat that yellow belly shit out of you.'

They had worked together for six months – it was Will who joined the gallery after the Frenchman and Gerard's antagonism and dislike had started from day one. Will was prepared to give the guy a chance but it did not last long when he realised he was a nasty and vindictive piece of work. When Will one day mentioned his military record and self-discharge, Gerard never let up. Mocked, demeaned and goaded him ever since, deemed Will a dishonourable soldier and not fit to call himself a man. Gerard made every working day a nightmare and it was not just him. He was as rude and obnoxious with every other member of staff and no one could understand why he was working here and what his problem was?

'What are you up to Gerard?'

'Working.'

'Seems like murder to me.'

'Whatever gets the job done.'

'You in charge of this operation?'

'It does not matter.'

'It doesn't matter to you that your colleagues are dead?'

'Of course not.' He smirked. 'It was I that killed them.'

Will watched his face for a moment and decided he could well believe the statement. Here was a man he had initially thought was only a troubled and cynical bastard but instead was a cold hearted murderer. The Frenchman really did not care and Will began to feel unnerved.

'Never liked them.' He continued. 'Especially you Booker! I had to put up with your terrible jokes and smug optimism. All of you were a poor excuse for masculinity. On and on, you all complained about the price of beer and taste of tea. Dead inside, the lot of you. I couldn't wait until the plan was initiated and I started putting bullets in each and everyone one of your pessimistic....' He emphasised 'pessimistic' with a hiss. '..... minds.'

He rubbed his head where Will had head butted it and checked his hand for blood. Satisfied there was none, he flicked his ponytail back off his broad shoulders.

Will wrinkled his nose; it wasn't broken, only very sore.

'I was the plant.' He bragged.

Will was disgusted, 'All this for what? A load of paintings?'

'Not the lousy paintings Booker. Sick of the sight of them. Overrated pulp. If I had the time I would burn the lot. No, not them. It's something much more meaningful.' He eyes seemed to glaze over at the mention.

The little curiosity Will had was set aside by the paramount urge to get out of here.

'You gonna kill me too? Just like the rest of our work mates?'

'I keep telling you, they were not my mates.' He said that sarcastically, mocking him the same way he always did. Emphasising with an over the top cockney accent. 'You are not listening Booker but then you never did, did you? Was always the self-absorbed failure! And yes, I am going to kill you and enjoy it. Its been coming since day one.'

'C'mon Gerard, I'm not like that at all…' Yet he could see it made no difference, the man had made up his mind. '…..Let me out of here. I left the Army because of….'

Gerard interrupted him 'Still crooning that spineless bullshit Booker. How many times you told me that.' He was enjoying himself now. This was his moment.

'Can you recall me telling you my past employment?' He didn't wait for an answer. 'Well I lied!' He winked and Will thought it was the most disconcerting expression he ever saw.

'Security is not my background, that's for lilies. I am a real soldier and have served my time in a real army. Not your pitiful outfit, which you British call a force.' His voice was louder now, 'I'm going to enjoy killing you. Tu es un lâche!'

He had been itching for a fight. It had been too long and this would be the closet he would get for awhile yet. The real thing would come soon enough and by God, he had been incredibly patient. He had yearned for the dust and dirt of battle again and the tastes and smells synonymous with war.

The odour of gun metal fired rounds and the shudder of the combat ground beneath your feet. Those situations were his home, even with the sight of his own spilt blood. There was nothing like it in the world that made you feel more alive and so close to your own mortality than the primary truth of kill or be killed.

Being away from the adrenaline and danger was akin to going 'cold turkey' he imagined and what better way to get my fix then to kick the hereafter out of this wimp. He thought of it as a workout before the real action began.

Gerard advanced, un-slinging the Uzi on his shoulder he threw it a distance away behind him. 'Make it fair. No weapons eh! A real fight!' He also discarded his two other handguns and his combat knife.

Will understood there was no changing this mad man's mind, he was itching for this fight that Will did not want and a part of him knew that the Frenchman could well make mincemeat of him.

'Leave it out.' Will raised his hands in surrender then quick as lightening moved forward and punched Gerard squarely on the nose, swiftly following it with a kick to Gerard's groin.

Gerard took it well but his eyes squinted slightly and a trickle of blood oozed from his nose.

'That's the spirit.' Gerard uttered then spat out blood onto the white floor. 'Dirty though Booker. Dirty.'

18

Meanwhile outside in Trafalgar Square and plodding his routine evening patrol, Police Community Support Officer Michael Costa was dealing with a bunch of skateboarding youths.

It was no big deal, he thought. They were not really causing much of a problem; it was just that they were using the concrete edgings that lined the end of the green and its National Gallery property for their leisurely stunts.

'C'mon lads, I've told you before...' Michael appeased. 'Please stay off the premises and be careful of the public.'

Good naturedly, as they usually did, they shuffled off and continued playing their games in the square. Often groups of kids would meet up and congregate in the area, hanging out and showing off their skills to any passer-bys interested. It was almost a showcase for them and the tourists who watched and marvelled at their tricks. In a sense, it kept these kids off the streets and out of real mischief, Michael viewed. They weren't drinking alcohol or doing drugs, if anything they took their skateboarding seriously. Every week they would meet, do their stunts, film them and then download them to YouTube where they had quite a following.

PCSO Michael Costa was a chubby little man who was often told that he looked like the actor Danny DeVito and to everyone's interest; he had the personality to match. He was easy going, relaxed, sociable and respected which made him ideal as a Community Officer. What hair he did have left was chocolate brown, side parted and clung to his head like its last days were nearly up. His black eyes twinkled mischievously on his content face and most people enjoyed the fact that he also resembled the 'Fat Controller' of a popular children's show in his girth and uniform. Because of these similarities, tourists often wanted their photos taken with him which he would oblige amiably. It was no big deal! While he was finishing giving directions to a Japanese couple, he heard what sounded like a muffled rumble coming from inside the National Gallery behind him.

'Now I wonder what that was?' he asked himself.

A little concerned, he decided to check with the night staff at the west door of the building. It was quite common for him or any patrolling Officer to do this. Call on them and ask if any assistance was needed as regards to kids, drunks or homeless people loitering or causing a nuisance on the Gallery's perimeter. The police and PCSO's like himself often worked together to maintain the security of these premises.

After ten longer than usual minutes he still heard no answer from his persistent ringing on the buildings intercom system. It remained silent. He even deliberately waved frantically a few times to try to get their attention on the CCTV lens by the doors but began to feel like an idiot.

He walked back out into the square and looked back up at the building and its pond like windows. Nothing seemed out of place and there were the odd occasions when it would take awhile for them to answer. He would try again shortly.

Then he heard another louder rumble and this time he was sure it emanated from the Gallery.

'Sounded like a bang.' He commented to himself.

He immediately put out a call on his radio to his superiors to report that he could not get in contact with the National Gallery staff at the west door and he had twice heard what sounded like unusual sounds coming from inside the building. Could they try phoning them, he suggested. Find out what was going on and then advise on his next course of action?

All he could do now was wait and wonder. Maybe they were carrying out construction work which could only be done at night and it was no big deal after all.

19

Gerard swiftly pounced forward with uncanny speed. For someone of his build he moved fast and in quick succession landed three punches to Will's face.
The blows stunned him into a smarting daze; he collapsed to the floor on his behind. That hurt, he groaned as something cracked in his face.
'Get up COCKNEY!'
He was using that annoying accent again. Gonna knock that outta him, once and for all, Will promised himself.
Turning over with his hands planted on the floor, Will pushed himself up and lashed out with a backwards kick to Gerard's knee and again with the same leg, this time higher to his groin area.
Now standing upright, he could see that last kick had hurt him. 'Man's Achilles' Heel,' Will remarked to himself. He almost sympathised with the French bastard.
Gerard's porcelain teeth were clenched tightly, lips drawn and his eyes fiery.
With the intention to keep punishing him in the same spot, Will kicked out again for Gerard's groin but he anticipated the move and catching Will's foot, he began to twist his ankle.
'You're hitting below the belt Booker. That is not nice. You want some?'
With his right leg, he went to return a kick to Will's groin but despite Will being held by his right leg, he managed to

twist his hips around slightly so the blow only struck his upper thigh. It still hurt.

As Gerard began to twist Will's ankle in frustration at not being able to return a similar blow, Will was able to reach and pummel the Frenchman's face.

As each punch brought more blood, Gerard was somehow still able to hold onto Will's leg and exert more excruciating pain. The blows to his face were not in the least weakening his grip. If anything, it seemed to spur him on more strongly with each punch.

Will had to stop him before he snapped his ankle.

Able to shift around with his body weight much closer to Gerard, Will's arm reached up behind Gerard's head and grabbed his ponytail.

He let out a howl as Will pulled, snarling like an angry dog that had had its tail yanked.

Gerard had no choice but to push forward, loosening the twisting of Will's ankle and lessening the length his hair was being pulled before it was torn from his head.

As Will was pushed backwards with Gerard's incredible strength, his back took the full bone jarring impact against the metal piping running down the wall behind him. He lost the grip on the Frenchman's hair and because of the momentum they both crumpled into a heap onto the floor. They both reacted immediately, trying to unscramble themselves and get the upper hand by grabbing any part of their enemy's body that was loose and vulnerable.

Wrestling now and rolling about the gangway, they gave each other punches, kicks, knees and elbows to each others legs, arms, torso and heads. Anywhere that would hurt the other and give himself the advantage. Grunting and growling at each other as they both continually escaped strangleholds and again landed blow upon blow like a no holds barred

wrestling match that even involved biting. There were no rules as each fought for their survival, anything went.
It was only a matter of time before the scrabbling fight was decided by who was the strongest and most resilient.
In a deadlock, they were both tangled together on the floor and against the pipe-lined wall.
Will was in a headlock and unable to free his arms, one was trapped on his front, the other held by Gerard, doubled up behind his back. Gerard's immense bulk behind him had him pressed up against the piping. He could almost taste the metal in his mouth.
Sweat and blood dripped and glistened of each other's bodies. Smeared claret graffiti-ed the white gangway.
The stalemate made Will realize how exhausted he was. He was panting heavily and Gerard seemed completely unfazed.
Gerard uttered, 'I'm short on time here Booker.' His hold tightening.
Will struggled desperately; he was losing air in his throat and his lungs.
'Need to burn more bridges.' Gerard chuckled at his own choice of words.
Will was losing vision. He was going to black out.
'Time to end your cowardly existence.'
'Fuck you frog!'
With reserved stamina that only comes with one last desperate chance, Will was able to pull up his legs, one at a time. The first giving his body some leeway. He was then able to plant both feet firmly against a pipe and mustering all the strength he had left in him and with a brute roar rising from his throat, he pushed.
It propelled both their bodies backwards across the gangway and through the skylight.

The window exploded and a thousand pieces of shattered glass followed them as they fell.

The Frenchman was behind Will, his thick arms still choking around Will's throat. Not seeming to care that they were plummeting to their possible deaths, he held on with intent on still squeezing the life out of him.

Will had resigned himself now to the fact that the end would come with a fatal impact.

He felt too tired and too hurt now. The rush of air passing him as they fell was strangely invigorating.

They crashed to the floor of the room with a sickening crunch.

20

He had to know who it was!
Initially Pawel was frozen to the spot. Unable to make a move, in case he made a sound that would bring about his demise.
But the questions persisted. Could it be a member of the night staff? That, he initially wished for. Safely giving himself up to a member of staff could be an option that he refused to rule out. One of them may even recognise him from his previous days working here. Yet he was afraid. It could well be that man on the bike?
Either way, he had decided he had to know. He felt he could not carry on unless he knew for sure.
Carefully, he eased over to the doorway of Room 8 and peered around the marble frame into the room that he and Joseph had been in earlier. The room that should have brought success but instead brought death. How quickly people's worlds can change and end in a flash of a gun.
He had to look twice before he was convinced there was no one in there. He must be next door, he deduced.
Again as silently as he could and even more cautiously, he approached the doorway to Room 9.
It was a larger space, a hall even and it's 94x36ft size added to the grandeur with larger paintings filling the extensive walls. The room had three other exits with the right eventually joining back up with Rooms 11 and 12 and the staircase of 13, areas that he and Joseph had also passed

through earlier. Straight ahead at the far end of the room, another archway led to the North Wing and to his left, the Link to the Sainsbury Wing and that was where the voice in question stood. With his back to him by the doorway he appeared to be watching or waiting for something in the Sainsbury Wing direction. In the centre of the room a motorbike was propped upright.

The man had his hand up to his ear which Pawel guessed was a radio piece. He definitely wasn't a member of the night staff and he was dressed in unfamiliar black army fatigues. A sub-machine gun was slung over his broad shoulders, resting against his back. He looked like a soldier, even a terro…and suddenly a memory awoke.

It was him, his mind screamed. Joseph's murderer!

And to confirm it, he looked back at the motorbike. Noticing this time, on its seat was resting a motorcycle helmet and he could make out the familiar markings. The white on a black background stood out blatantly and menacingly. It was a crudely painted swastika!

The man turned and Pawel quickly ducked back into his room.

Was I seen? He was afraid to move and make a sound. He prayed to whatever God he did not believe in, that he had not been spotted.

It was him; that was for sure. The same man.

Anger boiled up in him, his fists clenched. He wanted to run into the room and strangle the man but he knew a bullet would probably meet him head on.

He wanted revenge yet his conflicting emotions of anger and fear were intoxicating, confusing.

He didn't know how to respond and the uncertainty was making him more conflictingly enraged and frightened.

21

In Room 62 where paintings by Bellini & Messina hung, the silence was as still as a crypt.
The grey painted walls were a stark contrast to the main building, making it feel almost sterile.
Two bodies lay unmoving amongst the fragments of glass that twinkled like tiny diamonds scattered all over the wooden floorboards.
Someone stirred.
Will, groaning, untangled himself from the limp body of Gerard sprawled beneath him.
Getting to his feet, he noticed his surroundings and looking up; he saw the shattered open skylight that they had fallen through.
He rubbed his sore and inflamed neck and tried to comprehend how lucky he was.
Gerard remained unmoving; his muscular body inert. Considering the fall, Gerard must have taken all the weight of both their bodies on his back and broken it. The Frenchman had unintentionally and inexplicably saved him. He wouldn't have liked that, Will thought as a wry smile played across his lips.
'Christ!' he exclaimed, his voice echoing back to him. He ached all over and his bones popped with every movement. The sooner this ends the better. I can't take much more of this shit!

A 15th century depiction of Christ by Messina hung on the wall and appeared to stare back at him, disapprovingly at his cursing.

He stretched and limbered, checking himself while trying to avoid the glass that crunched underfoot. He noticed too that the lights were now on. Someone had flicked the main switch that lit up all of the rooms.

Taking some deep breaths, he still contemplated how fortunate he was. Part of him could not believe…. He heard distinct voice.

As he tried to tune in – his head was still ringing – he discerned the voices were not distant but oddly, tiny!

At first he couldn't understand, then realized they were coming from Gerard's radio headpiece.

Taking it off the dead man's head, he put it to his ear.

He was listening to a communication that had already started. '….. aware of it and keep a distance.'

Another voice came over the radio, 'Phoenix six, can you confirm?'

The radio crackled after a pause and another voice answered, 'Link all clear and ready.'

Then the initial authoritative voice replied 'Bring it down.'

Gerard had mentioned something about a bridge, Will recalled and with the mention of the Link, he put one and the other together.

He started running.

In 1985 Lord Sainsbury and his brothers made a donation to the gallery that enabled the construction of The Sainsbury Wing. It opened in 1991 and was a typical example of Postmodernist architecture in comparison with the opulent ornamentation of the main building. It's church like interiors were grey stone, a complimentary recognition to early Renaissance paintings that were now housed in this section.

The Wing gave the overall structure expansion and allowed the collection to breathe. With a single vista down the whole length of the gallery, it encompassed the old with the new and it was here that Will had started his run.

He didn't know how long he had. All he knew was that if he got to Room 9, then he should be safe. He wasn't even sure what would happen but he was not going to take any chances considering all the madness that had happened so far tonight.

Ignoring the aches and pains screaming in his body, he sprinted from the room into the next and then turning right into Room 60 and through Room 51, he passed the staircase on his right.

From outside, the Link resembled what looked like an enclosed bridge of sorts. Sometimes referred to as a 'Skybridge,' this was a type of 'Skyway' that connected both buildings on the second floor, giving access to each without ever having to leave both buildings.

He was able to see all the way down the vista; all the rooms fully lit now and could just make out the painting of 'Stubbs's Horse' in the furthest reaches of the gallery. That was his goal of sorts; what he was heading for. As long as he could see that horse, he should be okay.

His legs took long strides, increasing his speed and shortening the distance as quickly as possible.

The ground shuddered slightly under him, followed by an odd crumpling sound akin to the crushing of cardboard. The path in front of him suddenly began to disappear.

They had made certain all of the Link would come down by using huge quantities of C4 explosives which targeted the foundation supports.

A 15ft chasm gaped before him but he didn't stop running. He was committed now and the pace he had picked up spurred him on faster, to go and make the jump.

His right foot slapped down on the now crumbling edge of what remained of the Link's floor and he leapt with all his momentum and strength, willing himself up and over.

All around him the Skyway was breaking up, the deteriorating structure falling upon the thoroughfare below. Without any support, all the stone, steel and glass, all the materials that made up its edifice began to drop away like the ground had just opened up and swallowed it – and that was what was happening as all and sundry followed and tumbled into a yawning fissure.

A 14ft rectangular water tank with a capacity of just under 10,000 gallons resided part way on the Link roof and when that started to collapse, the tank shifted its mass which in turn began to tip. The steeper its angles became, it pulled and snapped from its connecting pipes that ran into the building. Escaping water began to spill downwards.

The vast container balanced for a moment, deciding whether it could right itself again but the roof edges it precariously balanced on crumbled away even more under the weight of the steel bulk.

There was no turning back. Gravity took over and the tank began to tip at an ever steepening angle. The heavy plastic covering that slotted in on top was pushed off by the overflowing water and shot down a few feet in front of Will in a blue blur.

As his body soared through the air, he was being drenched by the gushing, freezing water. Its sheer thrashing and volume thwarting his leap, pulling him downwards.

What remained of the Link walkway stuck out a little further on each side, narrowing the distance just enough.

His gut crushed into the jagged lip of the Room 9 doorway floor. He screamed as it bit into him and almost expelled all the air out of his lungs.

He had made it over the abyss even if he was dangling off the edge. The pain in his stomach, he tried to ignore. His upper body lay a little over the floor; his arms and hands clung and gripped for a lifeline while his legs dangled into space. He didn't dare look down. Found himself looking at 'Stubbs's Horse.'

From above the water still cascaded, pouring down upon him and now pooling into the room in front of him at eye level.

I need to pull myself up and over the ledge, he hastened.

Then a metallic groan was heard above him like the shriek of a ship's funnel.

Will turned his head and looking upwards, his eyes widened in terror. He saw the huge tipping behemoth that was the tank; fill his view, casting an eclipsing, threatening shadow over him.

He desperately began to pull himself up over the edge but he was slipping. Panic reigned.

His grip was hopeless against the pouring water that made the marble part of the flooring slippery. He was sliding backwards as he became heavier, his dense clothing soaked through by the constant downpour of water pulling and dragging at him.

He felt a breeze on the back of his neck and it made him shiver. Goosebumps followed.

He was practically outside of the building and under the night sky. It was a disconcerting sensation until the screeching of the impeding tank added to his desperation, an ominous block of death itself. He knew when the tank had approached its tipping point; it would inescapably come down upon him. Catching him prone on this ledge, crushing and bringing him and it to the deadly depths below.

He had to move quickly.

He was able to swing his right leg up to the ledge but to his horror, the shift in his body weight only sent him slipping off the edge completely.

The steel rods that protruded out of the concrete floor, he was able to grab with both hands. He hung on for dear life as the crass metal tore into his hands which were taking all of his body's weight. What relief he felt at saving himself from falling was short lived. That impending sound groaned above him again. Reminding him of the inevitable.

The frigidness of the water made his hands clinging on to the rods even more tender, the course steel cut into his hands like serrated blades. Water splashed off the ledge, stinging his eyes, temporarily blinding his vision.

His arms despairingly screamed at him to just.... let.... go and the pain will finally cease. That he wouldn't have to endure it anymore.

There was the sound of metal in friction with stone, a nerve scraping screech. Louder and louder it grew. It provoked him from the aches and pains that wanted surrender and mustering all his energy left in him and some, he pulled himself up again and this time hooking his left arm over a rod which gave him some leverage. For a few brief seconds he rested his weight under his armpit, relieving some of the pull on his weary arms. With that balance, he swung his right leg up and caught the ledge with his foot. Now with extra support and grunting with the effort, he was able to pull himself up over and onto to the reassuring solid flooring of Room 9. Just as a strong draft shot past him!

The tank fell, clipping and taking a piece of the edge with it, where he had been clinging onto only a few seconds before.

He heard it 'dong' oddly like an empty bell followed by a thunderous crunch. The vibration was felt throughout his exhausted body that lay collapsed on the puddled floor.

For more reassurance, he began crawling into the room away from the edge, too exhausted to pick himself up. Still on all fours, dripping wet and covered in a grey dust, he lifted his head and wide eyed, stared into the barrel of a gun aimed between his eyes.

It was being held by a soldier looming over him.

When will this shit stop? He whined to himself and pleaded to the man, 'I'm unarmed.' His mouth was so dry that the words came out thickly and hoarse.

'We all make mistakes mister.' The man smirked down on him. 'This is yours. Time to die.'

22

Pawel had made up his mind to confront whom he was convinced was his friend's murderer.
Do what exactly, he wasn't sure. A citizen's arrest was laughable in his position! Beat the 'gowno' out of him? The anger rising up in him again wanted to.
As quietly as possible, he started tip-toeing his way across the room towards the killer, poised for a showdown when suddenly an explosion rocked the building.
So startled was he, that he intuitively crouched down as if it would give him some protection from what felt like an earthquake. The whole building must have shaken because the room they were in certainly did. The paintings on the walls hanging from chains swayed a little and it was followed by what sounded like the tumbling of hundreds of bricks.
He was surprised to notice that the killer seemed to be expecting this commotion judging by his body language. He remained steadfast on his feet, watching whatever it was taking place with cool detachment.
Pawel could not be sure what was really happening. Had something actually blown up? The gut instinct felt right but the assumption was ludicrous.
Chunks of concrete bounced and scattered into the room followed by clouds of smoke and dust. Then oddly, water too began splashing into the room. Spreading and pooling over the floor; the quantity was increasing. Had a water pipe

blown? He even thought for a brief moment it might have been some storm or freak weather from outside that was causing this havoc.

Still crouched and not knowing what to do, Pawel watched the peculiar scene unfold.

The killer was still unaware of his presence behind him and was now moving towards the doorway that led to the Link, where this entire disturbance was coming from. He then drew a gun from his side.

Pawel couldn't move, frozen in fear. He was caught, he knew it. He's heard me and now it's my turn.

Yet the soldier did not turn towards him to fire that fatal shot. He remained watching something ahead of him and then lowered his gun arm, aiming downwards to floor level where a figure had literally crawled into the room.

The man was soaked and bedraggled and Pawel noticed the uniform. It was a member of staff. Being on all fours, he had the appearance of a drowned dog and as he lifted his head, he stared to the gun pointed at him.

The out of place waterfall seemed to abruptly end. Everything became dauntingly silent after the destructive clamour. The quiescent between each drop of water grew longer, echoing and almost drawing out the scene.

Something was said between the drenched, prone man and the soldier with the gun but Pawel couldn't quite make it all out. But he certainly heard the last sentence.

'…. time to die!' It was said loudly and boastfully.

It stirred something in Pawel. Be it an instinctive urge to aid this man in a uniform that he once shared and had a commonality with or was it simply seeing another human being in danger and he could not let another man die in his presence tonight.

At that moment, all he could see was Joseph!

Before he knew it, he was sprinting towards the killer with the gun, splashing through the floor, his plimsolls and trousers becoming soaked.

He heard him and Pawel expected it, his pounding on the floorboards and the slapping of water as each of his strides took him closer had alerted the man but he was hoping his pace would make the difference before the soldier had a chance to do what he intended.

Pawel was still fifteen feet from him when the killer had completely turned.

He had a thug's pockmarked face and his snake like eyes widened with surprise. But he recovered quickly and reacted, swinging his gun arm around into Pawel's direction.

Pawel was committed now; there was no turning back even if it was death by bullet. To continue running head on was his one and only chance.

It was the memory of what that man had done to his friend that propelled him further and faster and an uncontrollable guttural scream rose up from some dark pit of his stomach.

'Rrrraaargh....'

Then it dawned on him. He was not going to make it.

The killer had him in his sights and his reactions had been faster. Pawel's cry faded away.

The guard still on all fours and with dripping wet clothes sagging off him reached up and grabbed the man's gun arm.

The killer turned back to kick the guard in the ribs and he buckled up from the blow, clutching his body in pain but what he had done was enough for Pawel to reach the distracted thug and with a violent shove, pushed him. Anything to keep the gun aimed away from him.

The killer stumbled backwards, caught unawares and bumped into the injured guard on the floor. His legs flew out in front of him, his balance lost. He continued to topple backwards and over the edge of where the floor of the Link once was and disappeared from sight with a terror struck scream.

23

In the square, PCSO Michael Costa walked back and forth outside the West door, listening out for a call on his radio and waiting for instructions on what his next course of action should be. He had even tried the West door again but to no avail did he get an answer.
It was coming up to forty minutes now. Something was definitely up.
Initially, he had thought it may have been a power cut – it had happened before. No lights could be seen through the dark windows but that was quickly dismissed by the outside floodlights that lit up the building's facade. Anyway, even if it was an electric problem, the staff inside would have used the emergency release on the West door and shown themselves. No! This was worrying now.
Then it got more serious.
He heard a loud echoing crack from behind him. A fracturing like sound and turning his head, he looked towards the closed gates of Jubilee Walk that ran between the Sainsbury's Wing and the main building.
He witnessed the Link (the Skyway) above break apart and crumble into a newly formed crater on the street level.
It happened so quietly and orderly too, he would always recount. It was like a bag of rubble had been emptied and simply swept away into an opening in the ground.
In the end, nothing much remained to show of the structure that was once there, other than a slowly dissipating cloud of

dust from above the pit. Later, he would remark that 'It just disappeared. One minute there, the next gone.'

He did not know how long he stared in stupefaction until he realised his mouth was hanging agape. He then made the emergency call over his radio to all units of the disaster that had just occurred.

The radio airways would not be silent for the rest of the night.

Members of the public started to approach him with startled expressions and excited fascination. Jostling for a position where they could scrutinise past the gate to see what had happened and just as Michael tried to deal with this influx and had thought he had seen and heard it all, a scream pierced the aftermath silence.

He turned to Jubilee Walk again and briefly spotted a body plummet from the rupture of the main building's second floor, straight down into the shadows where the Link had disappeared into.

Some of the milling crowd congregating around him gasped and screamed; they had seen it too. Try as he did, he could not get another call out over the now frantic radio waves.

They had received his earlier appeal and soon all the available resources of the emergency services would be arriving. To confirm this; sirens began to wail in the distance already. The first of many more tonight.

He realised he was again gawping with his mouth open.

He had never in all his time as a PCSO experienced anything like it. If it was not for his uniform, he was just another member of public, bewildered and horrified.

'This was a big deal,' Michael scratched his balding head.

24

'Thanks.' Will said as he pulled himself up and proceeded to shake himself dry and brush himself down.

It was pointless. He was a grubby and drenched mess and his body ached all over. His stomach felt like he had been cut open from where it had slammed into the ragged edges of the ledge. He still felt winded and every time he breathed, he was only reminded of the pain in his ribs where he had been kicked by that goon. His hands had come off the worst and examining them he cringed at the red rawness of them where much of his skin had been torn and serrated by the steel rods that nevertheless had saved his life. Despite the soreness of them, there was not a lot of bleeding. All his inflictions were a small price to pay.

Eyeing his rescuer, Will registered little acknowledgement from the man. He seemed preoccupied with something and his eyes darted about furtively.

'You alright?' Will asked. Though he wasn't feeling alright himself after what had just happened. He hadn't been feeling alright since all this had started on his last cigarette break and he certainly wanted one now.

'Yes.' This stranger answered almost inaudibly.

'Worried if anymore of those goons will turn up? I know the feeling.' He wiped his brow with a damp sleeve. 'They seem to be over-running the place. Keep trying to kill me.'

'He killed my partner.' The man replied sombrely, pointing down at the killer's body.

Will did not know what to say to that and they both stood in silence for a moment, looking down at the destroyed Skyway.

'What a mess.' Will shook his head.

The goon that had fallen into what remained of the Link was facing upwards, splayed out over a large piece of grey wall. The back of his head had smashed open from the impact of his fall and from his shattered skull blood still oozed down the slab he lay on, darkening it. His eyes remained open, appearing to stare up at them with menacing intent.

The dripping of water dispersing from the room they stood in, splashed sporadically on the concrete rubble and made Rorschach patterns.

The public area that used to run under the Link was no more; the thoroughfare below had been smashed open. A rusty corner of the huge water tank slightly protruded out from the debris, so heavy it had almost buried itself with the rest of the Link's rubble as it pummelled its way further down through to the basement area below.

Even with the now revealed opening on each side of the buildings, there would be no access for any emergency services for some time. It was unsafe and inaccessible to the second floor levels until the personnel and equipment was eventually organized and only when they managed to get through the locked Jubilee gates, cleared the mess and then erected ladders.

About fifteen feet away from where they stood was the exposed opening of the Sainsbury Wing rapture. A large aperture in the building; distant and inviting, its lights still glimmered. Making it appear like some other unreachable worldly dimension.

It would be impossible to get from one building to the other now, Will understood.

A gust of wind swept into the rooms on either side of the exposed building, something that had never been felt before. By leaning out, Will could see the busy weekend traffic behind the left Jubilee walk gate. Members of the public had not been in danger when the Link had collapsed but now on both sides curious and concerned onlookers gazed upon the destruction behind each gate; eager to see what had happened to such an iconic part of the National Gallery. Cameras flashed and he could hear their animated chattering.

Damp from the soaking, Will shivered as he looked to the sky. He whistled dubiously at their position. They were a long way up from ground level here on the edge of Room 9.

What was the point of this? He mulled, rubbing his head. It felt like it was still ringing but then he realised it was a faint buzzing sound he heard and because it came and went, he did not initially pay it much heed. It could have been coming from inside or outside the building.

Still trying to shake himself dry and wringing his sleeves, jumper and trousers, he saw his rescuer follow suit by repetitively stamping his drenched plimsolls.

Will gave him a lordly arched eyebrow as if to say; I'm the drenched one here. But as he eyed the scrawny, pale and scared looking man, he noticed he was wearing the uniform of the shift staff. He also had a tourniquet tied around his upper left leg.

'Who are you anyway?'

The stranger was reluctant to answer.

The paleness of the man wasn't only because he was scared, Will recognized. He had that pasty, eastern European look about him. 'C'mon man. I only want to know the name of the man that saved my life.'

'Pawel Widzislaw.' He hesitantly revealed.

'Polish eh? I'm William Booker. You can call me Will. But never Bill!' He emphasised and held out his hand.

Pawel shook, noticing the slight wince and feeling the man's clammy and lacerated hands. Though he could not understand why this man had to differentiate between two different names. Surely it was one or the other?

'Sorry to hear about your partner.' Will was sincere but challenged him, 'What happened? What were you both doing here anyway?'

Pawel didn't answer. He felt this was the end of everything. He would either be apprehended by this man or murdered by these other thugs before he could get out of the building.

A distant mechanical growling sound interrupted the awkwardness between them. It was different to the earlier sound that Will tried to discern and more protrusive. Pawel knew that sound only too well and began to look around for an escape route.

Will sensed the man's agitation and queried, 'What is it?'

Pawel pointed at the dead killer's bike still parked in the room, 'More of them. We must go.'

'More trouble eh?'

The noise was getting louder and closer.

'C'mon.' Will led the way to an often overlooked door between Room 9 and 10.

Pawel knew this of course and briskly followed.

If they could hide away somewhere, they could then decide what to do, Will determined. They needed time to think and talk.

Another one of the keys on Will's large bundle unlocked the door and they both quickly entered, relocking it behind him.

The corridor only measured 10ft wide but ran with a right angle at one point to the doorway between Rooms 6 and 8. It was an emergency fire exit with a cramped elevator and a narrow stairwell but had since become used for unofficial storage too. Step ladders and picture moving trolleys lined the walls as well as spare rope barriers and domestic cleaning tools.

To Will's astonishment, they heard the roar of a motorbike pass by outside and slow to a stop not far away; its engine idling in what sounded like Room 9.

Pawel suspected the biker was probably observing the scene and the unattended bike. He may even discover the body of his deceased colleague, if he decided to check out the destroyed Link.

Will was still trying to grasp the fact that a motorbike was roaming around the gallery. Then he heard faint vocals and realised he still had Gerard's radio piece on him from earlier. He must have inadvertently shoved it into his trouser pockets.

Taking it out, he put it to his ear. Despite the drenching, it still worked.

'…….. mighty fine job of the Link there my comrades. 'Ain't nobody comin' or going from there, over.' It was an unmistakable Yank's voice.

'Received….' replied an authoritative voice over the airways. '…. and Hans?'

'See a bike but don't see….. Standby….' Static then, '…..Well, well. There he is. Looks like he fell with the Link. Hans is now kissing the hereafter.'

There was a prolonged silence on the airways until that same American accent came through again, 'You get that Phoenix One?'

'Yes.' was the curt reply. 'It can only be foul play. All units, be on the lookout for any remaining members of the buildings staff. Finish off the job you were all suppose to do. Find whoever it is. Phoenix One out.' The voice finished unsparingly. It sounded German, Will reckoned and slightly rankled.

The airways went silent.

'Poles, Germans, French, Yanks, South Africans. Is there anybody here that's English?' Will ranted. 'I've bumped into and heard the whole bloody United Nations tonight! No offence Polish!' He added.

Will turned to Pawel, who still had the appearance of someone whom the ground had opened up beneath him. He knew the feeling. The ground did actually open up beneath him and somehow he had made the jump. He recalled how after finally crawling into Room 9, a goon was waiting for him with a gun at his head. When that man gloated to Will that it was time to die, he caught the South African accent and he was convinced his time was up but salvation had come. Rescue courtesy of this man.

'Well Polish. All of 'em are looking for us now.' He shrugged, 'Makes no difference to me though. They've been trying to kill me since this mess started.'

Will regretted explaining it so bluntly. The look on the man's face was one of someone who had just been given their death sentence. He could plainly see the shock and despondency on Polish's face, seen that look a thousand times before in the army, at war. The look of someone who had just taken another person's life!

'You didn't actually kill him.' Will reassured.

Pawel was surprised at the man's intuition. How did he know I was thinking about that? Yet he could not get away from the undeniable fact that for the rest of his life – however short it might last here, he had to deal with it. Knowing that a man had died by his hands.

'It wasn't your fault man.' Will stressed. 'If anything, it was mine.'

Actually it wasn't mine, Will reminded himself. No one's but his own. That goon put himself in a perilous position, what he was being paid to do. If you're prepared to fight, be ready to die. All soldiers had to accept that! He told Pawel that.

Well, Polish and me had something in common, he reflected. We've both inadvertently killed for the first time today.

Pawel could see what he was trying to do. It was supportive and the consideration was appreciated but there would never be any getting away from it. How would he feel in time? Would he believe he had done the only thing anyone would have done? Or would the guilt slowly eat away at him?

The motorbike circling around the adjacent rooms purred and rattled like a mechanical animal prowling, hunting for them. Judging by the sound of the engine that reverberated up the corridor they were hiding in the biker lingered in Room 6 for a while.

Pawel knew with a heavy heart that the biker had discovered Joseph's body.

'They're relentless these bastards.' Will's comment interrupted the Polish man's poignancy. 'Do you know who they are?'

Pawel shrugged. He really did not know.

'What's happening and why...' he emphasised this. '...are you really here?'

He did not know what to tell this man?

'You're not one of 'em are ya?' he eyed him suspiciously. 'Gain my confidence with that rescue and when you get a chance, stab me in the back eh?'

Pawel fiercely shook his head 'No!'

'I'm in a situation here.' Will's voice lifted.

'I am not one of them. They murdered my partner.' His voice trembled.

They eyed each other as they heard the motorbike fade away. The original buzzing sound could be heard again. Whatever it was?

Will had a hunch that this guy was telling the truth. Alleviating the tone, he said 'They've already killed one of my colleagues and because no one else replies to my radio calls and I ain't seen anyone, I'm beginning to think the worst. I even called our control rooms earlier but nothing. External lines are dead too which puts the mockers on me raising the alarm outside and alerting the police. They may even have murdered the rest of the night shift.' He was running a hand through his damp hair wondering if he was going to catch a cold. He scratched his beard and realised he was getting anxious.

'Maybe I'm the only one left now….' He sighed. 'God, I hope not! Though after that explosion it won't be long before the police realise that something is going down and that'll bring 'em. Just wonder how they will get in? On my travels I came across entrances and exits already barred and blocked and some even rigged with explosives.'

As if on cue, a muffled blast was heard in some far off part of the gallery. 'What are they up to?' Will exclaimed while the faint buzzing sound resumed unabated.

'Have they come to steal the paintings?' Pawel hazard a guess.

'Just like you and your partner did?'

He did not expect that. He also had to admit, he admired the man's acuteness.

'I think you have one in that backpack under your jumper?'

Pawel grinned the grin of someone who knows he's been found out. It looked apologetic!

'How the hell did you get into the locked up building? How did you disable the cameras and alarms?' He shook his head disbelievingly. 'You know, I've got a hundred and one questions for you.'

Pawel just stared back at him, still unsure what he should divulge. Silence seemed the best thing to do at the moment.

Will saw that this was all he was going to get from him at present and that this guy wasn't one of them, he was sure. Why would he have come to my rescue? You could plainly see he was scared shitless, the look on his face made him feel sorry for him. Not surprising considering these goons murdered his mate. They were only burglars. Smart though to get in here, I'll give 'em that. But they didn't expect to run into a bunch of trigger happy terrorists. Of all the nights! Will was still intrigued though, 'Which painting do you have there?'

Pawel was uncertain about answering and then admitted, 'Madonna of the Pinks.' He had nothing to hide. By being honest, he hoped for trust.

'Good taste.' Will nodded. 'Shame though. It's just another copy.'

He stared Will straight into his eyes, not saying anything for a few moments then cursed under his breath, 'Bzdura!'

There was hardness in him that Will had not seen before. He initially looked like he was going to strangle him. Will had heard what he had uttered and appeased with his hands held out. 'It's only what I've heard mister. May not be 'bzdura!'

'You know Polish?' Pawel asked surprised.

'Only the rude stuff.'

'O Jezu!' He exhibited utter dejection as he looked down at his jumper where underneath the painting grated on him. My friend died for this, he cried to himself. What a waste!

'Look. It could be just a rumour. I don't know. I only work here!' Will was only trying to make the worst just that little bit better.

Pawel once again thought about leaving the painting behind. Just tearing the backpack off of him and chucking it away in disgust but a part of him told himself to hang onto it. Finish the job. Fake or no fake, at least still try to deliver it to Mr. G. He then dismissed his own hopefulness. Who am I kidding? This man won't let me. He's security and he'd only be doing his job. The same job I used to do. 'Gowno!' I might not even get out of here alive!

Another distant boom was heard, momentarily drowning out the buzzing. Again they shared quizzical looks.

Will addressed Pawel, 'You saved my neck and I will always be thankful for that. But the fact you were here to steal a painting, well, I should be hauling you in now....' He shrugged his shoulders. '...but because of this situation, it's not that important to me. I owe you and I don't really care about the painting. Surviving is the priority here!'

Pawel completely agreed with that. The little relief he did feel was called for and he wanted to leave now.

'Anyway....' Will was curious. 'How were you going to get out of this building undetected with that painting?'

'We had a plan.'

'Of course you did.' He teased. 'Been planning it for ages eh? How the hell did you get hold of the uniforms?' Then it dawned on him. He wanted to slap his forehead.

'Plonker!' he called himself. 'You used to work here didn't ya? Now I got it.' His voice was livelier. 'You left here five..., six months ago didn't you? My colleagues mentioned you. Quiet but reliable, they said. It figures now, I was your replacement. No wonder you know this place well, it's how you got around. You knew what you were doing.'

Pawel didn't particularly feel that way now after all that had gone wrong.

'But because of what's happened tonight our security had no chance of spotting you. All the cameras and alarms must have been down when you decided to steal. It was bad luck you attempted a robbery the same night a bunch of goons decided to take over the place. So of course you were taken for night security because you wore the uniform……'

He stopped, aware of what he was about to say. The guy didn't need a reminder of the events again. It had all been grim.

Will examined his hands. Cringing and gritting his teeth at their state, he decided that he'd better cover up the lacerations and give them some protection.

Looking around for something that could be makeshift bandages, he said 'Don't fool yourself though, thinking that you could have gotten away with it. Not without these fuckers showing up….' Mentioning them, another blast was heard. The same volume and distance as earlier, it sounded like they were concentrating in one area.

Will finished '… procedures have tightened up recently.'

Pawel pointed towards the door and remarked 'They got in. Not that secure.'

Good point! Will conceded to himself. There didn't seem to be anything appropriate to cover his hands, so he pulled off his damp blue work jumper and began to tear long strips from it. Flinching each time from the pressure and discomfit in his palms as he tore the jumper apart and water still dripped out of it.

'I know, I know.' Will continued. 'I'm guessing they must have had an inside man…' He gave Pawel a sceptical stare, letting him know he was not entirely sure about Pawel's motives even though he made up his mind earlier. '…. these goons are terrorists, I think. Different kettle of fish.'

Pawel was at a loss as to what 'kettle of fish' meant as a brief silence came between them. It only seemed to amplify the constant buzzing and it now came with faint vibrations under their feet.

On the floor of the corridor, Will had now laid out four torn strips of his jumper. What remained of it was thrown into a corner.

'That's a whole lotta noise just to steal some paintings.'

'Drilling?' Pawel suggested.

'You know, that's just what I thought. But I don't know why?'

Pointing at Pawel's tourniquet, Will asked 'What happened to you?'

'A bullet graze. Nothing much.' He dismissed.

'You're very lucky.'

'I know.' But it was said ruefully.

Will could deduce what the man was thinking about and added respectfully, 'I know. I know.'

They resumed a silence again. Both mulling over that sound with a mixture of intrigue and dread. Dwelling too on their personal predicaments and what could happen. Yet both strangers shared a common hope that they could possibly get out of this situation with their lives.

Will had taken one of the makeshift strips of bandages and began to wrap it around one of his hands. The dampness of the material was soothing and cooling.

With that one tightened and tied as best as he could, he repeated the process again with another strip on the same hand for extra protection.

'Technically I'm still on duty, so I should be guarding this place....' He shrugged his shoulders. 'But no! My duty mixing with guns ended years ago. That's why I left the bloody Army for this job. Looking after a bunch of paintings and keeping the building secure; it couldn't of been easier. Shit man! The only thing I ever had to worry about was whether I had my breaks on time.' He was annoyed and this was his tirade!

Pawel looked at him with some affinity. Maybe not the war stuff but the job, he certainly understood how important the small things were.

'Though I'm still curious as to what these goons are up to. Fancy a look? Failing that, we get the hell out of here.' He wasn't sure how yet but if he could get an idea of what these soldiers were here for and then escape, at least he would have something to report. There was still some aspect of duty in him.

'What d'ya think Polish?'

'Get out of here, yes. But my name is not Polish!'

'I know.' Will smiled. 'But that's what I'm gonna call ya. Okay? Tak?' He emphasized the Polish word.

Once again Pawel was somewhat impressed at the use of his language. Despite his weariness and mistrust of most people, he was beginning to warm to this Londoner who could well get them out of this. But can I really trust him? He asked himself.

Pawel watched Will apply the last two strips to his other hand. With those tied, he gave both hands some more tugging, pulling and tightening until he seemed satisfied.

He had observed the man throughout his task, trying to form an opinion of him with his long hair and unkempt beard. There seemed something of a 'rodnik' about him; a maverick and as he clinched and unclenched his hands, he looked up at him and uttered, 'Sorted!'

Pawel still fretted though, that this man, this member of staff could still turn him in!

25

The Sainsbury Wing had been taken out of the equation in respect to it featuring too many entries and exits that would have to be covered by more men, more explosives and much more work. They simply overcame that by destroying the primary connection; the Link. The main building was now their only concern.

After leaving the Head of Security locked up in the vault with the gallery's secrets, Jan, his two soldiers and the hostage Hannah had already made their way over to the East wing of the building.

Since the radio call he received that not only confirmed the Link had successfully been blown but he had also been informed that one of his men had perished with it. Immediately he knew that that was no accident. Hans was not that careless. What was going on?

It was too much of a coincidence that he had not heard from his number two in awhile. He could not get hold of Gerard and that was so unlike him, he always answered his radio. He had to consider the reality of the situation. It could not be dismissed that no matter how well Gerard could look after himself and the many battles he had been involved in and pulled through, there was the possibility that he had run into trouble. Had he finally met his maker? Did the consummate soldier screw up? He had never failed an order! Maybe he was only incapacitated, unconscious somewhere and would turn up like he always did.

Being irked by Gerard's absence led to an annoyance of some of his soldier's attitudes. Their actions and remarks left much to be desired. That Yank for example, who reported Han's death was unprofessional and disrespectful. Typical of their kind; loud and brass!

Though these foreign allies of ours shared the same objectives and beliefs, they had yet to show their true mettle. Were they prepared for the dangers that the coming months would bring? Did they have the commitment, nerve and 'stählern?' Would they die for the cause? The real war would begin when we succeeded tonight and then true colours and loyalties would soon reveal themselves. He waited for the day and it was eminent because when the new order began some of these cowboys would be weeded out. He may not like it but for now they would suffice and if they were immolated with their deaths to attain our final goal then he would not feel the loss unlike his number two.

Jan checked his watch. It was time to let the world know, he told himself.

He was the only member of the team with a mobile phone and it was specifically for what he was about to do and this reason alone.

The system answered promptly and he approved of that. This call would be very important.

He begun clearly and articulate, the delivery was significant. 'The National Gallery building in Trafalgar Square, London is now under our control....' Slight pause.

'... We are not ISIS, al-Qaeda, Hezbollah or even the IRA. We are EU Insurgents seeking to overthrow an ineffectual and corrupt governance.....' Another pause.

The receiver of the call tried to speak but Jan continued dismissively. He would be the only one talking. They only had to listen, he instructed them.

'Any attempts to access these premises will prove fatal. This is not a hoax and should be taken very seriously.'

Despite the fact that all the staff were dead, the authorities did not know that and Jan was still going to use the threat.

'Any ignorance of these warnings and the hostages, the staff will be eliminated. The many irreplaceable paintings on these premises are held to ransom also.' Mentioning the art collection was a red herring too.

'Our political determinations and demands will be relayed to you in due time.' He ended the brief yet seminal call.

Jan knew only too well that their demands wouldn't be transmitted, simply because there weren't any. They were only playing for time.

26

By now the crowds had increased as PCSO Michael dealt with the same monotonous enquiries from the exuberant and nosey Joe Public while keeping them from spilling over the barriers.

Even at this late hour, no one wanted to go back to their homes or hotels. They were afraid they were going to miss something exclusive. Something to tell all and sundry about and that they were there that remarkable night. So their cameras flashed as instantly as the images could be sent. Slaves to their devices, they wanted to be the first to Twitter and send photos of this absorbing event via their mobiles.

He had been assigned crowd control duties at the far edge of the square by the Mall at Admiralty Arch. A half mile no-go zone had been set up around the area.

As he repeatedly urged the throng back, he answered all their queries with the same, tired explanation. 'Move along now. It's no big deal!' They didn't believe him and neither did he himself but as a true professional, he continued to do his job.

The whole Scotland Yard and the Armed Forces had eventually turned up to assess the picture. They had tried the West door to no success and they observed what was left of the Sainsbury Wing Link. They continued to nod their heads at each other like that 'Churchill' dog from the adverts. Murmuring agreement and rubbing their chins before finally agreeing that it was a serious state of affairs. He could have told them that but he had been pushed to the back of the pecking order and forgotten as was par the way with PCSO. The real boys were taking over now; they reminded him. He was used to it and it was no big deal with him.

They then gave the decision to clear the area and set up barricades. Michael could have told them that too.

Surrounding roads had been closed and the hubbub of the usually busy traffic had now all been diverted away. Sirens from police cars, ambulances and fire engines pierced the night as they continually arrived and congregated around the Square. Television and radio crews had been tipped off and they all began vying for positions to set up for the best shots, some already interviewing wide eyed members of the public, all too eager to appear on TV. The authorities steered clear with the classic 'no comment.'

Numerous police and media helicopters drifted at a respected distance. Buzzing in replay circles like incensed dragonflies.

The sight of so much bullet proof padding and numerous assault rifles reflected the seriousness of the situation. Yet the public continued to squeal excitably as if they were at a concert. Smiling for the television cameras and saying 'How awesome' it all was. They acted like it was more a red carpet event then a terrorist's threat. Everywhere you looked their eyes were hypnotised by the phone light that glowed in their rapt faces.

Michael had seen this mentality of theirs all the time. The enticement of the internet was a kind of popularity status for some and that they would never be able to live it down if they did not let every Tom, Dick and 'hash dot com' know that they were there. They could not see or comprehend the severity of the situation and that their lives could well be in danger. They did not care. They were there and that was all that mattered.

Intense beams from the spotlights roamed over and around the National Gallery, highlighting it like a stage. It almost felt like a theatre backdrop and a show was about to start. Michael's sense of humour couldn't help himself and imagined he was expecting a troupe to burst out of one of its doors and begin singing.

Apart from the crackle of police radios and the indistinct drone of choppers, an eerie silence began to descend over this most emblematic of locations. Trafalgar Square was now deserted – a rarely seen sight.

27

Coming up from the basement area, she began to hear the steadily growing noise and the closer they got to their destination where this sound emanated from the louder and more sinister it became. Hannah could only speculate to herself on what was the cause but it did sound alot like drilling. What she couldn't understand was why? Earlier too, she had heard and felt what was like a detonation in some part of the building and glancing at the Colonel and his two soldiers, she saw no recognition on their faces that it at all seemed out of the ordinary. She was sure she hadn't imagined it.
They passed through the Sunley Room, a stark modernist space set aside for temporary and contemporary exhibitions. At present, a mish-mash of red and green paint filled the walls. Entering Room 30, they paused. Even from here the din was ear-splitting.
'Time for protection!' the Colonel said at the top of his voice as he and his soldiers took out ear-plugs from their pockets and inserted them into their ears. With scant contemplation, they had ignored Hannah.
As they entered Room 32, the deafening clamour reverberated all around and the acoustics of the room only amplified it.
The space itself was impressive with its classic Victorian interiors. Natural light was able to enter through the glass roof, suffusing the room and giving more space to its already

spacious 124x41ft. Over forty 17th century French and Italian paintings adorned the walls and Hannah wondered why the paintings hadn't yet hopped off with all the vibrations running through the walls and floor.

Two other doorways ran off from the room. One in the middle was more an arch; tall and wide with huge black marble pillars framing it, led to Room 37 and the splendorous domed ceiling of Room 36. The other doorway leading into Room 33 which was closed was again resplendent with the same darkly varnished mahogany red on its doors and doorframes.

The Colonel pointed to a far point in the room, 'Tie her up to that rope barrier.'

The scene in the room was appalling, Hannah gasped. What a mess!

A haze hung in the air and the domineering smell was of cut wood and damp dirt. Hannah sneezed.

An 18x15ft square cavity gaped in the centre and as Hannah was pushed over to the corner, she was able to glance into the hole. It went down approximately 40ft and she could make out its internal workings which were lit up with small portable floodlights. Men working below were blasting away at concrete with portable jack-hammers. Fragments of stone and brick bounced about in the small confines, joining the piling rubble at their feet. They wore PVC goggles and covering their mouths and noses were dust masks. She also noticed that the ear-plugs they wore were the large headphone type that fitted over their heads. With all the dust floating upwards and outwards, the floodlights gave the workers an eerie and ghostly form.

A vast array of equipment was scattered about the room; braided polypropylene ropes were securely tied to the marble pillars and trailed down into the hole, including dozens of cables snaking the floor that were plugged into the numerous plug sockets spread throughout the room.

To one side a heap of split and splintered timbers from the floorboards were piled and nearby two Raptor 52 petrol chainsaws lay on the floor with Jerry cans of spare diesel. Two portable compressors shook and rumbled noisily, their hoses also trailing down into the excavation where they hooked up to the pumping pneumatic drills that was causing the entire racket.

Two motorbikes were parked up in another corner of the room.

A thin layer of dust coated everything from the floor, sofas and equipment including some of the unprotected and priceless paintings and their frames. It was like a builder's site!

She was thrown to the floor and manhandled by her two ogling captors then handcuffed with her right hand, not to the rope barriers that lined the room but the metal poles itself that protruded from the wooden flooring and supported the ropes.

All she could do at the moment was sit there and observe the unbelievable scene taking place in one of the rooms of the National Gallery. It was all so wrong!

She coughed and sneezed recurrently and she was beginning to get a migraine. The overbearing noise was relentless and she found it hard to concentrate on what she was going to do. The din was akin to a dentist's drill in your head and Hannah wanted to scream out, as if somehow it would stop its abatement. Someway shout it silent!

She was an English Italian in her 30's and ever since she was a child, she stole things. From her family, friends, shops, schools, jobs and pretty much everywhere else. As she got older, she realised how talented she was at it because she was getting caught less and less. The only thing that had really changed in her compulsive habit was the items she now stole were much more valuable which in turn involved far greater risks. Yet she found it easy to gain access into locked premises and overcome their safety measurements and as security systems became more and more sophisticated, so did she.

Part of the profession was the thrill. She could never explain to anyone why she did it and she never really questioned the urge, she just knew she was good at it and it paid very well. Everyone was born with a gift she accepted and this was hers.

She told anyone who asked that she worked in acquisitions and fundamentally it was true. Apart from the usual hit and run burglaries, she had become a specialist in infiltrating companies and businesses, earning the trust of her employers by spending months in a job only to eventually get her hands on specific items of value by gaining access with codes, keys and manipulation. Deliberately using her gorgeous looks and intentionally portraying the dumb bimbo to get what she wanted. She played enamoured and gullible very well and she often thought she should go into amateur dramatics. She was a black belt in Taekwondo and 7th Dan in aikido and combining both these martial arts, she was very capable of looking after herself in most fights. She often took gun classes because sometimes in her line of work, a girl had to be cautious. She only ever had to use a gun once and it was not something she ever wanted to exercise again.

She could plainly see, as far as everyone else was concerned that she was just some 'Barbie doll' hostage that had the misfortune to be caught up in all of this and a threat to no one. But she was not afraid and she would not sit here and wait for these 'He-men' to decide her future.

She was in the gallery for that same item that the Colonel took from the vault and was furious when this happened. The diamond was hers! She had worked her way to it patiently by becoming Powell's secretary. Earning his trust and manipulating him with her sexual advances and seductiveness. The scheme had run its course and she had been waiting, biding her time for an opportune moment to act. She had been so close to getting into that vault and getting her hands on the diamond and then this 'Rambo turns up after all this time, only to take it from me when I had done all this work. Seven months worth of planning.'

Still, an opportunity would present itself. Her time would come, she was sure of it.

28

'Where there's a Will, there's a way. C'mon.'
They were making their way down the narrow corridor staircase. In the sparse confines the wooden steps creaked and their footfalls echoed noisily even as they treaded lightly. They had decided not to use the elevator for fear of attracting attention to themselves and their whereabouts with its clattering.

There were five floors that this often neglected staircase served and was only ever utilised as a fire escape for each level. The bottom of the staircase, the basement and staff areas they had decided to use where eventually they would arrive at another stairwell that would bring them back up between Rooms 33 and 34. It was internal and Will was counting on the terrorists deeming it unnecessary to cut off. He had not thought of it earlier when he first discovered the place under siege because at the time, all he wanted to do was get to the control rooms.

Will delicately rummaged in his damp back pocket as well as he could with bandages on his hands and pulled out a squashed and slightly damp packet of cigarettes. Most of them were ruined but found two that he thought he could salvage. Flicking his lighter again and again, he was finally able to get a flame which he used to dry one out as he rolled it through his fingers.

Throughout all of this, Pawel had watched him with scepticism.

At the bottom of the staircase with his cigarette dried and placed between his lips, Will slowly opened the door and peeked his head out. Looking left and right down the corridor he observed it empty and silent. The sensors then triggered the lights on, illuminating the drab corridor.

Will satisfied, nodded and they both turned right.

To Pawel's surprise, Will then lit his cigarette.

'You can not smoke here. It will set the alarms off.'

Inhaling in a long indifferent drag, Will said 'No it won't. Want some?'

'No.' Pawel answered offended.

'The alarms ain't gonna go off. Not sensitive enough. You worked here, didn't you know that? No! Okay. Guess if you don't smoke you wouldn't. Listen to this….' Will had a point to make. '…… I wouldn't be here now, talking to you if I hadn't taken a cig break earlier. Whoever said smoking can kill doesn't know it saved my life.' He took another satisfactory lungful. 'My luck was good. It could so easily have been bad.'

Pawel's face dropped. They were the exact words Joseph had used and he had had the bad.

He knew deep down in the bottom of his soul, he would be hurting for a long time. Joseph was his best pal, family.

'Anyway, a smoke helps me to think.' Will continued. 'Done my best stuff while smoking and at the moment I need this' He stressed.

Pawel didn't say anything. He was still in his own despondent thoughts as they walked.

'I killed a few men today. Not what I wanted to do but I had to. I'm ex- Army.' The cigarette had put Will in a pensive mood. He didn't know why he felt he had to share that. The more he thought about it, he realised it was probably something he needed to do. Confide in someone and share his feelings even if it was with a stranger. Yet he didn't want to divulge to Polish that it was the first time he ever killed.

He could see the man was relying on his experience as an ex-soldier to get them out of this mess. Polish wanted the reassurance and was probably glad of his support, as he was of his. He needed it as much as him Will admitted to himself.

No! Polish need not know that lack of experience in my ability. Let him believe as much as I need to too.

The sensors down here worked 24/7, always on and ready for activation. They burst into life as they progressed; its low lighting adding to the flaking, old yellow paint that dinged the corridor walls.

Even here in the lower levels of the gallery they could hear that ongoing buzzing sound but now a little distant and muffled like a generator.

Both men were continually aware of it and wondering if this was the cause of their predicament.

29

It was coming up to two hours and still they were not through.
He had hoped by now that this part of the operation would have been completed. Surely it couldn't be much longer, he brooded.
He was standing at the pit's edge, waiting and inspecting his boots. It was something he knew he often did when he became restless.
One of the engineers working down in the foundations climbed up the rope out of the depths to where he stood. Goggles and a face mask covered his face which in turn were caked in a filthy ashen powder.
Raising his voice; almost shouting, the man informed him 'It will not take much longer now.'
He returned a glare of irritation at him. 'How long is a piece of string?'
The engineer shrugged his shoulders and dust bellowed off his overalls, 'Ninety minutes at most.'
'Before most then!' He commanded then noticing particles on his boots, he proceeded to lift a leg and roughly polish each behind his trouser legs.
The engineer climbed back down into the pit to continue the hard and sweaty work. Four men – two engineers and two burly soldiers had the task of breaking through but because of the restrictive space and the thick hazardous dust, they had to allow for periodical breaks. Only two at a time could labour.

They had begun the painstaking work of pulling up the floorboards first then cutting their way around some of the existing pipes. Drilling and blasting into the concrete basement area followed until they eventually reached the bricked in part of the artificial foundation.

The measured to hole that had been chainsawed cut out of the wooden flooring was the easiest part. It was the concrete levels and metal obstructions that involved the difficult work. But the drills and small amounts of carefully placed explosives would see them get through. There were reasons for this unorthodox approach.

They had located the rear wall of one of the staff locker rooms where a section bricked onto it. This specific location had been meticulously researched by studying the blueprints of the building, the same blueprints that the old man had posted to him and their progress would not be hindered too much by the network of pipes and cables that ran underground. This was the fastest way despite the obstacles.

It was testament to German engineering that the extended brickwork done by their own men back in the forties remained so steadfast after all this time and it was because of this that they had not yet broken through. Their own sturdy workmanship was what was delaying them. The irony amused and annoyed him. Still it was a minor setback and the plan allowed for some flexibility in timings. Every successful plan had to.

After so much preparation there was still some nervousness that once they had finally drilled through the partition there would be no gold at all. He didn't show it of course, unlike some of his men waiting around in the room, checking their watches again and again. They did not fully understand what he had at stake. As well as his reputation, what they did or did not discover down in that hole determined the future of a lot of people. To most of these men they agitated because they simply wanted to get the job done and get out before the authorities could take back the place. His perturbations epitomised all of the Phoenix Project. At times the burden had weighed heavy but he knew with absolute conviction that he had the shoulders and backbone to see it through. It was another mission that he would accomplish like he always had done before. Not being able to shake this niggling doubt worried him though. Especially as more and more of the work progressed and the nearer they got.

And still no word from Gerard. He had to assume the worse. In battle you had to reluctantly accept that good comrades would die. The rest of the team, he expected it but Gerard, well that was harder to stomach. You may not like it and however much you admired and depended on certain individuals, it was an undeniable fact of war. You could not let emotions interfere. There would always be martyrs.

As he paced up and down at the far end of the room, his ear piece crackled.

'Phoenix One, you receiving?'

'Go ahead.'

'This is Phoenix four. Cameras show you got company right above your heads.'

'Military?'

'Ya! A stealth copter has dropped them! Looks like their ready to gate crash your party via the roof.'

'How many?'

'Eight, over.'

'Thanks for the warning Phoenix four.'

The Colonel addressed all his men in the room via radio, 'You all heard that. A Special Forces unit is about to come in from the ceiling above. Heads up, weapons ready but continue working. Let them think we are completely unaware of them. If they want to join this party, we will throw them a surprise.'

It's time to even the playing field, he himself decided. Let's have some casualties from their side this time.

They did not have long to wait.

The windows that made up the ceiling exploded in four different places and the mercurial shower rained down to the floor below. Shadows could be seen, fleeting movements swiftly followed by the eight SCO19 specialist unit forces on ropes, two at each entry. An elite cache of highly trained officers in body armoured fatigues, helmets, goggles and armed with MP5 machine guns.

The anti-terrorist unit had earlier established with infra-red scans that the majority of the terrorists in the building were congregating in Room 32 and their active heat signatures revealed that they were preoccupied with something. This was the time to act, which they hoped would give them the element of surprise.

As they repelled down their ropes and even before they could open fire they realised to their surprise and not the terrorists that they had been expected. The terrorist's weapons were already raised and targets picked.

There was a brief impalpable silence before all around the room was the flare and thundering of discharging guns. Blazes of light from the weapons skipped erratically across the walls and the portraits themselves seemed to shy away from what they were witnessing.

The Colonel and his men who were already wearing earplugs could not completely hear the onslaught the noise had on uncovered ears. Hannah did and she suffered the full intensity. Though the volume of the drilling earlier was horrendous, this sound was a different infliction. It came with shocking visuals that made it even more terrifying.

The British soldier's danced like pelted rag dolls, their bodies twitched and jerked on each impact of a relentless barrage of bullets. Blood erupted from multiple wounds down onto the room's floor. Their own weapons fell from their grips and hung from them on straps. Not one had had the chance to return fire.

To be witness to such atrocity, Hannah was utterly sickened. All the terrorists shared the same sinister expression in the flash of each of their weapons. Teeth bared, grimacing manically and their black eyes in the glare of the muzzle flashes made them appear like demons.

She could only cup one ear with one hand - the other being cuffed - and bowed her head in vain, averting her eyes from the slaughter even if the racket still pierced. Those poor wretched men, she cried. In her tightly closed eyes, she could still see the carnage.

The anti-terrorists unit had no time to counter attack or defend themselves before all eight of them were massacred. Their bullet proof vests could not withstand or protect the full might of the terrorist's arsenal; they were only designed to stand up to a few shots. Not this bombardment!

Like string puppets simply severed and mowed down. Their bullet ridden corpse's laid about the room; one soldier had landed on one of the portable compressors and on his back he hung abnormally over it, staring vacantly up at the roof that they had come through to meet their unforeseen demise.

Two remained dangling on their swinging ropes, hanging from the roof in a macabre scene of death. Lifeless! They had no chance, Hannah pitied. It was awful! The screams of those dying men would stay with her for a very long time.

The silence that followed seemed to resonate hauntingly as loud as even the earlier drilling and machine gun fire put together.

That was until the Colonel interrupted the uneasy atmosphere and remarked 'It's not for nothing that we Germans call an attack, a storm.'

The sick bastard, Hannah thought.

'We needed to open that roof. They saved us the job, ya!' The Colonel remarked without remorse.

As if in answer one of his lieutenants laughed ghoulishly.

30

Pawel still had trepidations about this man's wish to find out what the terrorists were up to - calling them 'terrorists' had now stuck.

Will had promised him that at any sign of trouble they would just hide it out until the authorities finally turned up or an opportunity presented itself. Still, he could not help but feel it was foolhardy. He only wanted to avoid more bullets and that seemed a rational plea.

They had lost count of how many times they turned left, right and ducked. Stooping more often as the ceilings lowered and the walls revealed its original brickwork. They were now deep in the basement sub-levels, avoiding the staff recreational area and sticking to the surrounding passageways and corridors. The network down here was vast and it was not unknown for new members of staff to waste time trying to find their way back to their locker rooms.

The unceasing and steadily growing vibrations of the drilling that bounced around the narrow corridors down here had become so regular that most time it felt like background noise.

They had walked in silence a lot of the time with Will pointing this way and that, forgetting that the man with him knew the way around too. But Pawel didn't say anything.

Both were deep in their own deliberations and unknown to each other they were the same; a mixture of apprehension, fear and urgency. In spite of them sharing a common enemy and a view that they were in it together, a little doubt still troubled both of them. Could the other really be trusted?

Before Will could register what was happening, a shadow swung out from behind a corner and dealt a powerful wallop to his stomach.

His ribs and stomach still ached from earlier, now it was excruciating. As he bent over clutching himself another blow swiftly followed, this time to the back of his head with the same solid object. Lights exploded in his eyes and everything went black.

How long he was out for he didn't know but barely conscious and with a headache from Hades he found himself lying on the floor.

His head felt like it was going to split open and touching the back of it, he felt a golf ball sized bruise had developed. It was extremely sensitive and released pain inducing fireworks to his eyes.

Looking up, his vision cleared a little more and he could make out a figure a few feet in front of him.

'No, no, no…! It couldn't be?' his thoughts panicked. It was Gerard!

His back to Will, the Frenchman was kicking and shouting at Polish who was sprawled on the floor. Pulling himself backwards with one arm and the other raised trying to futilely block the blows that came down upon him again and again.

Will managed to pull himself up off the floor. He had to do something to help Polish despite his delirium and discomfit. Everything moved in the wrong direction, disconcerting dizziness overwhelmed. His throbbing head felt hung-over and weighed a ton on his shoulders.

His hand found the wall that gave him the balance he was lacking. The passageway began to orientate itself and became more stable.

Polish was utterly defenceless and for a brief moment, Will was annoyed that Polish would not defend himself but each blow struck him so swiftly and relentlessly that he had no chance. Gerard was laying into him with his weapon, using the butt of his assault rifle like a club bludgeoning a seal.

Then Will noticed something. Peering at the back of Gerard's head, he realised with incomprehensibility that the man beating Polish was not Gerard. There was no shaven head or ponytail. It was not the Frenchman at all!

He swooned, almost fainted and steadied himself once again against the wall.

It was another terrorist that was attacking Polish. Not Gerard! The knock on my head has confused me, he told himself.

Still shouting at Polish, the terrorist was unaware of Will's presence behind him - probably believing he was still unconscious - and looking around for a weapon of sorts, Will spotted a shiny red fire extinguisher behind him.

Carefully he was able to lift it up without a sound or a grunt of pain.

The terrorist attacking Polish was caught up in his own rage to notice Will. Vocally expelling, '….and Germany is kicking pathetic Polish arse again….' He sounded like some kind of Nazi nut, Will thought.

He was becoming more coherent now, aware of his surroundings and movements.

He lifted the light weight but solid extinguisher and approaching Polish's attacker, he brought it back behind his shoulder and with all his strength swung it around and forward.

It caught the terrorist on the right side of his head and he fell like a sack of potatoes.

'Shut it.' Will sneered.

31

Directly outside the National Gallery and adjacent to the green lawns in front of the west corner of the premises was an open aired walled area that was known as the Director's Garden. Well kept with an abundance of colourful flowers and scrubs, the York stone patio also contained tables and chairs for whenever the Director hosted tea parties. Patio doors led back into his offices and the rest of the building but in one corner of the garden, a small nondescript door led out onto Jubilee Walk and the Square. It was a rarely used fire exit.

Here another anti-terrorist unit had disabled some of the exterior CCTV and the alarm between door and frame had also successfully been deactivated too. They were being very cautious and taking all the time they needed especially after the disastrous first attempt.

The authorities had still not heard back from them. No demands had yet been made and they were becoming very suspicious as to what they were really up to. Were they not terrorists after all and were only here in an endeavour to pull off an ambitious heist to steal the paintings?

Despite the earlier failed attempt to retake the building and the almost certainty that all the specialists team had perished they still believed the hostages remained alive. It was because of this that the powers that be had no intentions of waiting around. No terrorists were going to dictate to them on their very own soil and with a zero tolerance attitude they were simply not going to put up with it. These murderers had to be stopped whatever the cost. No time was wasted and this team had already been prepared and ready to go earlier when the initial effort had meant to succeed.

The four specialists made their way stealthily through the garden towards the locked patio doors. Making good progress they continually updated and relayed their movements and what they saw to their superior officers who held back at a safe distance outside the garden walls in the square.

Once again with patience and precision they were able to disable the alarm that ran between door and frame. It did not involve anything ingenious, only a thin rectangular foil strip between the points in the door where the magnets lay. This stopped the current and thus the alarm to sound.

The reinforced door now needed a little persuasion with a two man battering ram. This particular one incorporated a cylinder and firing piston, enhancing the impact significantly as it effected a breaching.

They took a moment to poise themselves, knowing that once this doorway was breached the storming of the building would commence. They would be followed by another team of soldiers waiting outside in the square.

The leader of the team informed their superiors that they were about to force an entry. Ready as they would ever be they nodded their heads at each other in confirmation.

On impact everything exploded!

C4 explosives are lightweight and could be moulded into any shape, pushed and pressed onto and into anything. Tiny amounts were powerful enough to cause substantial damage and it was considered the best in the business for both small and large jobs.

The garden was obliterated. It looked like the inside of a furnace, charred black and ash coated. Not a flower or scrub remained and the tables and chairs had become firewood.

Like a colossal fist had punched down onto the paved ground, a large crater had formed by the patio doors. Surprisingly the walls themselves which contained much of the blast - protecting those on the outside from the worst - remained standing although somewhat unstable in places. Cracks had appeared and some bricks had toppled outwards. The cast iron railing that ran along the top of the wall had remained intact but its paint had melted away.

The patio door and frame was no more and the surrounding wall had come down in the explosion creating a gaping arch the size of a car. Inside the Director's office, it was completely destroyed. What little remained lay under tonnes of concrete, brick and plaster rubble. Getting into or out of the building this way was now impossible.

Outside, the public gasped as one; all bobbing their heads back and forth to try and get a glimpse of the report that rang out over the square. The majority of the jostling throng weren't entirely sure at which part of the building the detonation had occurred but those at the front observed the black smoke drifting skywards, emanating from the small corner at the front of the National Gallery. They had watched the police enter via the outside nondescript emergency door and shortly afterwards came the explosion. They could not know the extent of the damage or the cost of human lives.

Only one of the four specialists had survived the devastating detonation and he had lost a leg, an arm, a kidney and his hearing.

The officers outside in the square quickly rushed in and managed to carry out their surviving colleague. Eyeing with horror at the sights of bloody body parts scattered around of the men who weren't so lucky.

They had underestimated their foes to a deadly cost once again.

32

Together they had tied up the unconscious terrorist using some discarded cabling they found and secured him to a pipe. The whole side of his face had blown up to a giant red welt and Will quipped he would resemble the 'Elephant man' for a few days to come.
The terrorist's radio was crushed to smithereens and the gun disposed behind a cluster of piping.
Will was still reeling from the blows and trying to regain some sense. He could not believe that for a moment there he was completely convinced that Gerard was still alive. That blow to my head had really done something to me to think that the Frenchman was back from the dead. Maybe because he had tormented and teased me for so long at work that I somehow could not let him go. It's like the fucker's haunting me! On reflection, he should have known it couldn't possibly have been him. How could Gerard have made it back over into the main building after the Link to the Sainsbury Wing was cut off? Anyway, the man was dead. He had seen the body.
He didn't share any of these thoughts with Pawel who was examining his injuries. Sleeves rolled up, there were no cuts or bleeding but his arm which had parried so many of the blows was black and blue with bruises already. Nevertheless he seemed more concerned with his possession, Will observed.
Lifting his jumper, Pawel opened the backpack underneath and partially pulled the painting out. To his disappointment a crack had appeared from the top to the bottom of the glass

protecting the canvas underneath. But it had not split and still remained intact. The work of art itself appeared undamaged. His shoulders portrayed a sigh of relief and as Pawel pushed the 'Madonna of the Pinks' back into the backpack and zipped it up, Will realised then that Polish had been protecting the painting with his arm rather than himself.

Pawel abruptly spoke up, 'I can't really let it go now. This is….' Pulling his jumper back down and patting it. '…..Joseph. It has come to represent him.' He sounded very serious. 'I cannot let it get damaged. Joseph will not let me.' He looked up at Will with a pained expression on his face. 'Do you understand?'

Will didn't exactly but said, 'I understand Polish.' Tell him what he wants to hear, Will understood. He didn't want Polish cracking up on him but he wanted to get Pawel out of his despondent mood. Get him to grasp the reality of the situation.

'We don't like being put in a position but sometimes you get in a corner and you have no choice but to fight. Being forced into these circumstances is horrible mate but if you don't make a stand, you don't have a chance.'

Pawel began rubbing his battered arm again, trying to ease the throbbing pain. He could see what this guy was doing. 'I understand. Thank you for helping me.' He said to Will.

'You would of done the same….' Will began to remark then remembered, '… Hey! But you did.' He smiled at Pawel who returned a better smile then earlier.

'Yes, I did. We are evens!'

'Yeah, we're even.' Will emphasised the correct pronunciation. 'You okay?'

'Yes…!' Pawel nodded boldly. 'We are going to make it.'

'I like that Polish. Good attitude.'

Will helped Pawel up, though he was cursing his own aches and pains. He felt like he had gone a full twelve rounds in the ring.

They set off again, knowing they hadn't far to go now. The drilling noise had gotten louder too and it didn't really feel that far away either. The vibration rose up from the ground and into the walls and dust could even be seen falling from places in the ceiling.

Eventually they emerged out of the pipe lined corridors, the underground area of the building behind them and were now back in the staff areas at the bottom of the stairwell to Room 33.

They looked at each other for acknowledgement that they both were ready for this next move and just as Will put his foot on the first step the drilling noise suddenly stopped.

They exchanged curious glances. The quietness was unsettling.

At any moment they expected a bunch of terrorists to come tearing in, guns blazing. But nothing happened, silence resumed.

'C'mon.' Will eventually whispered, urging them on.

They began climbing the concrete spiral staircase that would bring them back up to a swipe door, which would lead out onto the gallery floors on level two. These stairs always reminded Will of the narrow winding stone steps of a medieval castle and in his uneasiness imagined not soldiers with swords and shields of old but terrorists with automatic weapons trapping them in these twisting and turning confines.

Will worried too if the swipe door was still passable and not barred and blocked from the other side like so many he had come across.

A muffled explosion like sound was suddenly heard from a distant part of the gallery. They exchanged puzzled looks and both had the same question. What had these terrorists blown up now? They were even more anxious after what they were sure was another act of devastation.

They approached the doorway; Pawel behind Will, followed his every tentative step.

The light on the swipe system glowed green.

Will put his ear to the black wooden door and listened. Since the drilling had stopped the gallery had resumed its tomb like silence. Nothing was heard but his own pounding heart.

Will turned to Pawel and whispered 'Ready?'

Placing both hands on the door Will gently pushed and it began to open. He had to give it more effort because of its heaviness; it was a security door after all.

Air conditioned air rushed through the widening gap.

With the door pushed all the way open and holding it back against the wall, Will listened. Nothing.

He peered around both corners into both rooms on his left and right. They were empty.

He made sure Pawel took the door and he stepped into the small passage that linked both rooms. He then felt a sudden shift, a movement of air before he could turn.

Pawel had let the door go and because of its spring and weight it swung back and caused the loudest bang as it slammed shut.

The noise echoed in the rooms and without a doubt throughout most of the gallery.

Will's hand and arm was still outstretched into thin air where he never had any chance of catching the closing door.

Pawel had a silent and stupid gaping 'O' of a mouth.

Then they heard the motorbike.

33

Two miles away from the events unfolding in Trafalgar Square stood Chelsea barracks on the Chelsea Bridge Road which was only a stone's throw away from the River Thames. Originally built in the 19th century to house a battalion of troops it grew to its thirteen acres of land to accommodate four companies of the Guard's Regiment. Its residence by the British Army's Military of Defence went back 150 years, but now it was the beginning of the end of an era, as all its soldiers, vehicles and equipment were to be relocated. As the government reduced funding took effect, most of the land and buildings would be put up for sale. It seemed even the politicians were not against profits from defence cuts.
A base of sorts still operated as a small company of soldiers and vehicles remained until the final withdrawal and hand over to its future owners. Soldiers of the resident regiment that still held positions – albeit a skeleton crew - were the security for this evening's event.
Now at this late hour, a marketing reception for potential investors and bankers was coming to an end. In this promotional private sell-off and land grabbing by wealthy profiteers, the affluence was seen in all the designer clothing and three star Michelin food and drink being consumed.
Amongst this atmosphere of care free expenditure and capitalist greed, two men slipped away from their duties as waiters to attempt to steal the impossible.
They had infiltrated the hired catering staff and had been keeping up their cover by working four hours straight without a break and the Englishman was glad to finally see

the back of the chores and those 'stuck-up knobs.' As far as he was concerned he never wanted to see a glass of champagne or a canapé ever again.

He had slipped off to change into an RAF uniform that he had concealed in his duffel bag and as he now left the party he appeared as just another soldier heading back to his barracks.

'Had enough of this pompous bollocks!' He said to the guard who saluted him on the perimeter gate that enclosed the function area.

'Know what you mean mate.' The guard joined in. 'Bastards are ruining this outfit. Goodnight.'

He had been chosen for this phase because he was English and it would make passing the guards and gate easier. Most crucially, he was an experienced pilot of numerous airborne vehicles.

Situated behind the barracks were a line of familiar green military trucks, jeeps and parked further away; two helicopters. One of them was a Chinook and this was where he was heading.

A quick glance around the open grounds that used to be supplied with many a military vehicle and was now a shadow of its former force, he observed it deserted.

He walked briskly and purposefully to the vehicle. A CH – 47 twin tandem rotor helicopter designed by Boeing Vertol for the transportation of troops, cargo and rescue missions too. They had the nickname the 'Fat Cows' and could carry 12,700kg with a hook winch capable of lifting 20,000 pounds.

The cockpit door was unlocked and there was no alarm. Who would attempt to steal a helicopter in an Army base and with its security detail still in place?

It was said that it was impossible to 'hotwire' a Chinook but that was what the RAF had always stated. With any vehicle you only needed to know how to. It was a case of no one simply having the audacity to attempt it.

By now the second man that had infiltrated the caterers was climbing out of the staff toilets rear window and making his way to rendezvous with his colleague. Over the portacabin roofs which lined the perimeter fence separating the social event from the Army grounds, he stealthily moved across. He jumped down unseen on the other side and sprinted across the open tarmac to where the remaining copter was - an RAF Puma HC1. Instead of climbing into its cockpit, he flattered himself on the cold, concrete ground and rolled underneath it. He then attached something to the vehicles under carriage and just as agilely rolled back out again.

Getting back to his feet, he continued his sprint. This time in the direction of the Chinook.

As he approached it, the massive and impressive piece of machinery began to start up.

The pilot smiled a welcome at his passenger who breathing heavily clambered into the other seat beside him.

'G'day!' the Australian greeted.

'Ah! My co-pilot.' The Englishman remarked jovially. 'Welcome aboard. Glad you could make it dear boy. Strap in.'

He remembered the conversation he and the Aussie had had the night before. The Australian asking why he, the English of all Englishmen was doing this and was he not betraying his country.

To him, it was simple. Our once majestic island had become a refugee camp. The heart and soul of this great nation of ours has had the heart and soul ripped out of it. Siphoned off by Thatcherism! She had sown the seeds that had eventually sold our country down the river of privatisation and profit. Every leader since then was only prescribing the same bitter pill. Britain had become a commodity where its politicians had let every other greedy conglomerate and wretched exploitationists to sell, steal and suck us dry until we had nothing left to show or own anymore. We had lost our industries and reserves, our independence and our identity. I want Nationalism in our country again. Its time for a bloody revolution, he vehemently told the Aussie.

He continued to run through pre-flight checks quickly and efficiently. Checking lights and indicators on the complex screen panel as the Chinook began to produce more and more noise. Its powerful motors thundered all around them; its high pitch whine of the turbine generating the immense power for its eminent lift off.

The co-pilot turned to look outside through the cockpit window and uttered 'We got company sport.'

'And I believe we're ready to go.' The pilot pulled back on the stick.

Members of the security detail and some off duty soldiers had arrived too late in the base's open grounds to prevent the copter lifting off. The thump, thump of the blades rotating were in full motion now as it gave the lift that the vehicle needed.

As the huge machine slowly rose, its sound was momentarily muffled by the exploding Puma copter parked nearby.

The soldiers on the ground dropped to their feet, covering their heads. Some unfortunates were caught in the blast and blown backwards. Dead before they even hit the ground.

The discharge from the exploding copter buffeted the Chinook marginally but their increasing altitude was sufficient and its aluminium and titanium chassis was barely affected by the shockwaves.

'Woooo!' The Australian grinned. 'The bird has blown….. Get it? The bird has flown…!'

'Yes! Quite!' The Englishman replied sardonically.

The unscathed soldiers on the ground stood about helplessly. Their only chance of immediately pursuing the thieves was a burning wreck. They could only stare upwards through the bellowing black smoke as the Chinook disappeared into the night.

A call would go out and soon enough they would know where their stolen helicopter was bound.

34

The familiar engine of a motorbike came into Room 34 and pulled up right above the air vent's grill, its engine idling. So close in actuality that he could reach out and touch the hot rubber tyres if he dared to.

Only moments before at Will's hurrying they had lifted the grill cover aside. Will almost had to kick Pawel down the tight gap that had enough room for a maintenance worker to squeeze through. 'I'm coming down too, Polish. Quickly, their coming.'

Pawel needed no further urging, the thought of meeting another hail of bullets from another biker spurred him into action.

Once Pawel had climbed down, Will hastily followed and before dropping through the gap and with some effort he managed to pull the heavy grill cover back into place over their heads, just as the motorbike entered the room.

Here they were now. Both hiding in the room's vents that ran under the room's floorboards. Crouched down on their hands and knees in the dark, it was all they could do in these 4x4ft shafts.

Most rooms had one of these cast iron grills in the floor where cooling air or heating; depending on the season was pumped through from numerous generators working below in the basement. A whole network of these outlets ran throughout the galleries under flooring and considering their constant usage they were relatively clean. They had to be, Health and Safety regulated it. Yet some members of staff were convinced all kinds of dust and dirt that was blown up into the rooms were the causes of the oft quoted 'Gallery Flu.'

Despite many of these conduits there was not always a way to move from one room to another as Will knew only too well. It was only ever going to be a hiding place because at some point or another the vent narrowed to 2x2ft; making it impossible for anyone to traverse the whole network of shaft-ways.

The bikes engines were fearsomely loud above them as they waited. Its cacophony reverberating around their claustrophobic surroundings.

Exhaust fumes began to fill the vent and they tried not to cough from the intoxication but it was hard to hold your breath when you felt panic stricken and suffocated.

Glupiec! Pawel called himself. It was Polish for an individual idiot.

Glupiec! Glupiec! Glupiec! He was verbally berating himself for letting the door close shut like that. He should have known better, he used to work here! God knows what Will thinks of me?

Will wasn't dwelling on it. He was more concerned with what was happening above them.

Another motorbike could be heard approaching and it pulled up next to the other. More noise, more fumes and more danger.

They exchanged nervous looks.

The lights in the room above lit up a small part of the vent. Pawel could see Will's bandaged hands cover his mouth from the exhaust fumes and he did the same.

Once again I'm hidden away in a small, cramp and airless tunnel, Pawel anguished. The only difference now, it is with this man and not Joseph.

The thought sadden him. How everything had changed so badly.

He stared miserably into the darkness of the chute like it was his future. Glupiec!

The bikers conversed with each other but with the deafening din of their engines it was indistinct to Will and Pawel.

The exhaust fumes were getting overbearing and Pawel couldn't help himself. He coughed. Twice!

This is it, he feared. They were going to be caught like rats in a sewer pipe.

But the bikers had not heard the coughs above the running of their noisy engines. They were completely unaware of the two men hiding right under their noses.

It wasn't long before they revved off, to continue their search elsewhere and all became subdued.

Will and Pawel's drawn out sigh was immensely relieving. They had remained undiscovered.

After ten minutes Will decided they had waited long enough. The bikes were out of earshot and if they did return they would be heard in the distance and forewarned.

'Let's get out now.' Will prompted. They would suffocate otherwise and he would probably catch a cold. He was still damp from the Link explosion and the air circulating in the vents made him shiver.

Pawel continued to cough. The fumes from the motorbikes exhausts lingered unpleasantly in the vent.

Will reached up and slowly and cautiously pushed the grate up and aside. It screeched on its rigid metal frame but he didn't care if he was heard; they needed to get out of their fumigated hole.

Clambering out, Will began coughing too but at least he was able to inhale breathable air again.

Without warning he heard a bike's engine start up.

Looking up, he saw the bike pull out from around the corner of the adjacent room heading towards him. His Uzi raised and aimed in his direction.

'Shit!' he cursed under his breath. It must have been waiting. As Will crawled out onto floor level, he turned his head and whispered audibly enough for Pawel to hear 'Stay down and out of sight. Wait it out!' Pawel could still have a chance, Will believed.

Pawel's frustration at not being able to get out of this smog filled hole turned to guilt. Still on his hands and knees he retreated backwards out of sight, down the chute into its gloom again. 'This is my fault.'

Will stood up, annoyed with himself and his eagerness to get out of the vent.

The biker slowly approached him on his purring engine and with a wave of his weapon beckoned Will to move away from the opening. He then spoke into his radio piece. 'Phoenix Three to Phoenix One...?'

He received a reply in his ear and stated, 'I have the 'ratte.''

While he waited for instructions the biker was unwavering in his watch and aim over Will.

He could not understand why he had not been shot. What was the difference between him and his dead colleagues?

He stared apprehensively at the black mirror like helmet the biker wore. Not seeing a face made it menacing and there was no reaction to react upon. Will was seriously contemplating whether he could take this goon out.

'Roger that.' The helmet nodded after a long tense moment. 'Room 32. Lead the way.' He barked at Will and induced him with a wave of his weapon.

Another biker showed up then. Reinforcement. Will knew any chance of taking out the goon and escaping was missed now.

As he walked dejected, he was berating himself. Wherever they are bringing me it can't be good. I am such a fucking idiot!

At least they didn't check the vent, he supposed. As far as these terrorists were concerned they were only looking for one other person. What Polish was going to do now was up to him! He hoped that maybe he would somehow remain undiscovered and finally get out of the building, even with the painting. At least Polish has a chance! Me? I probably deserve what's coming to me. Why did I have to be so bloody curious? Stupid! Stupid! Stupid!

35

Those amber glowing blocks of sunshine. The aura was hypnotic. He had to see it for himself, touch it.
His men had finally broken through and personally relieved that the drilling had finished he threw away his sticky ear plugs. From the floor level looking down, the luminosity cut through the dust hanging in the pit. He climbed down.
The chamber itself measured 15x13ft and other then the four bricked up walls surrounding it; it was undisturbed since it had been sealed up at the end of the Second World War.
The gold rested on a metal pallet with rusting scaffolding poles slotted underneath, four on each side and the blocks themselves lay criss-cross on top of each to keep the stack stable.
The thick layer of decades old dirt coated the pile along with bits of concrete and brick debris that had fallen from the excavating. He wiped a line through it and the golden glow intensified.
A transcendent warmth began to flow through him and fill every vein in his body. It was epiphanic as if he had been touched by a God, if he believed in one. The smirk that spread across his face was one of immense satisfaction and he could completely comprehend the allure and hold that gold had always had over people, the love and death affair that always surrounded it.
He picked one up and like everyone else who ever had, was surprised at its weight.
He looked to the chalk caked engineers standing around in the cramped area watching him. Their masks removed he

saw their pale and sweaty faces. He could see they were relieved to be finished with the gruelling labour.

'Is it real?'

'Yes, it is.' One of them answered, elated. 'Tested and genuine.'

They all shared smug expressions.

Well, after all this time I have been proven wrong from beyond the grave of my surrogate father. I'm glad I am, he grinned to himself. Originally he had denied what Engel said that day at the wedding. Believed it was the ramblings of a senile man. 'Do the research if you don't believe me, it's in the documents I gave you.' Ever since then the old man's voice had invariably continued to echo in his head.

Of course, rationality had stopped him rushing in, he needed facts to follow up the so called revelation and discover for sure if Nazi history had some truth in what the old man had to say about this bullion. Eventually the intelligence, research and investigations proved it, leading also to the existence of the 'Phoenix Project.'

The antique photos which had been taken with state of the art military cameras of the time with printed dates and times on each, added to the evidence. They were all checked for authenticity including the aged blueprints of the National Gallery too.

Why would the patriarch lie about something like this after all this time? He may have been ancient and clinging to the anarchic dream but he was not crazy. Cretinous even but certainty no fool! Considering what the old man had been through, he still had his senses and was just as acute right up to the end. What little I knew about him and how wrong I was! Jan had to profess.

He picked up another block, weighing them both in each hand and then slapped them together firmly, discharging a cloud of dust. The dullish clap of gold felt strangely out of pitch but uniquely satisfying.

'Your estimate?' he addressed one of the engineers again.

He had already done the sums and promptly answered, 'Three hundred blocks. Twenty-four karat each. Todays worth, half a billion. At least.'

For a man rarely surprised the Colonel's eyebrows curved nonplussed, much to the amusement of his engineers.

Jan had been marked out many years ago when a wealthy charity set up by a subsidiary and discreet coterie of the Phoenix Project aided hundreds of homeless orphans. These unfortunates were taken in and cared for, even loved in some cases and given an upbringing of zealous education and grooming. Once they became adults they would gain positions of respect in many governmental offices. Eventually influencing and implementing new stratagems to the alliance's end. Initially the Phoenix Project was an idea of a few politically and elite like minded people; almost a men's club where the wealthy and influential socialised. It grew as similar ideas were exchanged on how the country and Europe should be governed. But the Third Reich's beliefs were out of date and times had changed. The Phoenix Project had evolved. Though the ideology of the party's original doctrines still thrived - originally rooted in a European German rule but not to such extremism. That's where the Fuhrer got it wrong in the end, he overreached his own ideals. The group now had new radical Reformist movements that embraced some of Hitler's early ideologies. One of them was an early idea of the European Union; then a truly German doctrine and Hitler had always dreamed of an EU long before it finally came about. That was his vision then and the Phoenix Project wanted to emulate that for the future. Ultimately their supremacy began to work its way into the very heart of its government; many holding high profile roles in European security and politics. After sixty years the seeds of German Nationalism were blossoming again.

Throughout all of his musings, Jan continually caressed the gold as if hypnotised. He did not realise how long he had been doing it before his radio broke his reverie.

He listened to the brief report on the British second failed attempt to get back into the building via the Director's garden - he had actually heard the muffled blast - and satisfied that there was still no threat, he simply replied 'Received.'

He then addressed his engineers, 'Get it ready.'

The old man was right about two things though, Jan had to respect. The gold was there and he knew I would take up the fight.

36

As he was led into Room 32, Will could not believe what he saw.
As if he couldn't be anymore appalled tonight, the place resembled both a building site and a scene from a horror movie. The hairs on the back of his neck tingled.
It was evidently the aftermath of an anti-terrorist team's attempt to neutralise the situation.
Immediately seen hanging from the glass ceiling that had been smashed opened was two soldiers suspended off ropes that would have propelled them to the floor. Gruesomely they swayed from side to side and Will was disgusted that no one had the decency to cut the dangling soldiers down from there.
Six other bodies lay about in the room in pools of their own blood. One was actually sprawled over a portable compressor where he must have fallen. It was a sickening sight.
While finding it difficult not to look at anything other then the dangling dead, he surveyed the chaos of the room. What had they done to the place? The grandeur of Room 32 did not seem so grand now, Will regarded sombrely.
Tools and equipment of various kinds littered the room and numerous cables snaked across the floor. Shattered glass twinkled all around and dust and dirt pervaded everywhere, over every surface. It looked like the whole place had been doused in talcum powder.
To his astonishment, in the centre of the room a large cavity had been cut through the wooden floorboards. From the

tinkering coming from down there – he couldn't quite see its depths or contents; this was where all the work was taking place. Was this where they had been drilling?

He surmised that it went right down to the basement area even possibly the depths of the foundations. What in hell were they after down there? He knew one thing for certain then; they weren't here for the paintings! They had no interest or respect for the antique and priceless collection that hung on all the walls.

Getting off their bikes, both terrorists waved their guns and led Will over to a corner of the room where a good looking woman was sitting on the floor. One of her wrists was handcuffed to the rope barrier post.

He immediately recognised her as the Head of Security's secretary. What was she doing here? He asked himself but at once, he knew the answer. She must be a hostage!

He couldn't recall her name but she was an unforgettable stunner. He had always wished he had known her better but because of their work patterns - she worked during the day and he on nights and both being in different parts of the building and departments too - they barely saw each other. On the rare occasions they passed and acknowledged each other with civilities but because of the nature of their jobs he never had time to chat with her. It was always a case of passing ships.

He smiled sympathetically at the woman and she unexpectedly smiled back. Whether it was in recognition, he couldn't tell but he was impressed at her lack of anxiety. She seemed to be taking it in her stride.

With one of the terrorists training his Uzi on him, the other shoved him down to the floor on his bum and with a pair of handcuffs shackled his right wrist and the other cuff onto another one of the barrier posts six feet away from the woman.

Then it dawned on him and he began to chuckle to himself. The fools! They were completely unaware of what they had done. These posts could easily be unscrewed by hand!

Will shuffled his sitting body as comfortable as he could in the circumstances, to ease the strain and pain on his wrist. He would wait, marking his time until he would make a move.

As the two terrorists walked away, Will turned to the woman he had joined in this dilemma and whispered to her, 'They don't realise these posts we're handcuffed to. They can be unscrewed.'

She simply nodded back at him like he was a stranger on a train remarking on the weather.

Changing the subject for now and in hushed tones, he asked 'How'd you end up here?'

'Working late with the boss.' She replied coolly. 'They've kept me as a hostage since. The archetypical damsel in distress, it seems.' She finished sarcastically.

She clearly wasn't in that much distress at all, Will noticed.

'What happened to Powell then?' he questioned.

'They locked him in the vault.' She smirked at him.

He laughed at that, a little too loudly and one of the terrorists came back over and rammed the butt of his Uzi into his stomach.

Will writhed with the pain, bending over and forgetting the cuffs which yanked and pulled at his right wrist and shoulder, only adding to his agony.

'Schweigen. No talking.' The terrorist stared down at him for a moment like he was a naughty child and returned to the centre of the room.

Hit a man when he is down. Will moaned to himself. That hurt, you bastard!

'You okay?' he heard the woman enquire.

He noticed that she was studying him; maybe trying to get the measure of him. She even noticed the bandages on his hands which were beginning to itch him annoyingly.

'I'll survive. Been getting this hospitality all night.' Will answered between gritted teeth.

He saw her smiling at his sarcasm and asked her, 'What's your name?'

'Hannah.'

'I'm Will, never Bill! Thanks for the concern.' He shook his cuffs, 'I'd shake hands with you, but….'

'Look forward to it.' She said genuinely and he was taken aback by the positive reply.

The terrorist that had delivered the blow to Will turned around and eyed them. They both remained silent.

Despite their perilous circumstances, Will realised that this was the first time he had been in this lady's company. If you can call being hostages, company.

He could not help noticing her shapely legs and thighs where her skirt had risen slightly. Modesty intact, she still did have her knees locked together and turned away. She was a fine looking woman, Will commented to himself. She had a comely figure to her, not like the usual skinny ladies that you could cut yourself on. He had to stop looking at her before he made her uncomfortable.

Both observing the room, they noticed a man climb out of the pit and dust himself down. He was attired similar to his men but for a traditional blue, grey officer's tunic which gave him the air of authority. He repeatedly stamped his army issued boots loudly on the floorboards.

Something was shouted in German by him and the body language of his hands portrayed a repetitive lifting motion.

'Germans.' Will mouth silently and old age stereotypes and prejudices came to mind.

While Will speculated at what it was they were going to bring up and the cause of all of this death and destruction, the man approached him at full height. Chest out, head held high, he had a firm stance and a confident gaze. Will could spot an experienced soldier and leader. Seen the type many times before; the man in charge.

Another soldier followed closely behind him and frequently turned his head, vigilantly watching the room.

'So you're the man that's been giving us all the trouble.' This leader spoke with a manner of those unchallenged.

'I was going to say the same thing to you mate.' Will returned.

A slight smile played over his lips. 'I was curious to see the man who was able to kill some of my men.'

'Me too.' Will replied coldly.

He regaled Will with a look of indulgence. 'Not only do you have the talent to take me on but you're funny too.'

It was a condescending comment, he didn't mean it and Will was in someway expecting the next question.

'Are you Army?'

Will shook his head 'Nah! Only security!'

'I think you are, Mr. Security.' he stated while looming over him. Will noted that that was easy for him to do with him handcuffed down on the floor.

'Maybe not Army now but you were. I can tell. There's no way you could have lasted this long and taken out my number two. That's admirable.'

'Lucky I guess.'

The Colonel nodded his head, 'Modest as well as humorous. No one's ever beat Gerard on luck. Come to think of it. Never, in all his battles!'
'The end comes to us all pal and he certainly had it coming.'
'I sense some animosity…...' He paused, looked at his boots. '…. You would have worked together. I see now. I understand. I know how Gerard loathed playing the inside man role and he no doubt made working with the rest of you…, challenging. He had a job to do and he knew that more than anyone.' His black piercing eyes looked away for the first time. 'A small part of me will miss him. He was an accomplished 'soldat.''
He stepped closer to Will and bent down, squatting agilely. Will was aware what this man was doing; intimidating him with his size and closeness.
'Tell me, soldier….' He was talking down to him now, even though he was on Will's level, their faces a foot apart and eye to eye. Will smelt him - some old spice!
'I'm curious as to how you affected my number two's demise?'
'I broke the spineless bastard's back.' Will answered sardonically. 'He was always heading for a fall.'
'I'm almost impressed.' The Colonel lied and followed it with a violent slap to Will's face.
Catching him on the cheekbone it felt like a punch. Ouch! Will cried to himself. He was convinced something cracked in him, the slap was that strong.
'That's for a good comrade.' The Colonel said and got up from squatting, rising to his full formidable height again.
Smarting from the powerful blow that was sure to give him pain for days, Will implored. 'Look mate, I don't care want you want here. Let me and the lady go.' His number two

meant more to him then a mere foot soldier. It had become personal.

'That's not going to happen. You're going to be my hostages.'

He was addressing both of them now. While Will could give the verbal just as good as the next, Hannah continued to watch calmly but vindictively.

'Consider yourself fortunate. I could have executed you both. Like the others.'

Will realised any hint of humanity that this man had shown throughout their conversation was now gone.

'At least, why don't you show some decency and respect as a squaddie and take down those men from up there?' Will asked, turning his head upwards to the dangling dead.

'Yes. You are right.' Jan nodded and turning on his heels, he walked across the room followed by his shadowing soldier.

With two well aimed shots from his HK Match, the ropes that were still attached from the roof to the British soldiers severed and the two bodies fell to the floor with unpleasant thumps.

The Colonel didn't even look back at them. He immediately started barking orders in German again.

Will shook his head in disgust and Hannah muttered, 'He's a nasty piece of work.'

37

It hung in the night sky above the building's roof with its soft hypnotic pulsations. The powerful searchlight beams that had been set up all around the square swept over the giant helicopter's camouflage green body. So much so, that to Michael, it looked like some CGI effect. Almost unreal!
Cameras from the media and the public incessantly flashed and filmed.
It was the second 'bird' that had flown over and hovered above the gallery tonight. The first was a smaller and stealthier machine which had moved quickly in, dispatching a group of soldiers onto the building's roof and then just as quickly departed. That had been an attempt by 'our brave lads' to enter the building via the roof. He had heard the distant rat-tat-tat of gunfire out here in the square and the gossip was that all of the soldiers had been killed.
Their second attempt was again fatal and disastrous. Michael knew this as fact because from the front of the cordon he had seen four specialists enter the Director's garden and after the explosion only one came out and he was on a stretcher.
This second copter arrived with much more aplomb as it thundered over the square to many gasps. Its swirling downward current rippling amongst the entire spectator's upturned faces below and nearly swept away the remainder of what hair Michael had left on his head.
The Chinook was British, that was obvious. He had glimpsed the markings but he was baffled though. Was this

another effort by the army to take out the terrorists? Surely they had backed off from trying to take the building back. Too many men had died and each attempt had been an embarrassing failure. What was going on? What were they up to now?

The shear size and tonnage of the Chinook seemed to hang in the air like it was a holographic image and its winch was now being lowered into the building, much to the excitement and intrigue of all watching.

Were they about to bring out hostages? Was it possible a deal had been made with the terrorists to finally release the captive staff inside the building? It was the only conclusion he and many could come to because as far as everyone was concerned it was a British copter coming to the rescue.

Michael was a mere spectator now and he had done his job, which was no big deal. All he could do was watch this riveting and incredible scene unfold.

He was just another expectant face in the crowd, he told himself but with one noticeable difference. He had no mobile phone!

38

They heard it before they saw it, amplifying to its stirring reveal 30ft above the gallery.

Looking up through parts of the destroyed ceiling, Will was always impressed by these elephantine machines and how they could keep themselves in the air like that while weighing so much. The steady thud of the two main rotors continued to spin a blur in the night sky. Operational lights from under its vast belly shone down into the room, bathing it even more brightly and intensely. Will thought the whole scene both fascinating and foreboding.

Despite the forces it was generating and manipulating, the downdraft was only a gutsy breeze, not at all like the micro tornados usually associated and felt with conventional helicopters. Its altitude caused only a mild disturbance in the room below.

The gold had been tied up in safety webbing, as it was found on the metal pallet. Hooked onto the ends of each scaffolding pole, it was now being hoisted up by the Chinook's powerful winch, rising out of the lower depths of the foundations for the first time in nearly seventy years.

Trying not to miss what was going on; Will and Hannah's curiosity was getting the better of them. They had to turn their heads to avoid the stirred up soot from the excavation which irritated their eyes but they wanted to know what tonight was all was about. Sharing the same thoughts: What was it that had caused so much death and destruction?

The two engineers that had been working down below to free the bullion held on to the netting and as it passed the edges of the torn up gallery floor they hopped off. They were covered in dust and their sweat had turned into a wallpaper paste like mush on their exposed skin. When they landed on the floor, clouds of the stuff floated off them. They resembled salt miners!

Will and Hannah's earlier questions were then answered when they saw the unmistakable glow.

Instead of the gold continuing to rise up and into the belly of the Chinook, the load was slowly moved over to the floor level and set down. Floorboards creaked and groaned with disapproval under the immense weight.

The two hostages exchanged speechless looks. They did not expect this at all. All that gold had been under the building, right under their noses all that time and no one knew. How long had it been there?

About a dozen soldiers began to unload the bars from the stack and proceeded to pack it into backpacks, boxes, containers and anything else that could hold the gold for its transportation by motorbike. They worked quickly and uniformly, it wouldn't be long before the pallet was empty.

Many of the gallery's rooms and corridor doors had been opened earlier in preparation for this planned evacuation of the bullion, allowing them to move to and fro without delay. Loaded up, each motorbike left the room using different exits. Either via Room 30, turning left towards the Sunley Room elevator where that was being utilised to bring the bullion down in large amounts on a flat trolley – essentially a wooden platform on wheels - or via alternative routes through the Barry Rooms, Central Hall and the Impressionist Rooms, all towards the main staircase.

In the main lobby more soldiers loitered, guarding the main doors in case the British forces had any idea of attempting to enter the premises again. From here, they watched the bikers come and go in what was like some kind of motorcycle stunt show. These bikers were expert riders, traversing not only the concrete steps of the grand Portico staircase but also the smaller ones on either side of the lobby that led down to the lower levels. One was used for going down, the other for coming back up.

Down in the lower ground level they would turn right past the cloakrooms and straight on through the opened staff door at the rear of the espresso area. Into these tight and narrow corridors they would weave left and right again and again - all these doorways remained opened too - until finally they reached the loading bay area where outside two ambulances waited to be loaded with the gold.

Back in the room, the Chinook remained hovering above the roof. The unhooked winch rested on the floor and with the terrorist's goal out of the excavation Will suspected the copter's use wasn't done with yet.

They were both becoming very uncomfortable now. Their right wrists hurt and their shoulders ached from being handcuffed for so long. They shifted their weight periodically by moving their legs into different positions. Will was still damp from the drenching he got earlier. His bum felt horribly dank and for some strange reason, he wondered if this was what nappy rash felt like?

'Once this man gets what he wants and it looks like he has, we won't be hostages much longer.' Will whispered grimly to her.

It was a sobering statement and Hannah had to agree with him.

'I don't know about you honey but I'm gonna end up just like my colleagues. Dead! Did I tell you that? All the staff here were murdered.' He had become very serious and Hannah could discern the change in his voice.

'No.' Hannah replied, 'But it figures. I've seen what he does.'

Will felt the bandages on his hands were loosening. They were also becoming soiled with sweat and dirt. Torn in places too and even a little blood had begun to seep through. His hands were suffering but there was nothing he could do while still cuffed. Anyway, his hands were the least of his worries. It was their lives, he was worried about.

He knew he could free himself of the post he was cuffed to but he was waiting for the right moment. The soldier who shadowed the leader watched constantly and it was hard to do anything without arousing suspicion.

As the terrorists worked and the motorbikes sped back and forth through the building, Will overheard the leader of this outfit being addressed as 'Oberst.'

He knew a little German to pick up on that. This 'Colonel' then walked over to Will and Hannah and addressed them. 'You noticed our deviation?'

He was referring to the fake cargo that had taken the place of the gold and was being prepared by the two engineers in the midst of the Chinook's swirling downdraft. A dozen boxes and containers that previously contained equipment and even one of the portable compressors were placed on the scaffolding poles and tied down with a green plastic tarpaulin wrap. The winch was then hooked onto it.

'Once we have taken all our gold out of here, the copter will lift this into its hold and lead the police and army on a bootless errand.'

Why was he telling us this? Hannah thought. Was he gloating? Showing off? 'You're never gonna get out of here.' She said. 'This place will be surrounded now.'

'Yes, yes....' The Colonel remarked flippantly.

'All this, for pure greed.' Will gestured with his head towards the gold. The terrorists had progressed actively. Motorbikes came and went noisily and frequently and most of the hoard had now been moved out. 'Its madness!'

'Greed is a terrible motive, I agree. But that is not what this is.'

'What is it then? Because it's not justifiable however you look at it.'

'There are many injustices in this world and we want to rectify that with.....'

Will interrupted him, 'By murdering men who were only doing their job. An honest day's work.'

'Revolutions tend to be bloody. Eventually, it will be for the better. The people realise this in the end.'

'You're full of fucking clichés mate.' Will rebuffed him. He caught a glimpse of anger flash across those penetrating eyes of his.

Hannah added to the insult, 'You're a terrorist. Plain and simple!'

The Colonel smiled condescendingly down on her. 'So were Nelson Mandela and Che Guevara. Their causes, beliefs and ours are really not that different. Governments and politicians all over the world are impoverishing our lives, stealing from us. Killing us softly with the distraction of ruthless capitalism. We want equality and nationalism for all but without those that corrupt and poison.'

'You think you're admirable but you're fucked up mate. Who do you represent?' Will asked out of curiosity. Though he knew these goons were all the same. Blood on their hands.

'The Fourth Reich.' He stated boastfully.

Will laughed aloud; he could not believe this guy. He looked to Hannah then back at this lunatic. 'You're Nazis. Dinosaurs that won't stay extinct!' He laughed again and shook his head in bemusement. 'You're out of your mind.'

The Colonel dismissing Will's outburst turned to check on the work's progress in the room and shouted something about time in German.

Was that a hint of impatience in his voice, Will wondered.

The Colonel turned back and scowled at them, his eyes like lasers. 'No. Those.... reprobates are long gone. Their oversight cost them. They made mistakes.....' His chest seemed to fill with air, '......We will not!' He finished arrogantly.

Will shrugged. 'Idealism is a narcotic buddy and you are addicted.'

Hannah added, 'A fanatic is a moral coward.' She had read Jung too.

Will and Hannah both turned to acknowledge each other's shared interest.

The Colonel turned his mouth up at them, revealing a grimace.

Will enjoyed that until the Colonel said, 'Did you know there was never a peace treaty signed between our countries at the end of the Second World War. So technically, we are still at war with England. You.....' he pointed a finger at Will, '..... I am going to kill.'

The Colonel stared Will down menacingly for a moment then turned and walked away. Once again barking orders, this time distinctly stentorian.

Will and Hannah exchanged raised eyebrows, both bemused by the odd comment and abrupt end to the conversation.
'Looks like Germany has declared war on you.' Hannah remarked wryly.

39

He heard the consistent engines of the bikers coming and going from the area nearby where he guessed they had been drilling earlier. It made it more difficult to get out and leave. Being so close, he was bound to be spotted. He really did not know what to do and for a long time that was the dilemma!
He had spent what seem like another age down here in this hole, deliberating on what should be his next step. All the plans tonight had only amounted to more and more trouble and he was not getting any closer to getting out of the building. How could things turn so badly wrong in one night?
The painting hung on him like a dead weight now, its frame continually rubbed irritably and sorely against him but he wouldn't give it up just yet!
Staying inconspicuous here would be easy until these terrorists eventually left. It would have been no different to his and Joseph's original plan to remain hidden until the next morning. Though he was getting itchy feet, the gloominess of the stark and empty vents made him feel more and more uneasy. However, he could not make the move.
He began to think of Will, the cockney who he had saved after the Link explosion and how he had become an ally of sorts. What will happen to him now? Should I try and find him? Help him? He had believed the man's army experience could well get them out of here unharmed but now Will had

been captured and he was on his own, unable to make a decision.

What was the matter with me? Since Joseph's death, I've not been able to take control of myself. It's affected me, I admit it. Not being able to save my friend has impaired me. I know I shouldn't but I feel to blame. Would helping Will once again somehow make the guilt a little easier? Isn't that why he came to his aid earlier? No! He didn't really believe that. The thought of putting himself in the firing line again terrified him and he definitely believed that. Nevertheless he did help, no matter the dangers and fear involved, he just did it. Wouldn't most people have done the same thing?

He heard the buzz of a bike and then it faded away.

He knew he would not be able to live with himself if he just remained concealed down here juggling with his dilemmas and dismay. He could not have another man's death on his conscious. He had made up his mind then. It did not change the fact that he was still afraid, still had that horrible sickly feeling in the pit of his stomach. As much as a part of him wanted to hide away, he knew he couldn't.

He crawled his way back out of cover from inside the shaft and peered up through the opening where the grill lid was still pulled aside. The lights of the room beckoned him to come out of his claustrophobic confines.

He slowly pulled himself up through the gap and made a quick check around the room. No one! The distant noise of bikers could still be heard but unless they got louder, he knew he should be okay.

Out and remaining crouched; he darted over to the door frame and pulled himself to full height. Stretching and moving all of his stiff and aching limbs, he felt his heart thumping frantically.

The doors here were open, as most of them had been for the bikers to get about unhindered and here he waited while taking a few deep breaths.

Whatever it was they were up to, he was now sure it was all taking place in Room 32. Every now and then he would peer around the door frame and observe numerous motorbikes going back and forth with regularity. Each time the bikes always seemed to be loaded down with something when they left the room and sped off into the distance of Central Hall. From there it looked like they turned left towards the main staircase and he could only wonder where their destination with their mystery cargo was then?

There was another sound too he briefly picked out. Different and not heard before, a faint beating. But the bikes drowned it out and he didn't pay it much heed.

Feeling ready he carefully took another peek around the door frame into Room 35. Seeing it clear, he sprinted on light feet to the far pillar and flattened himself against it.

Here was the circular vestibule of Room 36 with its striking glass dome ceiling and beautifully detailed motifs, carvings and busts of stone and gold. Two dozen black veined pillars bordered the four vestibules 35, 37, 38 and 40 - these were the Barry Rooms. The floor here was marbled tiles, its patterns mirroring the dome and the walls were carpeted with maroon velvety wallpaper. It was an architectural bliss that usually drew more attention from the visitors than the paintings ever could. The whole breadth of it portrayed a Victorian palace.

Other noises could be heard now in between the motorbike engines. What sounded like work in progress and the occasional voice could be discerned. But that other sound too - thicker, more powerful like and steady. He could not ignore it any longer. It was quite prominent now, almost draining out the motorbike's engine. This throbbing and pulsating felt like it came from above Room 32 and it was unmistakable to him what it was now. A helicopter!

Spying around the pillar, he saw it was clear and began to inch his way along the room wall that curved inwards and out of sight of any gaze that might be coming from the next room. His back was close to the carpeted wallpaper and barely brushed past a large portrait of Colonel Tarleton by Joshua Reynolds.

Reaching another pillar, he once again stopped while continuing to be cautious.

A brilliant marble white lunette of Queen Victoria representing colour and form rested atop the columns leading into Room 32 and a plain 7ft varnished wooden bench sat in the middle of the room but his attention was drawn to the sight next door. White dust like substance trailed out of the room, tyre tracks of it brought further into the gallery. He didn't believe what he saw at first and had to strain his eyes to make out what looked like a hole dug right out of the wooden flooring.

The hive of activity made him wonder if Will was in the room. It was a logical assumption and a better place than any. Had he been brought here? He really hoped so rather than the morbid thought that popped into his head.

He heard another bike rev up and he ducked behind the pillar just as it left Room 32 and like the others it zoomed off towards Central Hall. They were less frequent now, the intervals between each becoming longer.

Once again, he waited while the helicopter reverberations continued to beat. He could only speculate the reason for it. Furthermore he heard the unmistakable growling of yet another bike from the main entrance direction coming his way. For as long as he lived this sound would always be synonymous with death! He would never forget it.

If he remained where he was he would be seen. No doubt shot dead on this spot.

He caught a glimpse of the death machine and it was heading his way from the Impressionist Rooms. To get out of its line of sight Pawel had to move now and he swiftly side-footed into Room 37 and flattened himself as much as he possibly could against the wall and behind the pillar. Praying he had not been spotted by anyone in Room 32 as well.

40

The Yankee Tweedledum and Tweedledee were in their elements.
They were tackling the brawns of this part of the operation and as each new batch arrived they filled the ambulances with more gold.
Tweedledum unpacked each container, emptied each trolley load and proceeded to toss each bar like it was a breeze block into the back of the stripped out ambulance. Where inside Tweedledee would catch each one like they were bricks and evenly stack them out. Balancing and distributing the weight on the vehicle's modified and strengthened suspension.
With their loads emptied, the bikers immediately returned to Room 32 to retrieve yet another batch.
Tweedledee whistled and Tweedledum hummed while they both worked and they were glad to be doing something physical after all the time spent staring at screens that showed no cable television whatsoever.
Strangely, it looked like genuine ambulance paramedics were assisting in the movement of the gold too but they were only more of the Colonel's soldiers already disguisedly dressed in preparation for their escape. A pile of ambulance crew uniforms were laid to one side, ready to be used by others. These so called paramedics worked a flat four wheeled trolley which they pushed and pulled back and forth with each load that came down in the Sunley elevator.

Earlier the giant whale of the sky had passed them overhead in the loading bay as they waited for the bullion to arrive. Each thud of its massive blades reverberated with their heart beats and the ground beneath their feet seemed to fluctuate. They all had looked up at it and grinned at each other in respect. For each of them, it was a familiar chord often heard on the battlefield and reassuringly greeted. The sound of assistance and aid but in this scenario it was to be a convincing diversion.

Despite its impressive capabilities it was not for the gold that they had stolen a Chinook. For the bullion would be hauled by ambulances to rendezvous at a destination outside London. The ruse was to make the police and army believe that the cargo would be taken out by helicopter. Though the authorities could not know this at the time, as far as they were concerned it could only be paintings - a heist of the greatest pieces of art known in the world - hostages perhaps and likely escaping terrorists too.

It was a more believable ploy if they went to all that trouble to steal a copter from an army base and it was because of this that they hoped gave gravitas to the diversion. To lead the police and military on a wild goose chase for as far and as long as possible.

Picking up the already considerable pace they knew the culmination of the plan would soon be at hand and they would finally be leaving.

Tweedledee continued to whistle and Tweedledum continued to hum.

41

They were getting ready to vacate the building via the back gate. What gold remained was now being loaded onto the last motorcycles and most of them would not be returning; their job done.

More and more radio calls were going unanswered by his men and there were reports of death.

Someone else, a weaker mind perhaps would be of the opinion that the plans were going awry but not the Colonel. It did not come into his mindset. Despite more casualties the mission was far from lost.

Besides, he was sure it was only the last remaining staff member's handiwork being discovered and that 'ratte' was now handcuffed in the room with them. There would be no one else to concern himself with and soon he would put a bullet in that ex-soldier's head. For Gerard.

Over the radio, he ordered his men at the back gate to expect him in fifteen minutes and to have the gate open. Whatever transpires, proceed with the plan.

He then began the phone call to warn the authorities not to interfere with his escape or the hostages would certainly die.

42

While Will's attention was distracted by the Chinook's winch pulling up the fake cargo and the slight downdraft which every other person in the room shielded their partly closed eyes from, no one noticed Hannah until she was up on her feet and running.
He was surprised at the fact that she had managed to undo her cuffs from the rope barrier post. The post itself lay unscrewed on the floor, the rope still threaded through. Then he remembered telling her how easy they were to undo. But he never thought she would do something about it!
He saw the metal glint of her handcuffs cuffed to one wrist, swinging as she sprinted. What was she doing? What did she think she could do? What am I doing watching her? Move Will, Move!
Unlike Hannah, he couldn't unscrew the post quick enough. It didn't give immediately, so tight it was. It seemed to take forever but with an effort that he was sure sprained some hand muscles, he was finally able to loosen it.
He glanced back at Hannah who was running in the direction of the pit and the Colonel.
Then to his utter disbelief; she reached down and put a hand up her skirt and un-holstered a small KEL-TEC 9mm pistol that was concealed high up on her inner thigh. It was all done in one fluid and natural motion. Will gawped at this sight; the audacity of the woman. No one had thought to frisk this innocent bystander.

None of the terrorists had noticed her yet and the way she moved convinced him that it was innate to her. Still whoever she was, she was going to get herself killed, Will feared.

Looping the handcuffs down and off the post, he quickly got to his feet. The freed end of the cuff dangled from his hand as well as the loosened bandages that flapped about with every movement.

Moving quickly, he sprinted to the rope barrier's end where its tail hooked into a ring set in the wall. Unhooking it and yanking the rope, it threaded out of the post that he had unscrewed from the floor. Then running back, he picked up the hefty metal pole and sprinted to the nearest terrorist who was now turning and reacting to Hannah's movements.

It was one of the Colonel's lieutenants and he nearly had an aim on her when he then spotted Will out of the corner of his eye. The lieutenant turned to deal with him but Will was quicker. Pulling his makeshift weapon back behind him and using his shoulders, he swung violently.

Something cracked as the impact of the steel post connected with the side of the lieutenant's jaw below his ear. The goon spun 360' and was unconscious before he hit the floor.

But not before the Uzi in his hand fired as he fell back and the arc of gunfire sprayed skywards. Its trajectory soared up and through the skylight roof catching the Chinook's underbelly and then shearing its tail rotor.

It had been ascending and pulling away but now the helicopter began to lose control, spinning in slow impeding circles above the building's roof. The fake cargo on the end of the winch had just cleared the roof but clipped a broken part of the ceiling, showering some glass and metal framing to the floor below.

Grabbing the unconscious terrorist's Uzi, Will again saw another react too slow. He was one of the engineers and even he could not believe what was happening. The sight of this woman sprinting across the room, brandishing a gun looked absolutely striking and as far as they were all concerned was some harmless hostage who was supposed to be no threat whatsoever.

The interruption and this assumption had cost him his life! Will opened fire before the engineer could reach for his weapon. The round of bullets punctured his chest and the pit dust on his clothes burst off him into a lingering haze that hung in the air as he collapsed to the floor.

Had to be done, Will coldly calculated. Had no choice!

He glimpse back at Hannah. God, she was fast! She was now 10ft away from the Colonel and aiming right at his face. The gun she had, she handled skilfully, Will noticed. She had done this before.

The Colonel did not expect this. The utterly surprised look on his face represented his bafflement as he lifted his eyes from his phone. He had just finished the call to the authorities and still he held it. He had only a short lived moment to register that this lady wasn't part of the plan. That a hostage and a woman would turn on him with such lethal adeptness.

She pulled the trigger and the bullet entered the Colonel's left eye, through his head and out of the back in a plethora of blood and brain matter.

'There's more to me than meets the eye, buster.' She screamed.

'Jesus!' Will ejaculated.

The Colonel fell backwards into the pit, still clutching the mobile.

To add to Will's astonishment, Hannah continued running and leapt from the floor level down into the pit following the Colonel's falling body.

The remaining terrorist had already begun firing in Hannah's direction but she was already gone, down in the depths. Will took him out by turning his body left and with a well aimed swing - his loosening bandages flapped about annoyingly as well as the handcuffs - the round struck the terrorist's stomach and he tumbled to the floor.

Concerned about Hannah, Will run up to the pit's edge and stared into the depths. 'What are you doing?' he shouted down at her.

'Getting what's mine.' He heard her yell back up.

Unbelievably, she seemed unhurt from the thirty-five foot drop that she had just jumped.

With the portable floodlights that had been used down in the pit still alight, he could make out her frantic movements. Straddling the body of the dead Colonel, Will figured she must have used his body to cushion her landing.

He did not have much time to wonder what the hell that was all about when he had to react. Spotting movement out of the corner of his eyes and slightly behind his left side, he turned and took two long and nimble strides. The goon he had shot to the stomach moments ago was trying to pull himself over to his weapon he had dropped nearby. He would never reach it!

With his size nine boot, Will kicked the side of the terrorist's head like it was a football. 'Give it a rest.' He spat!

He did not care if the terrorist was now unconscious or dead but he kicked again, this time sending the terrorist's weapon spinning away against a far wall.

He was still trying to comprehend Hannah's actions. Without hesitation she had shot the Colonel with what seemed like cold professionalism. Who is this woman?

He looked down again into the excavation and was able to make her out fumbling with the body. She was searching the

Colonel, pulling at his tunic jacket until she found something and pocketed it inside her bra.

Shaking his head, Will deliberated. There's a lot I don't know about here. And I only thought she was some good looking secretary that worked in the building. What the hell's going on?

He waited for her as she athletically and impressively began climbing back up one of the ropes.

Offering his hand, she grabbed it and as he was pulling her up and out, a motorbike could be heard behind them.

They turned in unison; panic on both their faces as they saw an approaching terrorist on his bike with his gun raised and targeting them.

43

It sounded like the helicopter was moving away.
Then he saw figures moving through the room.
He saw a woman dressed in civilian clothing – short skirt and black hair - run across the room. She was brandishing a gun and then she was out of sight again and a gun shot was heard.
Was that her who fired? He asked himself before chaos broke out. Who was she?
More gun shots were heard and some terrorists scrambled in and out of his view of the room.
He was convinced that it was only a matter of seconds before someone spotted him and opened fire.
It was all happening too quickly for him to take it all in.
He saw one terrorist, his body twisting backwards and clutching his bloodied chest. His weapon firing pointlessly ceiling-wards as he fell to the floor, unmoving.
Then he saw Will run past, an Uzi in his hands. He couldn't help it, his heart lifted on seeing him. Was Will trying to save the day?
The increasing engine roar of the motorbike coming through the Barry Rooms was approaching close and he knew he had to do something right now. The biker raider would catch him and Will too in the next room.
He was staring at the wooden bench in the middle of the room and an idea sparked in his head. He had to be quick though; he heard the bike almost upon him.

In two sudden strides he leapt out from his cover behind the pillar and with the heel of his right foot, kicked one end of the bench.

It spun 180° on the polished floor, horizontally across the motorbike's path. At its considerable speed it had no chance of swerving to avoid the bench and hit the obstruction too fast to stop in time.

The bike's front wheel buckled like putty on impact and the whole bike flipped. The rider was sent flying off his seat and through the air into Room 32.

Pawel saw Will crouching over a gaping hole in the room's floor and the woman emerging from it. Together their heads turned.

The terrorist's Crash test dummy like body landed gruesomely with a lethal crack of bones and slid to a stop not far from them and their startled faces.

44

'You are unbelievable Polish.' Will was still crouched on one knee where he had been ready to pull Hannah up. 'And a sight for sore eyes!'
Actually his eyes did still feel irritated from the dust that had earlier flurried in the room. The Chinook couldn't be seen now but was still heard, beginning to whir defectively as it faltered away from the roof of the building.
Both he and Hannah had frozen at the sight of another biker, convinced that they both would be shot. Then they watched as Pawel made his move and the bike struck the bench, sending its rider sailing almost slow motion like through the air. It was a bizarre sight and the body had not moved since nose diving to the floor in front of them.
Will finished pulling Hannah up and out of the pit. They both stood there exhausted and relieved while Pawel walked into the room.
Will put out his hand to shake his, 'Saving lives again, eh Polish?
Pawel smiled moderately as he returned Will's handshake.
Slightly grimacing, Will felt the firm grip. It was much stronger than earlier. 'You're the hero tonight.'
Pawel shrugged coyly and said, 'I want to get out of here now. I don't care if I lose the painting.' He tapped it under his jumper and looked very sombre. 'I have become too attached to it. Since Joseph's death, it has clouded my judgement. It's not worth my death too.'

Pawel glanced at the dishevelled but good looking woman with Will and appeared a little abashed by his admittance in front of her. He was also a little weary of this stranger.

Noticing this, Will spoke up, 'This is Hannah, Polish…' He was trying to remember Polish's real name when Pawel said, 'Pawel.' He nodded response at Hannah and was unable to resist looking her up and down.

She pulled her skirt down some more, straightened her blouse and ruffled her hair. She felt a mess.

He knew who she was now, Pawel suddenly recalled. Remembered her from when he had worked in the building. She was the 'hot' secretary.

There was a brief silence between them all and Will tried to redo his grimy bandages. The make shift material was beginning to reek of dust, sweat and blood and the handcuffs got in the way.

Pawel stared aghast around the room's state. It was like a bomb had crashed through the roof and smashed it way through the floorboards before exploding and spewing up the mess that now littered the room. His gaze kept returning to the exits too. He was getting anxious, couldn't shake the fear that another biker could turn up. Justifiably so, they had been all night. The slightest distant noise and he was convinced it was another assassin on wheels.

All his thoughts were now on getting out of this cursed building. 'I am going to the back gate. If I cannot get out there, I will wait. Hide.' Pawel suggested.

'Sounds good Polish. Can't be too many of these thugs left. See if you can get the back gate open and let the police in. I'm gonna try the same at the front.'

Will walked over to a parked motorbike, 'I'm going by bike. You?'

Pawel replied, 'Walking.'

A few bars of gold still lay scattered on the floor. Gleaming but forgotten in the skirmish. Pawel approached them and picked one up.
He turned to Will and looked at him quizzically.
'That's what it's been all about.' Will explained. 'Nazi gold under the gallery. Who would have thought it eh?'
It was crazy, Pawel thought. Nazis were from another time, not this day and age. He speculated how much of it there really was and asked Will. 'No idea. Must be a chunk though to go to all this trouble. By the way....' Will remembered, '....be careful at the back gate mate. It could be where the rest of the gold was brought.'
Feeling the weight of one for the first time in his life was a revelation and he was immediately captivated. Like everyone else before him, he couldn't resist its allure and brazenly said, 'In case the paintings a fake. Yes?'
You couldn't take the opportunist out of him; Will regarded and chuckled. 'I like your style Polish. Go ahead! It's not like the authorities are gonna miss it. They never knew it was here in the first place.'
Hannah respectfully remained quiet while watching both men. She vaguely recognised the one called Polish but had not seen him for some time in the building. He looked tired, haggard and there was sadness in his eyes.
Will was beginning to come across as the typical happy go lucky cockney. Nothing could ruin his optimism and sense of humour. It was an appealing quality.
Both men were having a moment. Something had happened between them. A shared experience and it had formed some kind of relationship. God knows what they had seen and been through!
Pawel slipped the amber block into the backpack behind the painting and then looked ready to go.

He lifted his head and eyeing Will, he uttered 'Dziękuję.' Not lingering too long with eye contact, he turned and walked off.

'Hey Polish, thank you too, man.' Will yelled. He was kind of sad to see him leave like this. For a moment, he wondered if he would ever see him again. 'Do widzenia....' Will continued. 'Powodzenia.'

Without turning around, Pawel shouted back. 'Do widzenia, English.'

Will was still smiling when Pawel left the room.

45

He straddled one of the motorbikes that were left parked up in the room. The terrorists wouldn't be using these machines for their illegal activities anymore. Now it would be Will's turn and hopefully for a better end.
Starting it up and revving the throttle, he got a feel for the machine under him and in his hands.
He turned to Hannah. After all she had been through and the dust and dirt that covered her she still looked gorgeous, he thought. Part of her face glistened with small droplets of sweat.
He dismissed himself as a hopeless romantic and asked, 'You getting on?'
She arched a dark eyebrow, 'Where you going?'
'Getting out of here. My shift ended hours ago. Wanna go make some cheese.'
She wasn't sure if it was an expression or a euphemism? Either way, she didn't get it! He did look tired though, she noticed. Yet his eyes still gleamed with determination.
She began to feel it too, the ordeal and weariness was catching up. 'Just a minute…' she said and was off again.
'What now?' Will sighed under his breath. This woman continually surprised; the kind of lady to keep any man on his toes. Or exasperate him!
She had run over to the other side of the room where some of the gold had scattered and picked one bar up. Just like Pawel, she could not resist the allure too!

She glanced back at Will and looked like she was going to ask for permission, her almost innocent face seemed that way. 'Do you want one?'

He whistled, 'Tempted as I am, but all that has given me nothing but trouble. Nooo thanks!'

She shrugged her shoulders as if to say 'suit yourself' and with one in her hand, shoved it into an empty backpack lying nearby and slung it over her shoulders.

Coming back, she noticed Will frowning at her. 'What?' she exclaimed. 'It's not like their going to miss it….' She trailed off from his very own words earlier to Pawel, smiling at him playfully.

Will could not help but grin at that. 'C'mon.' he urged with a tilt of his head. 'Thought I'd try the main doors. Where there's a Will, there's a way!' He winked at her.

She rolled her eyes at his comment. 'That your motto is it?'

He chuckled, 'Nah, not really.'

She admired the fact that he could laugh at himself. He also reminded her of a big grizzly bear with his mop of dark hair and bristling black beard. She wondered what he would look like with a good haircut and a clean shave.

The main entrance seemed the best idea to Will at the moment. Maybe now all of these terrorists were finished or in disarray, he could somehow get through the doors to the authorities. He knew for certain that the police and army would be outside waiting. No doubt the world was watching.

He was having difficulty trying to retie his loose bandages when Hannah stepped closer, took his hands and assisted him. She didn't appear bothered by the blood and dirt on them.

She scrunched up her nose and he noticed this. 'You don't have to do…'

'No. It's not that.' She made clear. 'You smell of smoke.'

'Ah, yeah. Got a bit hot earlier.'
'And you're soaking wet.' She felt his damp clothes.
'Then I needed to cool down. It's been fun and games lady.' Will humoured.
Their handcuffs swung off each other with soft clinks as she tied and tightened his makeshift bandages up again. 'Once we get out of here, we'll tend to your hands properly.' she said considerately.
He was watching her as she worked and it brought back to mind her actions in the room earlier. How it seemed like a dream now.
He asked her what she would have done had he not been there to take out the other terrorists.
She replied, 'It was my only chance and I thought I could draw them down to me in the hole. Take them out then. As luck would have it, I had a soldier on hand to help.' She looked him in his eyes.
'You knew?'
'Not initially.' She smiled at him.
God, she was smart and beautiful. What man wouldn't fall for her? He had to control his rousing.
She said 'Thanks' and then hopped onto the bike with him without another word.
They left the room that had brought so much death and destruction. It was like the remains of a battlefield in a workshop. It was still difficult to digest what had occurred here and it had been a nightmare they would never forget!
In Room 30, Will braked sharply – the engine growled and the tyres squealed. Turning left to go through the Sunley Room he was essentially following one of the routes the terrorists had used to move the gold.
They were flying through the rooms now and Hannah had to cling onto Will's body more tightly for fear of slipping off

the back seat. She felt his lean frame as she held on and his body relaxed, accepting hers.

'You're quite a surprise lady.' He shouted over the engine's roar.

'Never a dull moment with me.' He heard her reply in his ear.

It made him smirk that she had leaned in close to him to say it. Even with all the grime on her clothes, she still smelt lovely. A cinnamon scent.

'Tell me. Why did you shoot the Colonel?'

Her reply was glacial, 'He was a bad guy. And as I said earlier, a nasty piece of work. He deserved it.'

He was both impressed and wary. 'I've seen that you can look after yourself. Who are you really?'

'A girl who gets what she wants.'

Did she just whisper that provocatively in my ear? Will asked himself surprised. It almost sounded suggestive.

He accelerated through the straight of the Sunley Room.

'Steady on. You'll get this old man excited.'

She laughed and it was a lovely sound. Something needed after all the madness.

'Just teasing big man. I'm actually a thief!'

'Woooo! Now you're gonna give me a heart attack.'

They were flirting with each other while the danger still existed. Both were wanting, needing to lighten the situation. He wanted to know more. How she learned to look after herself? Handle a gun? Was she single? But now wasn't the time for twenty questions. They weren't out of trouble yet!

As they rode through the rooms it seemed to Hannah that the paintings themselves were watching them, the crude eyes of the portraits following them with eerie intent.

They were now racing through the continuing straight of Central Hall and could see the open doors that led to the top of the main staircase.

'What is it, pick on the National Gallery week for you lot?' Will exclaimed, referring to yet another burglar in the building.

'What do you mean?' she shouted back.

'Long story lady.' He saw an opportunity, 'Tell you about it over drinks one day.'

'That we can do.' Was her genuine reply.

'Tell me, what did you take from the Colonel's body?' Will yelled as he swerved to avoid a wooden bench in the room.

She replied curtly, 'It belonged to me!'

He didn't push it anymore. Actually, he didn't really care. It was only a passing interest more related to who she really was. He was only trying to figure her out with casual queries.

Despite the threat of danger still lingering, a part of Will was enjoying himself. He got a buzz out of riding the bike through the gallery rooms. He felt quite liberated and naughty at the same time.

He applied the brakes, slowing down considerably as they came out of the hall.

He was about to tell Hannah to hold on even tighter as he intended to ride the main staircase down but what he saw made him hit the brakes and swerve the bike away from the staircase edge.

The bike responded to the sudden change and remained upright as it spun in a 360° turn, tattooing tyre marks on the tiled floor. The burning rubber billowed smoke and the screech screamed throughout the landing and lobby below where four terrorists were loitering.

Hannah had somehow remained on the back of the bike and its seat, clinging onto Will who somehow was able to take her weight and momentum too. How he did it, she did not know but the man's strength was impressive.

In the confusion of the spin, she did not see the terrorists below and once the bike skidded to a stop she was about to ask Will what was all that about when she heard him mutter, 'More of 'em! I'm beginning to hate these guys.'

When the tyre smoke began to dissipate, she saw at the bottom of the staircase who he meant.

46

Outside and aloft the National Gallery, the helicopter began to veer away from above the building's roof. Swerving erratically and beginning to tilt sideways, its spinning twin rotor blades pivoted and pointed towards the square. It made an off kilter kind of sound, a stuttering whirr that groaned against what the mechanics of the machine were not designed to do.

With the Chinook losing height, the load swinging beneath it began to bounce over the concrete ground. Again and again it bumped and dragged, each impact more violent until the fake cargo eventually began to fall apart. The tarpaulin covering it loosened and a metal box fell out, splitting into pieces and revealing its emptiness. The compressor which had been put in place on the make shift load shifted and one of its rear wheels slipped off the edge but so far the portable machine remained on the pallet.

A gust of wind then caught the tarpaulin and this time picked it up completely and flung it into one of the square's fountains.

Finally after all its upheaval and repeated knocks, the contents of the load and the metal pallet it was placed on smashed, disintegrated and scattered all around the square. Pieces of wood, metal and machine parts from the obliterated compressor lay about like shrapnel. One of the rusting scaffolding poles that supported the pallet somersaulted like a tossed caber, ringing out its hollow metallic tune on each bounce on the ground before finally embedding itself into the back of one of the giant ebony sculptured lions that guarded Nelson's Column.

There was universal disappointment from everybody watching outside the perimeter. The cargo was junk by the looks of it and it was not what the crowd, media, police or military expected.

To go to all that trouble of taking over the building, demolishing part of it and bringing in an impressive helicopter to transport the supposedly significant haul of priceless paintings out didn't seem right. Did they miss something? The authorities were at a loss as to what they gazed upon strewn about in the square, they could not understand it.

Inside the cockpit, the pilot desperately struggled to regain control. He took some encouragement from the fact that he had been able to steer away from the building underneath him but he could not escape the feeling of inevitability.

'I believe we've taken a hit on the rear rotor blade.' The Englishman said between clenched teeth, struggling with the shuddering controls in his hands. 'Difficult to control now…..'

The Australian seemed unconcerned considering the danger and peered out of the cockpit window, eyeing the approaching ground and spotting the cargo's debris. 'We've lost our goods sport.'

'Damn rotten luck.' He uttered as he continually fought with the failing instruments. 'Brace yourself. All I can try to do now is drop us into the square.'

'And you know what mate. It ain't gold our cargo.'

'What?' he cried out. The controls were fighting against him and winning. It was a losing battle.

'You must be mistaken my dear boy.'
'I ain't!'
Neither of them knew what the Colonel had planned. Had no idea that they were only being used; that they were only part of an elaborate diversion, pawns in the grand scheme of things.
'Double damned!' the Englishman exclaimed.
As they looked at each other, the realisation crossed their pained faces.
'Shit creek!' the Aussie summed it up.

The Chinook was now at an irregular 45° angle and it was never going to right itself again. It spun like a disorientated swatted fly in sluggish altitude decreasing circles towards the ground.
Then there was a horrible ear piercing screech as one of the main rotor blades struck the concrete and simply snapped in half like a chopstick. One end of the large blade whizzed lethally through the air, its sonorous swopping came to a stop when it took the top off one of the squares fountain's features like a katana through bamboo and finished its lethal journey, lodged inside an empty black Taxi cab.
Someone in the crowd cheered.
The Chinook finally crashed to the ground with a pounding crunch, coming down on three of the stone bollards lining the column and pulverizing them into sand.
A metal railing also ran 8ft around the tall structure and that was completely flattened as if it were made of tin.
The collision with the ground didn't stop it; it had too much momentum and the flying machine shifted and scraped its bulk over all that got in its way until it struck the base of Nelson's Column. Its nose wrinkled inwards which in turn buckled and popped its plexiglass windscreen outwards. Yet

somehow it still continued its final flight albeit on the ground. The Chinook's sheer weight pushed it further on and around, screeching metal on concrete. Sparks erupted beneath it until finally it came to a halt like an exhausted and defeated beast.

The Chinook's front was crushed up against the Column's base, lying on its concrete steps. Its fuselage tilted over like a beached whale.

47

At the foot of the staircase and in the lobby they had been covering the main doors while the bullion was brought down. Here they had been waiting for the last of the motorbikes to pass and then they would finally make their escape. But of course they had not yet come and still these four terrorists waited in anticipation, unaware of what had transpired in Room 32.

They heard the bike and initially presumed it was here at last, carrying the remaining consignment of gold. But when the motorbike braked suddenly and the smoke from the burning tyres had cleared, it revealed to them clearly that the passengers were not one of them.

In unison they turned, raised their weapons and began to open fire on them both.

Will and Hannah scrambled off the bike and darted for cover behind the marble pillars at the top of the staircase. Each behind one, as the bullets from the terrorist's guns began blazing away.

Over the cacophony, Will shouted 'How many more of these goons are there?'

'No idea.' Hannah shrugged. 'What are you gonna do?'

'Don't know. But I ain't dying for no gold.'

The barrage of bullets was constant as they began to shatter the marble work in an eruption of stone. The doors behind them that led into Central Hall were being ripped apart like papier mâché, the wooden frames dangling in sections and all the glass in each had already shattered to a thousand pieces, joining the rest of the heaping debris on the landing. Darting marble fragments pinched their exposed flesh and the floor was becoming a carpet of shards. To add to the blitz, the skylight above the landing began to explode in places. Bullets ricocheted through the glass, each time sending a scathing rainfall down upon their heads.

They felt like they were caught in a maelstrom. Not knowing which way to turn or cower from the onslaught of detritus that had become just as lethal as the bullets. They tried to huddle as much of themselves as possible while trying to move as little too, aware one false move from their meagre and deteriorating cover and a bullet would catch them.

Will figured, soon there wasn't going to be any more cover and then they would be sitting ducks. A cloud of dust had formed around them on the landing and it was becoming difficult to discern their surroundings. They tried vainly to keep their eyes and mouths closed as much as they could from the horrible taste of grit that invaded their mouths, often having to spit out the vile acridness. They're eyes stung with the particles and they flinched with every sliver of marble that lacerated them. Their bodies felt like they were being assaulted by a swarm of stinging bees and ravenous piranhas.

Then and even above the roar of machine guns, it was heard. From outside the entrance, a tremendous thundering shook the lobby itself. It was even felt under the feet of Will and Hannah on top of the landing where they crouched.

Their gunfire ceased, the goons turned their heads towards the doors in puzzlement.

Will and Hannah exchanged quizzical looks at the mayhem's sudden stop.

With trepidation, Will peeked around what remained of his pillar.

48

What the crowd had witnessed of the staggering helicopter crash prompted them to once again Twitter, text and phone all their friends and sundry about. They could be seen not to and it wasn't over yet.
Two figures were spotted pulling themselves out of the wreckage. The pilot and co-pilot, cut up and battered had miraculously survived the impact of the collision and began to sprint away from the scene. By running across the square separately they hoped to improve each other's chances of not being apprehended, but it was futile.
They were both quickly surrounded by armed police who stormed from numerous points around the square and were only a hair's breath away on their triggers from opening fire on them.
The Englishman and Australian knew they were caught, there was no chance of escape and thwarted, raised their hands to the shouted orders of the British forces ordering them to lie down on the ground. They were then swarmed, man-handled, cuffed, searched and led away to a waiting police van.
Once again, the excitement of the audience died down and the subdued murmurings returned. But it didn't stop their furious fingers from still sending messages.
Some stared at the downed helicopter like it was an art installation or a UFO had crashed to earth. Most remained absorbed to their mobile screens but it wasn't long before a

new sound stirred the masses into animated life again and with heads pulled from their devices they strained to see into the square what it was?

Constructed in 1843 at the height of 169ft on a granite column and base, the 18ft tall statue of Admiral Lord Horatio Nelson himself stood atop and gazed south towards the Admiralty in Portsmouth. It was a monument to Nelson who tragically died at the climax of the famous Battle of Trafalgar in 1805, where he masterminded the defeat of thirty-three French and Spanish ships without a single British vessel being lost.

Where the front of the Chinook's crushed cockpit had struck the foot of the column, fractures began to gradually appear and slowly spread all around the stone base like erratically drawn scribbles. More and more splits and cracks revealed themselves and pieces of stone began to pop and crumble out of the widening cavities. The column ever so reluctantly began to lose its integrity and stability and obeying the laws of psychics began to shift, toppling towards the National Gallery building.

Audible enough for most of the spectators, sharp snapping sounds were heard. Terrified screams then rose from the onlookers. Some began to scramble backwards from the cordoned off square. Pushing and shoving in desperation and fear, trying to get away. Yet many stayed and watched, ignorant of the dangers to their own safety.

Slowly and silently at first, like a falling tree in a forest the column tilted and it was not long before its weight picked up momentum and completely broke away from the foundations of its damaged base.

The statue of Nelson seemed to watch the ground rise up to him for the first time in his life. He must have felt like a mast on a sinking ship.

It smashed to the ground of the square in a canon like blast which echoed throughout the area and all the way down to Whitehall. The column broke into three separate pieces in a cloud of chalk. The impact pushed up the York stone pavement slabs like sea waves and the upper most part slammed into the wide staircase leading up from the square.

The sandstone sculpture of Nelson was thrown free from his plinth and obliterated on contact with the ground. His head - fully intact - snapped off above the staircase onto the public promenade, bouncing again and again towards the National Gallery. Indestructibly akin to Nelson's well documented resilience not to give in, a resolve to never accept defeat; it cleared the railing outside the Portico landing and hurtled with tremendous speed towards the closed gallery doors.

49

He was moving from room to room, briskly and as quietly as he could. Checking each room ahead was clear before sprinting off again.
The building seemed abandoned now. Not a sound was heard of those dreaded motorbikes, as if all the terrorists had finally left. How many could there be remaining? Nor he and Will knew for sure what number had initially entered the gallery.
He would be glad to finally see the back of this building. He didn't think he would ever come back to this place for as long as he lived. The memories would always be nightmares!
The backpack with its stolen painting seemed to weigh a ton now and its edges poking into him felt like blunt blades. Then he remembered he had a gold bar in there too. Nevertheless, he was prepared to put up with it for a little longer even if a small part of him wanted to be arrested, to be relieved of this burden. At least he would be safe in the custody of the police.
The scorch marks and nicks from the bullets in his lucky escape from the biker raider were bearable but his arm ached painfully from the battering he had received earlier trying to protect the painting. He rubbed and massaged it and wondered whether it would be worth it after all.
The grief of previous events he had to put aside and concentrate on his own self-preservation. Get out of this

building once and for all! What had occurred tonight had never even been considered as an outcome. No one could have known that this would happen, it was unthinkable!

He thought about Will and their farewell, impressed again with the man's use of his language. Contrary to what the 'rodnik' said, not all the words Will learnt were rude.

He could not turn back to acknowledge him at the end, avoided the eye contact. He thought if he did, he would never make it on his own and again his courage would fail him. So he had remained steadfast and kept walking.

Will had aided him in so many ways and if it wasn't for him, he wouldn't have gotten this far. Would certainly not have made it. He would forever be in debt to him and a part of him would miss the cockney!

The back gate gave him an option if he could make it there unseen, get it open and let the police in. Then he could possibly hide, wait it out and perhaps get away. He knew the building; there were other ways out once the gallery was regained and if he was caught by the authorities that did not bother him. Three meals a day in prison with a library didn't seem so bad.

He was now down on ground level situated close to the back gate after using the Sunley Room staff staircase and he could hear it then. The bombilation of firing weapons and screams of men, bullets wheezing, ricocheting and puncturing off metal and concrete. It sounded like a war zone; the racket was ear–piercingly assaultive.

Ever so guardedly, Pawel peered around the corner that led out into the yard. What he witnessed was pandemonium.

The ruthless terrorists and the cautious British were fighting it out. Everywhere he looked, men were running to and fro, taking cover, stumbling and falling to the ground. Bodies from both sides lay about in pools of their own blood.

Oddly, bits of paper and plastic litter from the dustbins that had been obliterated in the crossfire danced and floated about, their course being altered constantly by all the firepower. Numerous containers provided some cover until they were blown apart and a nearby skip only prolonged the advance of any side.

Some of the terrorist's motorbikes that had earlier roamed the gallery rooms lay discarded, thrown down on the ground. Silent and spent now, their usefulness finished with.

No one knew who opened fire first when the whole affair was later recalled but the back gate had been opened. By whom, Pawel had no idea. It could well have been the terrorists themselves in readiness to escape by using the two ambulances parked up with their rear doors open or even the authorities had somehow overridden the electrical controls from outside the gate. Whoever it was, had unleashed a battle.

He could just make out past the open back gate to the street where the blue lights of the emergency vehicles flashed repeatedly. Illuminating numerous police and military personnel attempting to manoeuvre into the loading bay area without being caught in the gunfire being returned by the terrorists. They too, took whatever cover they could but casualties were falling on both sides.

In the control room, all the glass of the windows had been shot out completely. Police officers were holding out as the whole room itself was a shower of electrical sparks. Bullet after bullet continually riddled the interior and the officers could only cower beneath the disintegrating control panel. To one side a body - Tweedledum – lay slumped over, face down on the panel. No doubt dead as the barrage of slugs still riddled his inert body. As for his partner – Tweedledee - he could not be seen.

The Colonel's remaining lieutenant was heard first behind the skip. Each time swinging out and unleashing a deafening blast from his SPAS-12 shotgun with deadly effect and catapulting another member of the British forces backwards with its murderous intensity. Their bullet proof vests were ripped open like paper bags, unable to withstand the shotgun's incredible salvo. Chests mutilated, they were already dead before any obstructions behind them ended their flight.

Four officers went down like this until the entire force turned their combined firepower upon the lieutenant and ended his tally of dead British with his own demise. The aggressive and vengeful onslaught of bullets tore his body to bloodied shreds.

With renewed optimism, the British forces resumed their effects on the remaining terrorists and attempted to finally put an end to this siege.

Though what Pawel beheld was appalling, he couldn't avert his eyes and still observing from around the corner of the corridor he was in, he knew it was unlikely that he would find a way out this way.

He saw one police specialist crouching behind an open door on the driver's side of an ambulance. The only cover he could find in the onslaught. As bullets tore past him in all directions and hammered into the ambulances' door, the window in it suddenly exploded outwards, showering him in glass. He was desperately trying to get a radio call out. Repeating again and again over the riotous deluge, '…. No hostages. I repeat. There are no hostages. And there is what appears to…..'

He never finished the sentence.

His head snapped back, a bullet to the cranium and as he crumpled to the ground, more bullets from the other terrorists riddled his body, making certain he wouldn't utter another word ever again.

The initial shot that killed the messenger had come from behind Pawel in the corridor. He turned at the rifle's retort and saw the assailant pointing his weapon, now at him.

'Don't shoot me! I'm only a burglar…' Pawel got out, not at all minding to the confession and realising how pathetic it must have sounded.

A momentary lack of confusion crossed the terrorist's face and it cost him. Blood sprayed from a gunshot to his neck and he fell forward, eyes stupefied and dead.

Pawel didn't wait to find out who shot him; he turned and dived into the opened ambulance. Anywhere to get away from all the gunfire. Going back into the building didn't feel safe after that last terrorist. There could still be more in there. In his panic, he somehow closed and locked the doors behind him.

He looked around and its interior was not what he had expected. If anything, it appeared empty of what he assumed an ambulance should accommodate. There was no emergency equipment whatsoever. But what was immediately seen, were the lines of gold bricks stacked on each side with a narrow gap - an aisle of sorts - running between each shimmering amber row.

'Jezu!' he uttered aloud, dumbfounded!

He said it again.

On the floor were what looked like a pile of ambulance crew uniforms and before he could decide on another thing, the ambulance itself began to sway abruptly accompanied by the sound of scrabbling in the front driver's compartment. He became afraid.

It was immediately followed by a bombardment of metallic like puncturing sounds and then the engine started and the vehicle lurched forward violently.

He wasn't ready and he fell towards the rear doors. Luckily they didn't swing open to allow him to fall out, they remained firmly locked.

He felt the ambulance collide with something outside with a momentous crunch and its violent shove sent him off balance again, backwards away from the doors and further into the ambulance's rear compartment. As he fell he instinctively covered his front with his arm, not to protect his head but the painting under his jumper.

He saw the golden glow rushing to his face before his head smacked it.

The last thing he remembered was that another collision of some sort rocked the ambulance and the unceasing metallic popping sound all around.

Then darkness reigned.

50

Hannah only heard the enormous crash. She was still huddled behind what was left of her pillar but Will witnessed the inconceivable occur.

The three foot boulder like object came pulverizing through the main entrance. The large 10ft high and 4ft wide thick Oakwood doors exploded inwards, splitting four ways dead centre. They hurtled in four different directions like giant projectiles spinning and crushing anything in its way including the skittle like terrorists who were gathered around the lobby.

The mass of stone bounced once on the polished marble floor, cracking and splitting it like china and snatched an unfortunate terrorist. He was powerless to free himself of it, as its momentum and incredible force of gravity kept him trapped against it via his back. Continuing in its wrecking bulk, it smashed through the donation box situated in the lobby, exploding it like a giant firecracker; its contents flying in every direction.

Finally the rock came to a crunching halt at the bottom of the staircase; its final wrecking act was to obliterate the first few steps of the grand staircase.

At least the terrorist didn't experience the terrifying flight first hand as both the donation box and the concrete stairs rushed lethally to meet him because the initial impact had already broken his spine.

An out of place silence that was so tangible after all the noise that had disturbed this building tonight, settled. All was quiet again.

Hannah got up from where she had been crouching behind the almost demolished pillar and observed the unbelievable scene.

A flat 4ft slab of marble was heard peeling away from the pillar high above her and she quickly side stepped in time as it fell heavily, smashing to the floor into pieces.

Behind her a piece of the wooden door frame of Central Hall clattered to the ground, joining the mass of debris that covered all of the landing. The tiled floor and a lot of the stone staircase could barely be seen beneath all the rubble that covered it.

The skylight above their heads had been completely destroyed. Not a piece of glass remained in it, it was all crunching underfoot.

She saw Will staring transfixed down into the lobby at the foot of the staircase and her gaze followed his. Her eyes widened in astonishment, 'Oh my God!'

They both eyed the large, grey object in disbelief. It did not seem possible. It was the granite sculptured head of Admiral Lord Horatio Nelson.

They both shared the same implausible assumption. Had the column in the square actually fallen? It defied belief that such an iconic monument could have been demolished. How?

Looking up above them, part of the splendid dome ceiling had caved in. The night sky could be seen winking with some stars.

Nothing at all was left unscathed. Every part of the lobby staircase and main landing outside Central Hall was damaged to some degree or another. Every piece of stone, marble, metal, wood and glass not obliterated had been scarred and inflicted by the ricochets of bullets. Each fixture, signage, ornamentations, lights and fittings, wallpaper and paint chipped, marred or wrecked.

It was a sombre sight!

They surveyed the sight that filled the Portico foyer. The four terrorists laid unmoving; perished in different circumstances. The one that had been caught by the immense weight of Nelson's pummelling head was sprawled beneath it. His chest, ribs and internal organs must have been completely crushed. Another suffered a similar fate but squashed by a large piece of the splintered main door, it still lay across his lower body and blood could be seen pooling outwards from underneath him. Half of the main door had even buried itself into the Information Desk, destroying it.

One terrorist had suffered a grotesque demise; coins and shards of the plastic and glass that the donation box was made of had embedded themselves into different parts of his body. A coin protruded from the side of his forehead. Blood trickled from out of his gaping mouth and one of his ears. Each coin an offering, had become lethal weapons!

Through the smashed opened door, flashing lights of the emergency services could be seen on the far side of the square. Big Ben too could be spotted and there it was amiss. In validation to their earlier assumptions, Nelson's Column stood no more.

They both looked at each other with disbelief.

Will began to hobble down the main staircase. He was feeling all his pains now and they were punishing him. He needed rest, healing time. The most sensitive and intense was where he was sure he had cracked a rib or two. His head throbbed with the large bump on the back of it. All his other wounds were tolerable but no less painful. The dirty blood stained bandages had become loose again, the hands stiff, raw and numb. A cold bath appealed.

Everything crunched underfoot, debris slipped and tumbled and he had to step painstakingly so as not to miss each covered step.

He glanced over to Hannah by his side, who was also treading carefully. He could see all the nicks and specks of blood on her face and skin. Bits of white dust in her black hair and her white blouse was smudged all over with dirt. She somehow still looked pretty and poised after all she had been through.

'Horatio wins the day again.' Will commented.

'I'm almost tempted to say 'Kiss me Hardy.'' Hannah engaged.

'Oh, get out of here.' He laughed off the corny comment.

She smiled back enjoying the light relief between them and the fact that this nightmare was finally at an end. God! She'd never known anything like it. The job had gotten out of hand and turned into a war that she had been slap bang in the middle of. Nazi terrorists, lost gold, another burglar and the destruction of parts of the gallery and Nelson's Column. She had entered into this simple job of becoming the Head of Security's secretary and getting her hands on the jewel. She had never expected this. But then, who would?

Malcolm Jameson Powell came to mind and she questioned how he faired in the vault but the thought did not last for long. He did not deserve the empathy.

Killing the Colonel gave her mixed feelings, immoral and exonerating at the same time but she had no choice. He would only have murdered her and Will.

A part of her thought she would get out of this stealing game, it was becoming dangerous after what had occurred tonight and maybe she should finally take up amateur dramatics. Though, give it time and the urge to steal that she always had, would probably get the better of her.

She and this man, Will had their own wellbeing to consider. What would happen now? Everyone would almost certainly be rounded up and questioned. As far as the authorities judged, everyone no matter how innocent or circumstantial would be a suspected terrorist. She did not think she had much to worry about though; she would stick to her story about being the Head of Security's secretary and lover. And a hostage! They did not have to know about the Cora Sun-Drop Diamond. She patted her bra and reassured, still felt it there.

And Will, well he was only doing his job. He would be in all the papers tomorrow as the hero and she, the damsel in distress that he had rescued. It was the only motive that made her decide to leave with him. He was a good man and he would be her hero. That's how the authorities would see it and she would play along with that. Was counting on it! As long as her cover continued that would suit her. She also wondered if the Polish man had made it out. She didn't know him but she hoped he had, for Will's peace of mind.

A gust of wind from outside blew through where the gallery's fortress like doors once stood and it was a welcome, invigorating breeze they began to feel it rid them of some of the dust and dirt that covered their grimy and weary bodies.

A scraping sound was heard to the left of the lobby. Hannah saw it first; a terrorist on the floor by what was left of the destroyed Information desk. He was moving his body to adjust his aim of the Uzi in his hands which was aimed at Will.

Hannah yelled a warning just as the weapon fired.

It was too late.

Will tumbled and fell the last few steps onto his back.

Hannah screamed angrily, it was so unjust. It wasn't fair dammit!

At that point, soldiers came pouring through the main door and immediately a barrage of guns roared and downed the terrorist before he could fire again.

Hannah began to run over to where Will's body had fallen but was shouted at by the soldiers not to move. Their guns were trained on her, prone and ready.

She froze but Will did not.

He got up. 'I slipped in the panic. It was your scream, your warning....' He coughed, winced, clutching his ribs. '...I'm okay. He missed.'

Hannah laughed nervously. Absolutely relieved.

More soldiers rapidly spilled through the smashed opened main doors into the lobby. Weapons swinging in all directions as they swooped and covered every spot, stepping over the debris and bodies of the dead terrorists and taking up tactical positions.

Will and Hannah were now surrounded by at least fifty uniformed and armed personnel - Police Special Operations, the Force Firearms Unit, Anti Terrorists Branch, with the Counter Terrorism Command and SCO19.

'Don't shoot. We work here.' Will shouted. His voice sounded croaky.

Both he and Hannah raised their hands above their heads, handcuffs still dangling from one of their hands.

'Get down on the floor.' All the soldiers seemed to bark as one. 'Now, now.....'

In compliance and with utter exhaustion, Will dropped to his knees on the Portico floor followed by Hannah.

Under his breath, he uttered the words 'Welcome to the National Gallery.'

EPILOGUE

It had been over a year and for most people, the incidents that unfolded in Trafalgar Square that night had become a distant memory. People soon tired of the repetitive news coverage and yesterday's news had a habit of being forgotten very quickly.
Regardless of all the reportage and scrutiny, the real truth of events that happened were never fully revealed or admitted. The government informed the world, terrorists were to blame – everyone knew that - but which group never owned up or was ever disclosed and so the speculation continued to this day for those that remembered or even cared.
Yet one online rumour persisted more than any other of how a Far Right group with considerable European influence had tried to seize power and control from an ineffectual British government. A failed coup d'état! There was even gossip of Neo-Nazi factions and lost gold which was dismissed as ludicrous and fantastical by the government. However, it was pointed out, why the government would issue a statement to something deemed preposterous. The denial itself had aroused suspicion.
One thing was certain. The security guard on duty that evening and the only one to survive out of all of his shift colleagues - Will Booker, was the hero. He even saved 'the beautiful secretary' Hannah Ellis from the 'evil terrorists' that had held her hostage and the public loved a story like that. It sold a lot of papers and online activity was abuzz like

it never had been before. Everybody from all around the world had something to say.

In Will's eyes, the real saviour was Polish. He saved my life twice and in more ways than he would ever know. But because of how it resolved, no one else could know the truth about Polish's existence there that night. Will had to remain silent about that.

He had found it difficult to come to terms with the events despite the training he had received years ago as a soldier to help him cope with bloodshed. I paid a price for my survival; I subsequently relinquished something I can never get back. Still, he had no choice and he had all his previous combat experience to thank. Without it, he and Polish would not have made it out of the gallery alive. Nevertheless, he was beginning to deal with it his own way. It had been his personal war and it wasn't on a battlefield in a foreign country but of all places, right here back in Blighty!

Will couldn't go back to work at the gallery, it did not feel right. He received a decent compensation package from the government and that helped him to pursue his cheese making to some success. Security work was now history despite turning up in his occasional nightmares.

The Head of Security, Malcolm Jameson Powell was not so lucky as well as the rest of the staff on duty that night. To the authorities shock and disgust, they had discovered there were never any hostages. All the employees had been professionally murdered. The terrorists had lied. A memorial had been placed in the Annenberg Court of the building in the victim's honour. It seemed in death, Powell still got hero status much to the chagrin of all who knew him only too well and didn't believe he deserved it.

Will and Hannah were questioned again and again for days afterwards and both their recounts of the events remained the same. Finally satisfied that they had nothing to do with the terrorists, the police officials finally released them. They had confiscated her gold bar though but they never discovered the 'Cora Sun-Drop' diamond still concealed in her bra. Much to Hannah's relief, they had not even discovered her true identity and she soon disappeared from all the media attention despite offers of silly amounts of money to be the new 'pin-up' celebrity girl.

It wasn't long before she was no longer recognized as the National Gallery's 'Damsel in Distress!' She now had a new name and a new look.

Even Michael Costa, the PCSO who had first discovered that something was amiss in the gallery that night became a celebrity of sorts. He still continues to work and patrol the area and is now even busier with visiting tourists with requests for photos and selfies.

The National Gallery itself which had faced so much drama was slowly but surely getting back to normal after a year. The damaged rooms, main staircase and other areas that were devastated had already been restored and opened to business as usual. Because of the establishment's new worldwide notoriety, visitor numbers were up and for many, it wasn't for the appreciation of the art collection.

The destroyed Sainsbury Wing Link was still being rebuilt and soon Nelson's Column which more than ever would represent the country's resolve would soon be unveiled, restored and with a new unofficial media moniker – New Nelson!

Of the painting 'Madonna of the Pinks,' which hadn't been seen since that evening? Well the gallery statement was 'Due to damage caused by the events of that night, it is still undergoing repair and restoration works.'

The gallery could not afford to let it be known that not only was one of their paintings missing but it was one that the public themselves had raised the cash to keep in the country. How long could this pretence carry on before there was a public uproar and inquiry? It was only a matter of time.

Only a handful of people knew the truth.

Pawel did deliver the painting to Mr. G via Mr. Ipsen and he had collected his and his ex-partner's fee of ten million Euros.

Once the authorities had taken back the building, Joseph's body had been discovered and they knew exactly why he had been there. Evidence on his body at the scene and the eventual discovery of where they had concealed themselves in the public toilets at closing time, proved it. An unfortunate burglar killed by the terrorists who had also illegally entered the premises the same unfortunate night. The government had showed some sympathy considering the murder but knew this deceased man had had an accomplice who got away with the painting. The investigation continued and of course, none of this was general knowledge either.

Of his involvement with Joseph's murderer, Pawel did not feel a lot of self-reproach and remorse like he imagined he would. In fact, he was quite surprised how he wasn't suffering any kind of post traumatism. Will had helped ease his guilt at the time and the cockney was right; the terrorist had brought it upon himself. He was the soldier and he died for his evil cause and Pawel looked at it no other way. If a little more callous, he was glad he had done it. Willingly, he had avenged Joseph's murder and at the least, it was honour for a friend.

Joseph's body was eventually sent back home to Poland to be buried by his family who would later receive small but regular amounts of money from an unknown source for many years to come. With the help of Mr. G's associate – Mr. Ipsen that total would eventually be five million Euros, Joseph's share.

The ambulance that had escaped the building and finally eluded the pursuing British forces was never found. The chase had ended when across the river via Westminster Bridge; it had cleverly entered the busy Accident and Emergency district of the St. Thomas' hospital and lost its many pursuers by road and air amongst the other ambulances coming and going.

The authorities still couldn't believe all that gold had been under their building and noses all that time and had slipped through their fingers so easily. They hadn't stopped slapping their heads since. That was the heads that didn't roll!

Sunlight had woken him in the back of the vehicle that was completely riddled and perforated with countless bullet holes. The rays of light shining through had made him feel he was in a giant sieve. He had a thumping headache, felt hung-over and his battered arm was barely moveable, stiff with pain.

Pawel found himself lying on the floor between the two separate rows of gold bars. He later laughed at the absurdity of that. He had taken one bar from that room in the gallery and now he had a van full.

Amazingly, it was these same blocks that had protected him from the relentless barrage of gunfire that must have completely ravaged the ambulance. To this day, he would often shake his head at how incredibly lucky he was.

Opening the rear doors, he got out and the sunlight pouring in from a non-existent roof blinded him. He found himself inside an abandoned warehouse. Looking at his watch, he discovered that he had been out unconscious all next morning and into the afternoon.

In the driver's seat, he came upon the body of the driver. A huge, well built man with a blood-soaked 'Indiana State Fair' cap resting in his lap and equipped like all the other terrorists that had infiltrated the building. Unknown to Pawel - it was Tweedledee - he was slumped dead in his seat which was saturated from the blood that had poured from each of the man's many, many bullet wounds.

Somehow this soldier, terrorist had escaped from the gallery and police but eventually died from all the shelling that he and the ambulance sustained. It was a gruesome and sickly sight!

Ironically, he had this stranger to thank for his escape and freedom.

'Good luck and bad luck...' he heard Joseph's words and I had the good; he silently acquainted his late friend.

A part of him believed his partner would be pleased for him. He was missing him terribly and he would for a very long time.

He had no idea where he was. Not another building could be seen when he finally found his way out of the abandoned and dilapidated steel mill that the ambulance was parked in.

It wasn't long before he knew he had to decide to do something. The initial decision was the easy part. What followed would be difficult. He had to remain off the grid, lay low, find a hiding place far from home and the city and most far-reaching of all, call in a friend for help.

'I'm not interested in writing a book. Blimey! How many times have I got to tell you guys?' He let out a weary sigh. 'Anyway, how did you get this number?'

'You're a celebrity English. It was easy to find you.'

There was a prolonged silence on the phone and Pawel filled it in, 'What should I do with an ambulance load of gold?' The answer that came back was an exasperated cry, 'Oh shit Polish!'

THE END

COPYRIGHT©2014

Author's note -
I would like to thank…..
Roll-ups and alcohol - my ink.
Bruce Springsteen, Vangelis, John Williams, Hans Zimmer and numerous other movie scores (the modern day classical symphonies) for the background momentum.
Bob and Charlie for always being interested in my hobby-writing.
Caroline D'Souza for her vetting appraisal, advice and enthusiasm.
And of course my Geeky Girl, friend and beloved for all her laptop trouble-zapping, proof reading, unflagging support and having to patiently put up with looking at my back for so many evenings and late nights over the last two and a half years. To be honest I could not have done it without you.
I thank you, Darling Blue.

Printed in Great Britain
by Amazon